MW00848875

BAD NATURE

BAD NATURE

A NOVEL

ARIEL COURAGE

HENRY HOLT AND COMPANY
NEW YORK

Henry Holt and Company
Publishers since 1866
120 Broadway
New York, New York 10271
www.henryholt.com

Henry Holt® and Ⓗ® are registered trademarks of
Macmillan Publishing Group, LLC.

Distributed in Canada by Raincoast Book Distribution Limited

Library of Congress Cataloging-in-Publication Data

Names: Courage, Ariel, author.
Title: Bad nature : a novel / Ariel Courage.
Description: First edition. | New York : Henry Holt and Company, 2025.
Identifiers: LCCN 2024026501 | ISBN 9781250360885 (hardcover) |
ISBN 9781250360878 (ebook)
Subjects: LCGFT: Novels.
Classification: LCC PS3603.O88647 B33 2025 | DDC 813/.6—
dc23/eng/20240614
LC record available at https://lccn.loc.gov/2024026501

Our books may be purchased in bulk for promotional, educational, or business use. Please contact your local bookseller or the Macmillan Corporate and Premium Sales Department at (800) 221-7945, extension 5442, or by e-mail at MacmillanSpecialMarkets@macmillan.com.

First Edition 2025

Designed by Kelly S. Too

Printed in the United States of America

1 3 5 7 9 10 8 6 4 2

For Catherine

BAD NATURE

I

THE NOTHING AGE

1

Turning forty was nothing special. I was an unmarried, childless lawyer living in one of Manhattan's many nondescript condos. The memorable figures in my life were my secretary and my medical professionals: the dermatologist, the cosmetic dentist, the gynecologist, the allergist. I was not a hypochondriac; I just had a lot of time and money to spend on myself.

The only one I never saw was a psychiatrist.

"I'm allergic to psychiatry," I once told my allergist.

"Very funny," he said, with no change in facial expression. "Please remove your jacket."

My only birthday plan was an appointment with my primary care doctor. The office had a Third World aura: too many people trying too hard to get too little attention from the bored and vaguely Slavic receptionists. I'd been seeing my previous doctor since I was in my twenties—I joked to her once that she was my longest relationship, and she'd visibly shuddered—but she had recently retired. She'd referred me to this new office, maybe as a joke of her own.

With the toe of my boot, I worried a chip in the gray linoleum, a hole with some unnameable brown material beneath. I thought about the person who laid that material, who probably knew it had a specific name, and how you can be mistaken about these things. How things seem unknowable only if you don't take the time to learn. The television in the waiting room was playing a story about a mudslide somewhere in the South, shots of an RV park mired in dishwater.

The doctor was a man. I hadn't expected that. He had a unisex first name, and I hadn't bothered to look him up before coming, accepting my old doctor's recommendation on faith, not wanting to anticipate her punch line. He had a fatherly manner, or at least what I think is commonly considered fatherly; I wouldn't know. He called me into a crowded cubbyhole of a room, gave me a paper johnny with a plastic drawstring, and then left. The string broke. The doctor came back too soon. My body was partly revealed, my naked chest to the plaster wall.

"The tie," I said.

"That's fine," said the doctor of the string, waving his hand dismissively. He spoke with a slight untraceable accent that made his voice seem kinder, softer. More patient. I folded the paper johnny over my body, then gave up and let it flutter open. It was ridiculous anyway, with him about to examine me. I wasn't sure if those johnnies were designed for the benefit of the patient or the doctor, so that they wouldn't have to take in the problem of the patient's body all at once.

"Lie back," the doctor said, and I did. He leaned over me and fidgeted his gloved fingers over my chest. He had very brown skin. I looked up first at the thick hair in his nostrils and then to the ceiling lamp. I stared until it burned white circles into my vision that faded when I finally blinked. The doctor's eyes were fixed at some point far from me, like he was looking at sheet music.

"Hmm," he said, my stupid body his instrument.

I snorted. "Excuse me," I said, and then, mortifyingly, "I'm ticklish."

When the exam was over, the doctor sat in front of the computer, face blue.

"Oh, happy birthday, Hester," he said absently, rapt in my chart.

"Thanks."

"Forty was a good year."

"Forty is an old year."

"Just wait until you're my age."

He could've been anywhere from forty to seventy. He had one of those illegible faces.

"Hope you're not in any rush," he said.

"To get old?"

"No, I mean right now. I'd like to talk to you about taking some images. There is something. Or possibly nothing. I don't know for sure."

Leaving the doctor's office, I called my building's super.

"Can you come over? The sink's leaking again," I lied.

"For you?" he said. I could tell he was grinning. "For you, anything."

Within an hour, I fucked my objectively repulsive super. Technically, he was only responsible for communal areas of the building, but he often performed free labor around my condo, mounting picture frames or moving heavy furniture. The kind of free labor usually performed by husbands. I didn't have a husband. I had a policy of jettisoning any man I dated around week six, fucking a lot of borderline-grotesque strangers in between. I hadn't had anything I would describe as a romance since college and preferred it that way.

I always came early and silently, with no real effort on the super's part. Maybe because it was debasing to fuck someone like him and therefore erotic, or because the rounded part of his gut pressed against me just so. Or else it was daddy issues. I don't know. He never seemed to notice what I did or didn't do in bed. I liked to lie there, waiting for him to finish, counting in my head the white paint flecks on his forearms. The building seemed to have an endless supply of newly empty condos that needed painting.

The super was deeply incurious. He never asked questions. I liked that, too. I'd never been to his apartment but I imagined his walls were bare except for a shawl tacked over a combination wall safe. I didn't want to know his tastes. His politics were probably appalling.

"I'm leaving," I said to the ceiling in the quiet aftermath. I wasn't sure of it yet but wanted the practice of saying it.

The super was on his back next to me, breathing heavily. I accepted the risk of his having a heart attack on top of me. His skin was as white as the walls, and he, too, had a faint accent. Threatening violence was his form of humor, idle and with only a hint of real trouble behind it. "Sublet," he told me, "and I'll break your kneecaps."

Maybe I should have found it hard to work with my mortality up for debate like that, a big italicized question mark leaning on the next sentence of life. I didn't. If anything, I was more effective under duress, more extroverted the worse I felt. I appreciated the busy-ness of work. It was hard to see the future over the stack of venture documents and asset purchase agreements for review on my desk. I was tired, and my breasts felt leaden, tender especially where I jammed my fingers into my uppermost left rib, but these were not unusual feelings for me, to the point that I thought they just came with the territory of being a woman.

I was deputy in-house counsel for a large, storied company that had grown over the past century to encompass subsidiary interests in several sectors, ranging from shipping and logistics to grocery delivery and AI. They had locations in New York, Seattle, Los Angeles, London, Dubai, Shanghai, Luxembourg. They tried to affect a start-up ethos by allowing dogs in the office. We were all compensated in stocks and options on top of generous base salaries, and the work was easier than my firm days, though

I still stayed late more often than necessary. I made more money in a year than my parents had in their lives, but this did not give me as much satisfaction as one might think.

Around the time I visited the new doctor, much of my day-to-day involved settlement negotiations with the EPA over unregistered pesticides imported from Malaysia and sold on the company's platform. The offending items had promising names like Miracle Chalk 100% SAFE or Super-Magic Dreamland Indoor Bait Powder. My work entailed reviewing reports from something called the Environmental Fate and Effects Division.

The week after my appointment, I opened the file and pulled out the stop-sale, use, or removal order and ran its thick paper between my fingertips just for the feel of it. I'd never really appreciated that: the simplicity of a fresh white sheet.

"Magda," I called to my secretary. Administrative assistant, technically. New name, old concept.

She appeared in the doorway.

"Feel this paper, Magda," I said.

"What?" she said, squinting the way she did when confused.

"Come here."

Having no alternative, Magda approached my desk. She felt the corner of the paper. Her hands were wrinkled and freckled in contrast to the paper and her smooth, pond-surface nails. She never deviated from a murder-mystery red, was never tempted by sage green or midnight blue.

"Very nice," she said. "Miss, is something the matter?"

"It's fine. Thank you for humoring me."

Magda had been at the company for decades, passed from department to department. Her old-world mustiness ran counter to their attempts to seem relevant and cutting-edge, but she couldn't be let go; she'd seen too much. I think she was suspicious of me. She would've preferred a man. Not because she thought men were competent—she complained eloquently about classic male idiocy, their inability to function without women to straighten their ties or organize their cabinets or make small talk with their clients or, in her longtime ex's case, get them a visa—but because she felt her dynamic didn't work with a woman. She was a single mother of two boys and was accustomed to men serving as ersatz fathers, slipping them candy and money, asking them what they'd be when they grew up, giving them errands when Magda had no choice but to bring them to work with her, perhaps someday writing recommendation letters for schools or jobs.

"They're working you too hard, these people. Let me bring you some coffee. You look tired," said Magda.

"Tell me I look young and fresh, Magda," I said, sliding the form back into its file. "What kind of sycophant are you?"

"An honest one," Magda said, and closed the door. She came back a moment later with coffee and a paper-wrapped, beribboned rectangle together on a tray.

"What's this?" I asked as she transferred the cup and gift to the edge of my desk.

"For your birthday. A bit late, I know."

When I first took this job, I'd gone out of my way to tell HR that under no circumstances were they to celebrate or otherwise disclose my birthday, as I viewed this as a gross breach of privacy. I had no idea that Magda knew, much less how she knew. She'd never mentioned it before. Then again, this was a milestone year. I felt unexpectedly touched. I am not a sentimental person. I used to squash spiders and dispose of poisoned mice for my mother without fuss.

"You didn't have to do that, Magda."

"It's nothing. You know what would be something? A vacation."

"You should take one."

"I mean you," she said. "*You* take a vacation."

"We should both take one."

"Girls' trip," Magda said, smiling with feigned enthusiasm.

Her teeth were stubby and translucent and dark like tea, her sons' orthodontia having received priority over her own care. She let the smile die, coughed, adjusted the hem of her skirt, and then looked at the package on my desk. I've never liked receiving gifts, the gratitude rendered performative by virtue of having an audience, no matter how genuinely felt. I looked at the package too. We both sat there looking for a long time until Magda pointedly handed me a letter opener from my desk caddy.

Beneath the wrapping was a journal bound in fine matte leather. It clearly cost too much relative to how little it would be used. I'd received a few journals or diaries in my life from people who knew me hardly at all and had never used them except as kindling in my condo's white-bricked fireplace.

I opened it to a random page and felt it. "Now this," I said, "is great paper."

Magda smiled again. Her teeth were too short for her lipstick to ever stain them. "I'm glad you like it," she said, and then left.

It was getting to be late in the day. In my office were two low leather armchairs, slick and somehow sexual, just birthed. Case files piled up on their cushions. I had floor-to-ceiling windows with blinds I could control with a button beneath my desk. I never closed them, preferring the light even when it slanted in and made me sightless. When night fell, I'd turn on my arced floor lamp with its buttery glow and work in silence, staying long after the rest of the office had emptied out.

I tapped my pen against the desk and looked out the window. My view was of an office across the avenue, empty but with the banked fluorescent lights still on. I could hear my mother's voice: *Turn those off, it's lit up like Vegas in here.* Her plump wrist curved around the doorjamb, hand groping for the switch. Her fingernails were never painted and always thick as boards, permanently thickened from her pregnancy with me.

I turned back to my screen and let the autofill complete the address for my father's site. My father and I had been estranged for decades, but I liked to check on him once every six months or so, like doing a breast self-exam. He was an artist and wanted everyone to know it. My browser used to show me my most-visited URLs until I turned the feature off, and my top three were LexisNexis, my dad's site, and the website of the restaurant where my ex—there was but the one—now worked.

To my surprise, Dad had moved. He was in California, trading the stony fields of our home state for saguaros and red rock. He and his new wife were living on the outskirts of a desert town. I still thought of her as the new wife though by that point they'd been married for years. They took selfies. They raised chickens. They hiked.

His move offended me. For years he'd stayed more or less in place. Who the hell was he, I thought, to change?

Magda appeared in the door again, her parka buttoned up and a scarf tied over her hair, the knot nestled under her chin. I'd forgotten about her and nearly startled out of my seat when she appeared.

"Good night, Miss Hester."

"Good night."

A few days later, I had my imaging done. I was too gaunt for the lead apron, with hardly enough flesh to pinch into the machine. The technician at the imaging center had to tie it closed. She placed little pink stickers with metal studs over my breasts, areas marked for further investigation. She kept guiding me roughly, pressing my back and pulling my arms.

The technician left me in the grip of the machine and said, "Okay. Do your best. Don't breathe, don't move. And again."

When the results came, the doctor called me back to his office.

During that time, his waiting room had descended further into squalor, overcrowded and for some reason full of crying children though no pediatricians worked there. In the exam room, I started to remove my shoes, force of habit, but then the doctor appeared and told me to sit.

"I am sitting," I said, because I already was. I tucked my feet under the chair, out of his view.

"Yes. Listen. This is difficult. I am going to refer you to an oncologist who can explain in more detail. We will need to do more tests. I do not want you to worry. We are going to take care of you."

He leaned forward and rested his hand over mine on my knee. I understood that this was a gentler delivery of bad news than many people receive, but still, I hated him. I hated that he had this intimate knowledge of me now. That he knew the vulnerability of my body, which was as susceptible to failure as any other. He had confirmed for me my total lack of specialness, the irrelevance of my intelligence and character. People talk about human life as the universe's aberrant miracle, but it's hard to sustain belief in its importance at scale, repeated with every second of every minute of every day.

"I just saw the doctor last year. I was fine," I said.

He withdrew his hand. "Things can be hard to see and may worsen very fast."

I accepted the information he gave me without comment or question. In the weeks to come, there were more tests, more long waits, more excuses to "work from home" so I could go to appointments without attracting attention. My oncologist was an ultramarathoner with a head too narrow for the width of his grin. All around his office he displayed finisher medals and participation trophies and pictures of his races, along with a framed poem he'd evidently written and self-printed about his experience of running a 10K. I still remember one particularly bad couplet: *we run from the fear / that pricks our hearts severe.*

"How long do I have?" I asked him.

"Without treatment? Six months," he said.

It struck me later as strange that he mentioned going without treatment. Like he knew that was an option for me. I'd seen what chemotherapy and radiation did to my mother, the way the illness ate away her dignity. Death seemed the less terrifying option.

He continued, "With treatment? Two, three years. It's unlucky to get something so aggressive so young. But between therapy and lifestyle interventions, you could well prove me wrong. What do you do?"

"What?"

"For a living."

Something about the phrase "for a living" made me smile.

"Lawyer."

He frowned and said, "You need to avoid sources of stress. Take a leave of absence. Be outside as much as you can. My advice? Whimper no more, postpone no more. Be done with indoor complaints, querulous criticisms."

I blinked at him. "What is that, fucking Thoreau?"

"Whitman, actually."

He asked if there was someone I might call to pick me up.

"Do I seem upset?" I asked, nearly yelling.

"Not particularly," he said. "But people sometimes are."

"I'll call my mother," I lied.

I drove everywhere, even in Manhattan, because I owned a car too nice not to use and loved the petty competition of parking. Heading home, I experienced a total absence of feeling. Everything seemed more vivid for lacking the filter of mood. I sat at a traffic light, fixated on the glowing red eye, and when it turned green—something that had happened thousands of times in my life without being in any way remarkable—I felt it physically, like a switch had been flipped at the base of my skull.

I idled in my car at the light too long, but I was somehow the only person on the road at this hour on this day on this bright, wide avenue, and so I was able to let it run through several cycles, red-yellow-green, staring until my eyes watered and each discrete dot of light blurred into the next, all gone to glittery refractory gems.

A car drove in front of me across the grid, a sedan with a family inside, mother and father and girl about seven. I had a brief disorienting moment of imagining the family reconfigured and jumbled like some impossible puzzle, the girl in the driver's seat and the mother in the back and the father strapped to the roof like a Christmas tree.

The moment passed. I drove on.

The supermarket near my condo provided single slices of cake in wedge-shaped plastic tubs. I'd never seen a soul buy one, and in that way they seemed theoretical, abstract. It was no longer my birthday, but I bought myself one. I took down all the art I'd hung up over the years in hopes of looking normal for my guests at the dinners I once hosted for senior associates. I've come to learn that people find art-free walls strange, borderline psychopathic. I stacked the frames on the floor like building a pyre and then sat cross-legged next to them, eating cake and staring at the wall.

The bare wall was painted as white as the frosting but at that moment bore a slash of clear gold from the late-afternoon sun filtering through the window. I sat and watched it darken into a deep amber, like tea left to steep too long, and then darken further into grayish blue.

I sat there all night, sugar stiffening on the tines of the fork. I wanted my mind blank and awash in color, too.

2

I was always going to kill my father.

Or at least the idea came to me very young. I never had a specific plan. I knew I was going to kill him the same way you know that sooner or later it's going to rain. It was a natural fact.

"We hate you," I seethed to him on the phone when he called the house once, sometime after the state removed him from our lives and divorce proceedings began. I was thirteen and speaking for my mother and myself. I didn't know why he'd called, to torment us or seek our forgiveness or ask if he could get his record collection back. I didn't wait to find out. His reasons were irrelevant.

"Don't call us. I'll kill you," I said, feral and fiendish, and hung up.

"Who was that?" Mom asked from the other room.

"No one," I said.

So he had his fair warning.

I was told the anger would fade. As part of my parents' divorce, I had to go to court-mandated therapy for traumatized children, though thirteen barely qualifies as a child in my estimation and I did not consider myself traumatized. The doctor's office had a gumball machine in the waiting room. At my first session, I rigged it to dispense pocketfuls for free, then, under questioning, refused to speak. This behavior got me branded as emotionally troubled. The psychiatrist, a man with a ridged baldpate like a horseshoe crab I'd once seen washed up on the beach, told Mom I'd mellow over time. Later in life, at a client dinner, I heard a sommelier say the same about an immature wine.

I never did. The anger was TV static, too diffuse to be separated from my personality. It didn't exhaust or distract; it invigorated and verved, routine and harmless like coffee. I just grew more strategic by never talking about it. I'd only ever told two people about this homicidal urge and hadn't spoken to either of them in years.

The best revenge is a life well lived, Mom often said, but she didn't live life well. She cobbled together several jobs to afford my care and died young of a cruel illness before I finished high school. When she was healthy, she'd talk about the future. She wanted to buy a car, drive west, meet friends and other, better men. This kind of future existed only in movies. She never did those things. I'm not claiming my father put a gun to her head, but, to my mind, she started dying the second she met him.

I knew men did worse, put literal guns to literal heads and pulled literal triggers. I knew women were capable of the same. It didn't matter. The feeling was beyond logic; I couldn't reason my way out of it.

I occasionally looked him up to confirm he was alive and therefore still killable. The first time I checked, I hadn't expected there to be much. I figured that, being older, he'd have a relatively low profile. That proved not to be the case. He was an artist, easy to find because he wanted to be found. He curated and presented information about his life and work for some unknown audience.

We were not Solanas and Warhol for many reasons, first among them that my father was no genius. He was a heterosexual mediocrity. If you worked in certain small circles during a narrow range of years, you might know his name. His art consisted of huge canvases abstracting the female body into loud colors and lines: pink breasts, blue legs, yellow vulva, orange anus.

He cast himself as a misunderstood genius of category-defying talent. My mother bought into a variation of this line: He could've been great, truly special, but he never really tried. It's possible she said this only to make me feel better, so I wouldn't think I'd come from irredeemable trash. Or maybe she only said it to justify her attraction to him. I never asked what prevented his trying or what she thought the trying would've looked like.

You'd never know what he'd done by looking at any of his online avatars. They looked like photos of any man on the downward slope of advanced middle age. The one on his website was taken at the beach. He was wearing sunglasses, but you could tell he was still squinting. He had an awkward sunburn from unevenly applied cream. It troubled me how many people were out there with pasts like his, looking harmless and deserving of no particular evil.

At some point when I was in my twenties, he acquired the new wife. She was only slightly older than me, slender, her dark hair free of grays. She had no children of her own, and they had no children together. He painted portraits of her in which she looked even younger than she was, almost adolescent, and in which her gold crucifix necklace featured prominently.

It wasn't enough to have lived in rebuke of him by choosing a practical, remunerative, and anonymous life in opposition to his impracticable, unprofitable, and recognition-seeking one. His apparent happy remarriage, lack of real job, good health, chances of outliving not only my mother but also me: It all made me sick.

Maybe the wife knew about my mother and me. Maybe she forgave him. Like in a Christian way.

3

I resigned, effective immediately, from work, citing a "family emergency." This must have confused them because both Magda and my bosses knew I had no family. I did not offer to help with a transition. I did not express gratitude. I felt no guilt. I'd given them, and the firm before them, years of my life. My last vacation was three years ago. I'd spent the whole time ostensibly reading a mystery and drinking margaritas by the pitcher but really just responding to work emails, sober and watching teenagers mock-drown each other for fun in the hotel pool. My salary was lower than the other deputy counsels, who were all men, though that never bothered me as much as it probably should have. If anything, we all should have made equally less.

I've always been prickly and standoffish, selectively sociable, largely humorless. I hadn't had a friend since I was a teenager. Being a "career woman" had been a good fit for me, and I'd enjoyed it in my way, but it was ultimately easy to let it go.

I packed a bag. I took very little. My wardrobe consisted of suits, blazers, and shift dresses in corporate gray, black, and beige. You could examine this closet and know nothing about its wearer except her measurements. I took the urn that held Mom's ashes, which I'd never scattered, and the gun, which I'd acquired years before. People freak out about guns, but there are more civilian-owned firearms in America than domestic cats. They're barely worth mentioning, like lamps or alarm clocks.

This was the plan: drive west, find Dad, kill Dad, then self. I didn't even want to try to get away with killing him. I was dying anyway; I might as well end it there.

I liked the simplicity of my plan, its extremity. I liked the way it echoed my mother's desire to travel in that direction, though I am not, as my mother was, a person who wants to see things just to see them. I liked the way I could take my time, controlling how quickly or slowly I got there. Flying would have been faster, but wildfires out west were diverting flights.

All the hand-wringing about the dying planet was overwrought, I thought. Embarrassing, even. Still, the fact that my father had blithely relocated to a hellish conflagration—that his plans weren't at all impacted by the world's demise—bothered me. He gave no indication he knew the state was burning around him, that people were losing their homes and fleeing in cars with melting tires. He was oblivious to misery to the point that I wondered if he hadn't somehow caused it by virtue of his presence.

I called my bank to let them know I was going on a trip. I was connected to a woman with a syrupy accent. I pictured her with a curly, colorless mullet; I pictured her saying *debutante* all round and thick, lipsticked like chicken in gravy.

"Where to?" she asked.

"California. I'm driving."

"A road trip," she sighed, like her traveling days were long behind her or had never existed. "Goin' with family?"

"Just me."

"Aw. Nice that you can treat yourself."

Treat yourself. What a disgusting phrase.

"I'm going there to euthanize my father who's dying of brain cancer."

"Oh," she said, with a satisfying degree of dismay. "How long will y'all be gone for?"

"Forever," I said, and hung up.

I then took my cell phone, placed it with ceremonial deliberateness on the patio at my condo, and bashed its face in with a hammer. Just for fun. It shattered like ribbon candy; I almost wanted to eat the shards.

I bought a new one. The clerk at the store asked if I wanted to keep my old number. "I've never had a phone," I lied. When the clerk tried to reminisce about landlines, I for some reason went even further and said, "No, I mean I've never had a phone of any kind."

I felt so good that I wondered if I really was going to die. How often were doctors wrong about this kind of thing? Maybe I'd misunderstood him. Maybe I'd dreamed up the whole experience.

I called the oncologist again.

"Is this a new number?" he asked.

I ignored him. "Six months?"

"Only if you do nothing. I hope I didn't unmoor you. I was only trying to convey a sense of urgency."

"Have you ever made a mistake? I feel healthy."

"There's a certain amount of guesswork to all prognoses, but I am usually on the mark. As for 'feeling healthy,' I would remind you of Bashō's eternal words: 'In the cicada's cry is no sign it will soon die.'"

"What is it with you and poetry?"

He seemed taken aback. "Many of my patients find comfort in the eternal wisdom of the bards."

I paid up my bills, moved some money around, canceled various accounts. I slept soundly, a perfect eight hours, and had no dreams. A good sign, I thought. I've never been a good sleeper.

I went to the condo's underground garage and got my E-Type. Once I'd worked at the firm a few years, it seemed somehow embarrassing not to own a car; an insult to people who would've loved to own one, and an insult to my mother, who always said that if she'd had the money, that's the kind of car she would've bought. I'd never understood this desire of hers, which seemed imported from another phase of her life, before Dad and I brought her so much trouble. I'd never asked her about it, one of many questions that occurred to me too late to ask, and so in lieu of an answer, I just bought the fucking car.

I sat in the front seat, taking my time to adjust the mirrors, to reapply lipstick I'd put on minutes before, to make sure my driving sunglasses were accessible in the center console. I felt protected, in an armored shell in a shaded bunker, my connections to the outside world destroyed and new ones never to be forged. I've always liked times like those the best: when you're not at home or at your destination, when you're beyond the places that define a life and give it shape. In biographies no one ever mentions time spent in train stations and waiting rooms, bus stops and airport gates, because these experiences are boring and universal. But that's why they're so pivotal. They're the times you can become anyone.

It was the first of May. The past month had been full of unseasonably cold, bright days with sunshine so acidic it scrubbed surfaces of their texture. I cut briskly against the moderate press of Sunday traffic. Outside a Bank of America, a homeless man played a reveille on a dented trumpet. The patriarch of a tourist family, camera draped over his torso like an ammo strap, jaywalked in front of my car.

The tunnel out of Manhattan and into my future was a glimpse of low-budget hell, wanly lit and pressurized from water rushing above unseen at thousands of cubic feet per second. My path was smooth and unimpeded. I turned on talk radio, letting it fuzz for a full minute until I reemerged into daylight. Any voice would do.

It's not just a matter of questionable taste anymore. You're now toeing the line, and it's hypocritical because they say they want to give the people what they want. But when you try to do that, they say, "Not like that." There's this distrust, that people think they know what's better for other people. That giving them what they want is bad.

A moral panic over taste.

Yeah.

The tunnel spat me out into the land of sand and gravel and ready-mix concrete and fuel storage, of shipping containers like children's blocks and cell phone towers poorly camouflaged as evergreen trees. Billboards advertised gambling only legal farther down the highway in another state. The orange-tan marshland, spiked with reticulated transmission towers and dying trees, looked rinsed in gasoline. Trucks merged onto bridges over Point No Point Reach. A sign told me in electric letters PREVENT A TRAGEDY, but I didn't get to read the rest before I passed, so I never learned how.

Over my shoulder I could see Manhattan's scutal skyline sinking into the earth. The city cast a sprawling shadow of distribution centers and waste-management facilities and freight offices and acetylene factories and chassis depots. The place couldn't exist without depleting a thousand others, but whatever, I wasn't from there, wasn't even from a place remotely like it; I was from a place all fields and nothing. I had a resolvable injustice to correct. If you can't beautify ugliness or remedy inherent inequalities, you can at least rid the planet of one irredeemable asshole.

Correction. Two irredeemable assholes.

The first time I went abroad and returned to New York—the first time I saw the place from above—the overwhelming impression was of grayness, of gridded streets and cemeteries and creeks interrupted by methane flare stacks. I swore I saw garbage bags piled at the curb from twelve thousand feet. The experience was like a photograph taken from an unanticipated angle that reveals every flaw of its subject, a phenomenon I'd experienced at work holiday parties when the camera's flash stripped away all my effortful beauty and made me look withered and nonnutritious, like a burnt french fry at the bottom of a carton. I couldn't believe I'd been living in it. But it was too late to change tack; I'd just been admitted to law school then, with my future mapped out.

Many might've given up, given into despair, said a radio interviewee. *But not me. I persevered.*

4

Near Philadelphia, I pulled into a rest stop. I hated having a body with needs, resented that I couldn't exist as pure will alone. I barely deserved my physical form anyway, using it as I did for such a limited and unimaginative range of pleasures. Plenty of people probably would've put mine to better use.

I'd prodded around for my tumor but hadn't been able to feel it myself, even when I demanded that the oncologist demonstrate, which he did, his hand over mine on my breast in a pantomime of intimacy. I couldn't believe I was being so betrayed by my own matter. I looked around the rest stop parking lot at every other body. People got sick and carried on, forgetting the insult. I knew I'd never.

Both the car and I stood out in those drab surroundings, I in a skirt and faux-fur vest that was as expensive as a real fur one and big sunglasses and a laptop-laden handbag in the flattened, still-cold early haze. I wondered what my tumor was up to. My breast was such an inhospitable place, meager and thin. I pictured my tumor like a goat on a cliff's face, hunting for roughage to gnaw on. You almost had to root for it, the underdog. I called it Beryl, a name I'd given a lot of my dolls growing up. Poor girls love gems: Crystal, Ruby, Amethyst. Later I learned beryl is an acute carcinogen.

The rest stop still had pay phones in the lobby like massive reliquaries, plastic phones instead of dead saints' arms. There was a kiosk where I bought a pack of cigarettes, though I hadn't smoked in years, and a McDonald's, where I hadn't eaten since my father left us. I'd loved to pick tiny onions like diamonds off the bodiless red-slick bread. These were meals I begged for and sometimes got from him, never from my mother, who usually insisted on eating what we had at home. When he left, I was weirdly as angry about the end of our secret, infrequent tradition as much as any of his other misdeeds.

"One Happy Meal," I said when I got to the counter. "Please."

I expected some pushback since I was clearly an unaccompanied and unhappy adult, but the bored middle-aged woman behind the counter punched it in with no remark. I'm always expecting a sneer and not finding one. This should be good, but instead I'm disappointed, like I'm not even worth the minor effort of derision.

I got my cardboard box and sat in a corner with my sunglasses still on. A child at the next table stared. My lipstick stained the bread of the burger, which was likely full of polysorbate 80 or whatever else was produced at one of the nearby chemical factories and piped directly into a sludge tank out back. The toy was a dinosaur made of oil derived from its ancestors, and when you turned its tail, its jaws wound up and chewed, chewed, chewed.

The kid's eyes on me became unbearable. I smiled at it with a mouth full of bready debris until it turned back to its mother, frightened. I crinkled my food back up in its paper diaper and stood to go back to my car, upholstery be damned.

When I got back to the parking lot, I couldn't find it. For a moment I thought I'd gone precociously demented. I hit the finder on the fob but heard no answering beep. I stalked the rows, assuming I'd just forgotten where I'd parked. It would be easy to forget; the rows were many and indistinct. But that car stood out in a crowd, and it was gone.

"Fuck," I said.

I had my cell phone and my laptop and my wallet, at least. But the car was gone, along with Mom's ashes and the gun. I wondered what I was going to do about my plan now that I had no weapon. Maybe I didn't need it. Anything can be a weapon if you're persistent enough. A car, kitchen knives, fire pokers, golf clubs, a pair of sweatpants, a wine corkscrew, a pillow. A dessert spoon smacked with correct pressure against the basilar artery. Life is a pretty fragile business.

Another person might've taken this early bad luck as a sign from the universe, but not me. I am the single-minded master of my own destiny.

I called the police. The cop who showed up an hour and a half later had maybe once been handsome but now had a face creased by wrinkles and overgrown nose hairs. It depressed me to think of him wasting away in a patrol car, alone, pulling over other Black people in cars with out-of-state plates, though I doubt he felt that way about it. His eyes traveled from my heels to my fur to my lipstick, appraising the type of person he was dealing with.

When I approached him, he asked, "Cheering yourself up?"

I was still holding my half-finished meal, its contents now cooled and soggy. I chucked it in a squat trash bin with a brown flap.

"I was gone for ten minutes. Who steals a car from a rest stop in broad daylight?" I asked.

"Rash of problems at this particular spot. We think it's all the same crew. If you're lucky, it was covered by the cameras."

I frowned. I'd parked it all the way at the end to keep it from other drivers I didn't trust not to scratch it.

"Well, it's distinctive, at least," I said. "Easily found."

"They usually strip 'em for parts, chop 'em up so you can't tell what they were one way or another."

I glanced around the parking lot, doubtful. Tearing apart a car like that would be sacrilegious, I said to myself in my mother's voice.

"There someone you want to call?" asked the cop.

I shook my head no. Why were people always asking me that?

He drove me to the police station. I'd been in a squad car before under no happier circumstances, but sometimes it's hard to tell if my memories of it are real or implanted from some dream or old film. My mother standing in the door, talking to officers, their jackets backlit by headlights and the dizzying swirl of cherry tops that were the only lights but the stars and moon.

"Where you headed?" the officer asked, driving a road he'd driven a thousand times before, trying to fabricate conversation out of thin air. "*Were* you headed."

"Visiting my father."

"Folks local?"

"California," I said. It's always strange, pretending I have a normal family. That it's at least in the same spectrum of relatability.

"Long drive."

"Not too long, in the grand scheme of things."

"Well. Hope you get back on the road soon."

I had an insane impulse to tell him about my plans. Just to give him something unexpected, a story to break up the monotony of patrol. Instead, I reached into my purse and pulled out my lipstick and a compact. Applying lipstick made me feel like a rich woman. Much of my life was affected based on what I thought a rich person would do in a particular circumstance. Exhibit A, the contemporary abstracts I'd hung in my apartment on the advice of some idiot interior designer, mimicking what I thought other people in my position did.

"I don't," I said, popping the tube's cap back on. "He's a real bastard."

Bastard is an underutilized word, a rare pleasure to pronounce. The officer glanced back at me in the rearview, alarmed.

The police station was a gray building, low to the ground as if designed for withstanding a nuclear event, which, depending on the decade it was built, I guess it might've been. The cop had me fill out forms and call my insurance. Another woman at the front desk was telling her story to an officer who wouldn't look her in the eye, keeping his gaze trained on a logbook he slowly paged through. "It just isn't right," she kept saying.

"Can I get a lift to a dealership?" I asked.

The cop looked confused.

"Used. Whatever's closest. I don't care."

"You don't want to wait for the insurance?"

"I'm in a bit of a rush. My father is a very sick man."

"You can't just buy a car in a different state. You gotta get it plated and registered in the state where you live. It takes like two weeks to get to your mailing address," he said, looking at me like I was unwell.

Having a lot of money, a sustained remove from practical life outside my narrow expertise, was probably on par with a kind of brain damage. After all the waiting and paperwork and calls, it was getting to be late afternoon. No natural light penetrated the police station; the building seemed to deny the possibility of sunshine.

"Let me worry about that."

"I know this is all a shock. But think it through."

"Okay, to a hotel, then. I'll sort it out in the morning."

"Best you'll find is a motel, and speaking from experience, most have a hooker problem or a drug problem or both."

"I'm sure you know a place that's not too awful."

"Call a cab," he said, feigning interest in a landline phone that was muted but still screamed red with incoming calls.

"You really can't help me?"

"I'm a cop, not a concierge."

His curtness didn't deter me. "Please," I said, raising my sunglasses and smiling.

I know it sounds ridiculous but this worked more often than you'd think. For a person my age, I had very white teeth (the handiwork of Dr. Remsen) and very clear, wrinkle-free skin (the handiwork of Dr. Corbett). I kept my hair brutally shiny, my body wincingly trim. Short of surgery, I did every violence I could to myself to look conventionally attractive. My mother hadn't had such luxuries. When she was my age, she'd already fattened and sallowed, her body ravaged by a difficult pregnancy and a difficult marriage and a difficult job she supplemented with difficult ad hoc work, scraping together what she could. She was not a vain woman, but maybe only because she couldn't afford to be.

I was pretty certain my self-discipline suited me, though I sometimes felt unsure of how others perceived me. I once heard a male associate at the firm describe me as an *ice queen*, which felt like what I'd been going for but also not. It's possible I looked like a person not quite at ease with themselves, someone who hadn't reached their final form. But I rarely looked at other adults and felt this way. Everyone seemed to have arrived at a terminus that made sense for them at the time.

In the end, the cop gave me a lift to a motel. I didn't immediately move to get out. By then, it really was late, the showy sunset blasting its pink trauma all over the landscape. The sky's upper deck was a dark, rich blue, its lower rungs golden orange. Gantry cranes at the distant port stood skeletal and Jurassic, the stars above like lights over a museum diorama.

There were four bars embroidered into the sleeve of the cop's uniform, and when I asked him what they meant, he said you got one for every five years on the force. A tear in the stiff leather of my seat revealed yellow foam beneath. I hadn't reported my missing gun, though it was legally acquired, though I had every right to report it. In fact it was my responsibility to do so.

"When's your shift over?"

"If I make an arrest, it's anyone's guess."

"Come by for a nightcap when you're done," I said, resting my hand on his forearm, just over the tenure stripes.

He could get my number from any of the forms I'd filled out that day. Being this brazen—not vulgar, just direct—sometimes backfired, but usually not. Usually the reaction was surprised interest.

He laughed. "Are you fucking with me?"

"What, you don't think I'm attractive?"

He shook his head and laughed again uncomfortably. He ran his left hand over his mustache, and I saw he wore no ring.

"Is this some kind of test? Some kinda sting?" he asked.

"No."

He leaned back and looked at me. I looked back blankly and steadily, not trying to sway him in either direction. I fucked aging or misshapen or mean men like him for a sense of escape, a vacation from myself and my standards, and for a kind of managed risk, like a controlled demolition. His rejection or acceptance made no difference to me.

He abruptly leaned over me. For a moment, I was pressed back by his weight, enveloped in the starch of his uniform, but all he did was open the passenger-side door and then withdraw back to the driver's seat, putting as much distance between my body and his as possible.

"Suit yourself," I said, and got out of the car.

5

The motel looked worse in the morning. Its three separate buildings with mildew-tinged facades circled a parking lot, crumbling like too-dry cake. The walls of my room were yellow as butter. The bedspread and drapes bore a chintzy gold-maroon pattern common to dollar-store fabrics. Even the tarp on the pool was offensive, a plain, desaturated brown. A chemical odor hung in the air, highway petrochemicals and marshland salt.

There was no comfortable sleeping position for my breasts, which ached. Sometimes sleeping poorly made me feel compensatorily more alert and alive. I rolled onto the grossly textured carpet and did fifty push-ups and two hundred crunches, just to prove I could. Something was wrong with the shower, the water too hard to lather, and I felt dirtier getting out than I did getting in. A mass of hair not my own swirled in the tub drain.

I found a car rental place within walking distance. I crossed the parking lot under the eyes of two women in Lycra dresses sharing a cigarette outside a room with drawn curtains. *Hooker problem.* I wondered if they thought I was competition.

The woman who checked me out of my room wore a blue salwar threaded with gold. A man, her father or much-older husband, sat in a plastic-covered armchair next to a light-starved potted plant, playing a cell phone game that involved digging a deep hole with a pixelated shovel at high speed. Maybe she dreamed of killing him. I'd lean over the counter and whisper in her ear my secret. I'd slowly build a network of women with the same unspoken wish until the whole nation was liberated of bad men.

Who was I kidding. He was probably a nice guy.

Dad was both worse than most people would imagine and also not. In the suffering sweepstakes, the catalog of human cruelty, what he did would barely register. Squalid little dramas like it played out every day in real life or on the Lifetime channel. This just made me angrier, like a teacher who learned a favorite pupil cheated on assignments, bullied the disabled kid, killed the class hamster, all the typical signs: disappointment that he didn't even put in the effort to be original, alarm that he'd ever been the favorite at all. I didn't enjoy being aggrieved, exactly, but neither did I relish words like *healing* and *trauma* and *survivor*. Blah blah blah, Daddy hurt me, boo-hoo, who cares. I'd rather pluck his eyeballs out with a fork and eat them jellied on toast than endure five minutes of therapy.

The sun was pinchingly bright and hangover-cruel. I began to walk to the rental place but realized that the narrow curb next to a four-lane highway was not exactly walkable. The hard heels of my shoes sounded obtrusively loud on the pavement. My gait was too fast and strident; a Manhattan pedestrian-pushing walk, a hopelessly out-of-place, I'm-important walk. I drew a sidelong stare from a squat, brown-skinned guy with a backpack who passed me on a creaky bicycle, riding against traffic on the shoulder. A semi honked at me suggestively. I looked down over the railing of a concrete bridge and saw that below there wasn't more road, as I'd expected, but a thin, crooked creek bed, more mud than water and strewn with plastic shopping bags that said THANK YOU! to the murk.

Leaning against the railing on that bridge was what my mother had euphemistically called *an urban outdoorsman* and what in college I would've called a *crustpunk. Crustpunk* seemed more apt than *bum*. He looked to be in his twenties, which implied a certain degree of choice and future. He had a long beard, probably grown to make him seem older, that led all the way up to his eyes and the tight pink-tan skin of someone who spent a lot of time in the sun. He looked like a Russian serf, like he'd eaten nothing but beets since birth, a maniacal fervor in his eyes like he thought he could cure children of hemophilia. On a piece of stained, floppy cardboard, he'd written *TRAVELING* in black ink.

I looked at him intently because he reminded me of my ex, but that was a long time ago; I was a different person now. I would've crossed the street to avoid him if I could, but there was no other side. I'd just have to plow ahead.

As I walked by, he said, "Fur?"

"Faux." I'm not sure why I bothered responding.

"So, plastic."

By then, I'd moved past him. I turned back to look at him. He had his palm bladed over his eyes. I couldn't tell if he was squinting from the sun or disgust or both.

"Get a job," I said, then added, redundantly, "Loser," and kept walking.

The car rental agent had one cloudy blue eye that was difficult not to stare at. He seemed likewise bemused by me and my interest in a one-way trip to California and my impeccable credit and bottomless cash reserves. I understand being well-off is a hateable quality, but it's true, and, having once been poor, I will not apologize for it. It didn't matter what I spent; I'd be dead soon anyway.

What an exciting idea. For years, once or twice a day—often during interminable compliance trainings—I'd pictured my skull exploding in raw flora of blood, brutal relief for thoughts that had been pressure-cooking in there for decades. I occasionally sought out gruesome snuff or quasi snuff online to be able to imagine this in more realistic detail. I felt queasy after each session, but also satisfied. The closest emotional analogue is how I felt as a child when I was permitted to resume normal relations with the world after being punished. Flirting with evil and being redeemed; sorry for being part of the world's imperfection but also perversely craving the chastised state. If this sounds Catholic, please know that mine was not a religious upbringing. It's just that being a child is, in essence, a religious experience.

"You don't have a Jaguar, do you?" I said.

"Jaguar?" The agent sounded confused, like I was asking for the literal exotic animal. I left the lot with a sedan in a shade close to flat ginger ale. It wasn't exactly the chariot I'd hoped for. I'd wanted Dad to understand from my car and my well-tended appearance that I was giving up a life of riches and beauty for the higher moral pursuit of vengeance, but maybe it was better this way. I needed him gone; everything else was just noise.

"That's a pretty color," lied the agent.

The interior of the car had a hot, clean chemical smell. The car had once been delivered from overseas in a shipping container but bore no distinctive markings of its journey. It came to me clean, storyless and context-free. It could have been manufactured in China or on the moon.

From there, I drove to a thrift store for replacement clothing for what had been lost. It was the closest option and also familiar, Mom and I having slunk into similar charity shops in my youth. I say *slunk* because Mom didn't like to be seen shopping there. When I got to college, I was surprised to meet people who thrifted out of preference, not poverty. The shame of it stuck with me, though I perversely enjoyed that shame, because it reminded me of her.

Midmorning on a weekday and the place was full of old women and the children they were charged with watching. Babies sat in drifting shopping carts while nannies and grandmothers appraised chipped dishware and lumpy, out-of-season sweaters. I chose jeans softened and stretched by another person's body, hiking boots with the dark imprints of someone else's soles on the inserts, a rayon dress and low heels, three sports bras, hoodies and T-shirts and a zip-up puffer jacket with a hole in the partly deflated sleeve. My choices were random; I didn't know what exactly I'd need.

I bought underwear at a pharmacy in the same strip mall as the thrift shop. The elastic threads were already unspooling from the waistband, and the cloth looked dingy before it was out of the package. Then I went to Dunkin Donuts and, though I'd taken my coffee black for years, ordered an iced sugary concoction taller than my torso. I changed in a restroom reeking of dextrose and palm oil and washed the bras with pearlescent pink hand soap in the sink and then pinched their straps through the car's windows to air-dry.

To get back to the highway, I had to backtrack slightly in the direction I'd come. The crustpunk was still there but now seated with his back to the lip of the bridge, his sign resting on his shins and his rolltop backpack on the ground next to him. I pulled over. In all my years of odd sex with odd people, I'd never encountered this particular kind of oddity. I was interested in adding to my collection. He was so slender and reedy, I figured I could take him in a fight, if it came to that. Besides, I've been a kid stuck on the side of the road before.

I rolled down the passenger-side window. The bra I'd hung up to dry fell into the footwell. He'd already sauntered over with his backpack hoisted onto his shoulders when he recognized me.

"You lost your fur," he said.

"Don't worry, it's in the trunk. Where are you going?"

"Where're you headed?"

"California."

He shifted his backpack to one shoulder and from the top

extracted this huge bound atlas thick with sticky notes and folded papers. The year on the cover said *1998*. He opened it and flipped it over to a dog-eared page covered in ballpoint scribbles.

"I'm trying to go here," he said, pointing with one exceptionally dirty finger.

"Is that west of here?"

"Yes."

"Then get in."

He hesitated, hand over the door handle. "You know how many times people have told me to get a job?"

"Probably about as often as I get comments on the fur," I said, though in truth, before then, it had only ever drawn compliments.

He got in. Once I was in an enclosed space with him, there was a faint funk, salty and mushroomlike, detectable under the VOC odor of the car's interior. I found it unexpectedly pleasant. He seemed not to notice the sports bras dangling around the car.

"John," he said, reaching across the console to shake my hand.

"Hester. How long've you been waiting for a ride?"

"Two days."

"That's a long time."

He shrugged. "I've had worse."

"Probably because you keep heckling people who offer to pick you up."

He knuckled the side of his nose apologetically but otherwise ignored my remark. "You're just driving straight a couple miles," he said.

I put the car into gear, and then we were on our way. I saw the man on the bicycle again, heading in the opposite direction, handlebars now laden with plastic bags.

"What are you doing in these parts?" John asked.

"How do you mean?"

"Like, in this shithole."

His use of that word surprised me. It sounded like me before

I learned to choose my words more carefully. Before an older, wiser lawyer, a partner at the old firm, told me that I had to stop talking like I was poor. That in my chosen profession, I needed to sound like money, whose vernacular was just as ugly but more refined.

This lawyer was also the one who taught me how to shoot. But I'm not at that part of the story yet.

"You don't think I'm from around here?" I asked.

"With that fur thing? I don't think so."

I took a sip of my coffee, which had started to turn to watery milk soup. "No, I'm not from around here."

"Well, neither am I. I've been on the road a long time. Working on this project."

"Oh?" I said, eyebrows raised, fully expecting him to be a flat-earther or a Marxist alien hunter or some other variety of roadside nutjob.

"I've been going around visiting Superfund sites. Taking photos, poking around."

"Uh. Why?"

He continued without acknowledging my question. "I just came from this place. Drums of chemicals stored right on the river. Acids, mercury, arsenic, you name it. All those unstable compounds started a fire so big it released a fifteen-mile cloud of ash. This was in the eighties. They let the fire burn down and then hid all the contaminated soil under a slurry wall. The road leading up to it now is petroleum sites and oil terminals for refining or asphalt, and then it ends at a dead bridge and there's this tiny, normal-looking house down there, like with a hound on the porch and an old lady in a rocking chair and everything. I asked her for a glass of water, and she gave me Dasani. How do you feel about the government? I mean, where are you politically?"

I blinked at his abrupt pivot. "Mostly indifferent. And tired."

I expected him to harangue me, but he just said, "I'm tired too."

"That's what your project is about? The government?"

"I'd say it's more about capitalism and its attendant degradation of our ecosystem, but insofar as our government facilitates that, yes, it's about the government."

"Uh-huh," I said, skeptical. "And you hitch?"

"I did the math. I've saved .33 metric tons of greenhouse gas since I've been on the road."

"That doesn't sound like much."

"Picture a football field," he said, gesturing with his hands out at either side. "Picture a big balloon from the goal line to the ten-yard line. That's one ton."

"I don't watch football."

He brought his hands down. "Neither do I," he said, like it had just occurred to him.

"You don't have money?"

"A little. Sometimes I beg."

I thought he was an idiot. Surely any suffering he put himself through was an elective romanticization of a life some people were forced into. His mannerisms were broader than mine, the gestures of a person in a large, wide-open country with room to spread. He seemed to belong to an earlier America, when men hopped trains to meet their Western destinies and hobos slept in barns unmolested by teenagers with cell phones and bad intentions.

"How old are you?" I asked.

He squinted at me. "Well over twenty-one. What's it to you?"

"The way you say that makes me think you're younger."

"Well, I'm not."

"It's nothing to me. You just sound like a kid."

"What does a kid sound like?"

I shrugged, slowing to let a speeding driver with pumping bass pass us. "Forget it," I said. I regretted my impulse to pick him up. I didn't want to fuck some scrawny, unwashed twenty-six-year-old with ideas. I continued, "Where am I dropping you? Let me put it into the GPS."

"Don't use that. I mean, you can, but it won't be much help. It's not like the place has an address."

"Then give me a cross street or the coordinates. Or whatever, fine, we can do it the old-fashioned way if you navigate."

Every time he moved, shards of mud shook off his boots. He reopened his atlas, which he'd never fully put away, spreading it over his knees like a blanket. This seemed another young-person quality, an affected desire for the impractically old. Maybe that was why he'd accepted my offer of a ride: I was vintage.

"You're one of those tinfoil hat types, aren't you? Paranoid about being tracked by the government," I said.

"I'm not, but for the record, it's not *that* paranoid to think that. You're going to want to make a left here."

Our interaction bothered me. He was getting the wrong impression of me, thinking I was the kind of loose, softheaded, messy person who picked up strangers habitually and unthinkingly, the way you pick up venereal diseases. Truthfully, I was that kind of person—maybe not softheaded, but I'd gotten chlamydia more than once—and he didn't need to know that. Worse, I couldn't explain why I cared.

I flicked on the radio.

She got screwed, I mean truly. Her parents were getting death threats, and she got fired from her job. And it's like, if that's what she wants, if she wants to go and post that online, who cares? Who are these people to care? Who are these people who think their feelings matter?

I turned the volume up high, almost painfully so.

6

The place John wanted to go to was forty miles off, an hour in the car but more than a day on foot. Beyond the occasional directive, he was dead quiet for the rest of the ride, any attempt at conversation eclipsed by my radio.

The place he wanted to go was at the end of a one-way road that turned to foam-pale gravel before dead-ending at a few concrete barriers. A chain-link fence at the side of the road separated us from a grassy hill and knobby, short shrubs that were possibly aspiring trees. A sign zip-tied to the fence said NO TRESPASSING. Off in the distance lurked a power station or a groundwater treatment plant, some municipal service like that.

"There's nothing here," I said.

"Yeah. What's eerie is that the badness is hidden. And it kind of has to be. But it makes it hard to see what's going on. The place that used to be here kept arsenic salts in uncovered piles that seeped into groundwater. Worst-case scenario was four cases of cancer for every thousand exposed at the worksite, one in a thousand who lived nearby."

Those numbers didn't sound bad to me. Not good but not catastrophic; nothing that couldn't be explained to a judge or six civil jurors. Of course it was always catastrophic to be the one or four in a thousand. Maybe I'd lived in a toxic plume without knowing it. Maybe the plume had caused an error in my cells, planted a seed that grew into a tumor named Beryl. Maybe my childhood home had been an isle afloat in a sea of poison. It'd be funny, almost, if everything that happened in that house had been a result of chemical porphyria.

While I was thinking, John had busied himself with removing a smaller back sling from his bag. He unzipped it to reveal a camera. I'd never had an artistic hobby of any description and couldn't tell a shutter from a lens, but I thought it was a pretty object, all licorice-black body and silver-capped angles.

John had continued his monologue: ". . . a lot of plant life in the surrounding area. The owner was found shot to death. I think they said it was murder, but they never solved it."

"Will you? Solve it, I mean."

"No. What?"

If I were him, I'd have been more interested in the murder than in the landscape, but maybe that was just my macabre cast of mind.

He turned to me and said, "Well. Thanks."

"Do they have security, usually? At these places."

"Occasionally."

"Like, booby traps? Alarms?"

Once in law school, I'd read a case where a farmer rigged up a shotgun in an abandoned barn and blasted the legs off a trespasser. You need a good memory in law school—case names, years, precedents—and I found vivid imagery more helpful than any mnemonic device. That one I recalled as blood seeping through old hay and gapped floorboards.

"Alarms sometimes. Booby traps? Not yet. Occasionally cameras or guards or other employees."

"I'm coming with you," I said. I'd spent most of my career defending companies like the one John described. I'd never actually been to one of the affected sites, never seen what lay on the other side of the fence.

"I'd actually prefer if you didn't."

"What, I'm good for a free ride, that's all?"

"That's not what I mean."

"Don't worry. I can handle myself. I won't cramp your style."

I was an educated and experienced white woman. My life was insulated from interference, police or otherwise. I tended to discount the likelihood of problems, at least ones from which I could not easily extract myself.

I pulled over to the right, where some overhanging boughs created enough cover that it was unlikely the car would be seen. We got out. The fence needed to be scaled. I was limber and fit for my age—the work of a well-compensated personal trainer with a doctorate in kinesiology, which I hadn't known was a career possibility until I hired him—but jumping felt juvenile, delinquent, foolish in a way that was, at this advanced stage of my life, not in keeping with my idea of myself. Still, once John was over to the other side, I hooked my fingers into the links and jammed my toes into the gaps with little thought for propriety.

We kicked our way through a carpet of dried orange pine needles and crisscrossing surface roots until the noise of the highway faded, the hum of engines and wheels replaced by wind. Through a break in the trees, I saw a pale strip of sand leading out to sky-blue water. I had the sensation that I was looking at an image cut perfectly from an advertisement for a tropical vacation and pasted onto a suburban billboard. The water was unnaturally, flawlessly round.

Dad had been obsessed with the story of Giotto's perfect circle, drawn freehand to impress the Pope. The simpler and purer the object, the more elusive it becomes. His sketchbooks were full of his attempts. His obsession with clean circles and other geometric forms did not reflect any greater orderliness; his studio was a mess of turpentine-soaked rags and brushes left too long in jars of dirty water. While he plodded after genius, making no financial contributions whatsoever, Mom worked and tried to keep house. He aspired to culture, but he didn't have to go to school and confront the social reality of being poor the way I did. He didn't see that we were backwoods trash.

John took a few pictures. Birds I couldn't identify chirped.

"What is this?" I asked.

"A blue hole."

"I can see that."

"Abandoned sand mines filled with water. They're all over here. Teenagers sometimes drown in them."

"Why's it so blue?"

I'd asked Dad why the sky was blue once, that classic kid question, and he'd pretended not to know what I was talking about. Had insisted it was green.

"Nothing lives in it. No algae. Nothing to make it murky. Look." John grabbed my shoulder and guided me closer to where he stood at the water's edge. He was so gentle I forgot to protest his hand on me. I was particular about who touched me, depending on the type of touch.

The beach was narrow, more shelf than shore. I looked where he was pointing and beneath the surface could see the rusted-out husk of an old VW Beetle, its orange darker for being surrounded by such pure blue. I imagined the stripped Jaguar in there, hollow-framed and adrift. I couldn't believe after so many years of carrying Mom's remains close I had lost them so easily and so quickly. I should have had them made into jewelry, something I kept on my person.

"How deep are these?" I asked.

"Deep. Who knows what all's at the bottom. People dump things here."

"Bodies."

"Don't be morbid."

He returned to the trees, his feet clearing a path through the duff. I stuck my tongue out at his retreating back. I hadn't done that in years and felt briefly alarmed at myself. I followed him to a strip of cleared land that stood in sharp contrast to the knotted trees and shrubs located on either side. The loamy soil seemed reluctant to support our weight.

"The facility was demolished and the leaky lagoons filled years ago," John said. "It's still technically being monitored. I bet if you tested this soil, though . . ."

He trailed off. His camera's mechanism made an arthritic, grinding pop-and-release sound. The earth seemed to bear no wound from where it had been injured. It looked ordinary unless you knew better. I didn't understand what John hoped to capture on film when there was neither obvious beauty nor evidence of wrongdoing. His portfolio must have largely been pictures of dirt.

I turned back to face where I thought the road was, idling away from him. I could hear the skitter-wheeze of trucks again. I came up short in front of a raccoon carcass, curled on its side and deflated, fur dark and eyes cloudy. I used to see roadkill often where I grew up, garter snakes squiggled to match crack-sealed pavement, possums splatted and sprawled, a skunk sacrificing its final stink. I was often able to observe them up close, my father having kicked me out of the car and told me to walk.

I heard a shout.

I looked up to see John wave his arms at me, then take off running with a gait like a glitchy video game character. I saw what spooked him shortly afterward: A man was approaching, his orange safety vest bright against the muted landscape.

I thought about running. I thought about tearing through the pines, sap-coated needles sticking to my clothes and cheeks. It would be difficult to run on the soft soil here, my calves burning and my one bad foot aching, my ears attuned to the heavy boots behind me crushing the sprouts of spring.

A memory, sudden, forgotten, called up from some abandoned well, of running as a child, sharp, reedy grass and brambles whipping the skin on my legs and leaving a dozen tiny, shallow cuts dotted with jewels of blood. In that memory, my vision was unsteady and carbonated like a shaken bottle, every breath torn violently from me.

I wasn't going to run. Not because it didn't make sense to, and not because I couldn't outrun this man, who looked like he'd secreted several sandwiches up that safety vest for later. I wasn't going to run simply because it wasn't my style.

"You're not supposed to be here," he said once he was within spitting distance. "You didn't see all the fences around?"

I shook my head credulously. "My dog slipped his leash and went in a gap in the fence. I just adopted him, and he's so skittish. The shelter said he was abused, it's really sad. Anyway, I've been running all over looking for him. He's a pit mix, brindle coat, about this big, have you seen him?"

I've never owned a dog. Or a cat. Not even carnival fish. The closest I came to having a pet as a child was a wood frog that took up residence in the shady leaf litter under our deck one winter. Those things have antifreeze for blood.

The man was probably in his fifties, with skin the texture of dense bread. I liked looking at older people because you got to puzzle out what they were like when they were younger and how that might've shaped their lives. Not biographical physiognomy, just small things, like if you got teased for having eyelashes too thick for a boy or had a nose you wanted to fix but could never afford to. You didn't have to be good at this game to enjoy it.

He looked at me for a moment. "What happened to your friend?"

"Who?"

"The guy who ran."

"No idea. He's not my friend," I said, which was true enough.

"You're telling me that after two years working this site without incident, I suddenly got two complete strangers in a single morning?"

"So you haven't seen my dog?" His disbelieving half smile only made me dig in harder. "It's not funny, sir. He could be hit by a car or mauled by a bear. He's cute, but he's not smart."

"I haven't seen a dog. You need to leave. This is US property."

He escorted me off the premises via a sandy, unpaved drive that led to an unpadlocked gate. I had the distinct sensation the man was a figment of my imagination, a compilation of every hideous man I'd ever slept with. My greatest hits. John was a figment too. I was in fact dozing in one of the armchairs in my office, with Magda about to bring me a cup of coffee pressed from a plastic pod.

"Please keep an eye out," I told him. "I'll give you my number, and you can call me if you see him?" I recited the landline number to my childhood home, which he didn't write down.

At first I was unsure where I was relative to the car. I turned in the general direction I thought I'd come from and walked along the side of the road until I glimpsed the blue hole through the dense trunks of pine. I breathed in deeply. City living had made me forget the comforting scent of soil and leaf rot and dew-damp grass, worms hard at work underneath making new earth. Even in parks, you're only ever so far from asphalt.

The car was still there when I returned. John was not. It was not even noon.

It had been stupid of me to pick him up, to follow him. Beryl was conspiring against me all the time. Maybe I had even less time than I thought. Maybe Dad would choke on a chicken bone or have a heart attack on the toilet, time eclipsing my plan.

I wouldn't necessarily be disappointed at that outcome. I just didn't trust the universe to provide that kind of justice.

7

I drove without stopping for hours. I passed the baby blue Ben Franklin Bridge, I passed Petty Island and Strawberry Mansion; I passed metal and alloy powder factories and parking garages and tollbooths run by robots and highway barriers aproned in kudzu. Beyond a certain point, everything smelled like manure. A general menace was in the air. An eighteen-wheeler passed me with mudflaps that read PASSING ON THE LEFT, SUICIDE TO THE RIGHT. Another that said HEY STUPID. Faded ribbons threaded into overpass fences spelled out the names of sports teams or couples long since broken up. The farther from Manhattan I got, the farther from my recent existence, the better I felt.

As these immigrants are crashing over the border, you know what they're singing? "Do You Know the Way to San Jose."

Not going to go down that way with that one. On to the next caller. And by the way, Dionne Warwick is just a knockoff Gladys Knight.

And Gladys Knight is just a knockoff Aretha Franklin.

That's right. Nothing original in this world.

I stopped for the night in Pittsburgh. This was not accidental. This was the city where my ex lived. He'd become a chef. The news described the restaurant he worked in as a world-class establishment that was going to help elevate Pittsburgh to a true cosmopolis. I'd never visited the city before but found the reports of its revitalization overblown. Downtown was a tiny brutalist box. Its outskirts were overgrown empty lots sandwiched between small buildings with split-shake siding or weathered brick or stone cladding. Delis advertised cigarettes sold at state-minimum prices. Two senior citizens sat on rollators outside the Byzantine cathedral where Warhol had been eulogized with sprays of white roses and asparagus fern.

I parked in a garage and clambered into the back seat to change clumsily into one of the thrifted dresses, hanging spare clothes in the windows for privacy. I gave myself a whore's bath with a packet of premoistened towelettes and applied orange-red lipstick. Most of my lipsticks had been my mother's; she had several that she never used. They showed no beading or fading, and though they smelled of must and had a claylike texture I had to augment with balm, I never had a bad reaction to them.

I was apparently early for the dinner crowd. The dining room was empty but for two tables. At one, a pair of old men in expensive suits held snifters of brandy and fussed with a slate of artisanal cheeses. At the other, a woman sat alone, like me. She was barefoot under the table, taking a break from her four-inch Manolos, the kind with crystal buckles over the silk toes.

At some point I'd bitten the inside of my mouth and kept running my tongue compulsively over the ribbon of swollen skin. The maître d' hardly looked at my clothes but nonetheless exuded disdain for them. A busboy poured water into a glass that immediately clouded with condensation. I pretended to regard the menu, ordered the second-most expensive dish from the list of entrées, asked for directions to the ladies', and then, when I reached its door, turned sharply and walked into the kitchen.

The space was arranged to maximize efficiency, with long rows of counters, few walls, and open chrome wire shelves. Everything was visible, surveillable, except where clouded with hot white steam. A black-shirted waiter slid behind and around me as if

I weren't there. On a table near the back were several denuded rabbits, pink as kissed mouths, next to a huge stockpot. This was the restaurant's signature dish; the rabbits were procured by local farmers, then marinated for forty-eight hours in herbs and oil, then cooked in broth over low heat for another six.

In front of the rabbits stood Caleb. This was my ex. If I hadn't found him in that kitchen, I would've gone to his apartment, which I'd found on LexisNexis, or to the office of the lawyer who several years ago had helped him file for bankruptcy, records of which I'd also found on LexisNexis. He'd acquired more tattoos and scars, and the contours of his face had rutted and sagged. He hadn't been clean-shaven when I knew him and now he looked vulnerable, overexposed. He drank from a jar on the counter that contained clear liquid, water or vodka, I wasn't sure.

"Caleb," I said.

He looked up slowly, like he could avoid being recognized if he drew it out as long as possible.

He said something under his breath.

"What?" I said. Other sounds seemed momentarily distorted, some muted, others loud: the line cooks' Spanish, the hiss of steam, the pert chop of a knife against a butcher's block.

We stood staring at each other for a moment. I stifled an impulse to smile.

The maître d' came to escort me back to my table in the cooing, capitulating tones one uses to coax the mentally unstable. When he tried to hold my elbow to steer me, I pulled it away and hissed, as if it were a threat, "I am going to spend two thousand dollars."

8

Until my junior year of college, which was when I became academically serious, I used to go to parties, drink from a bottle I brought myself, and find a boy to mishandle in the dark. This was my education. I didn't much likc school. I thought my professors were coddling and condescending to me, shepherding me into a normative vision of adulthood. I never claimed to know everything but sure acted like I did.

Everything except men. I wanted to learn about them. How they tied ties, talked about women when women weren't around, fought, sweat, stank.

I'd avoided boys until that point. My only friend in high school, May, had once told me a boy liked me. I didn't believe her, but even if I had, I would've said that poor kid was mistaken. I was preoccupied with Mom's illness; when I thought of boys at all, it was only to hate them. I thought I'd be like that forever, but in college my ideas of celibacy predictably backfired, the way deprivation always leads to excess. I reframed my exploits to myself as enemy reconnaissance. I wished I were gay, asexual, a monist, anything other than what I was, which was very straight and very, very lonely.

I was studying politics for whatever reason, and the boys—technically men—drawn to that subject were either insufferable nerds who thought life was a game of chess or broad-shouldered, white-bread jocks destined for actual political office. Kid Kissingers, baby Bushes. I don't think they took much notice of me except as a representative of my sex. The girls in this circle could tell I didn't belong, that I'd never so much as seen a lacrosse field or owned even fake pearls. For the boys, it was like I'd found a flavor their palates couldn't detect and therefore couldn't reject. All it took was a padded bra, picking a few arbitrary opinions to defend in an amusing way, and never talking about my family.

They all moved in the same fashion, the mechanical pushing of the hips, beery grins and groping hands and vague eyes, always dirty and quick and stupid, and they hardly spoke, or if they did, what they said was unmemorable. I couldn't recall any individual face, only an amalgamation, a type. This cut both ways; I could easily imagine any of them describing their experience of me in similar terms. I thought a lot about Mom in those days and how she'd managed to find my father in a similar environment, to pick him from the pulsing masses, and how she'd gotten so singularly unlucky in her choice. Her death was more recent then, the spring of my senior year of high school, so I was thinking about her a lot anyway.

Despite my promiscuity, it still took me a long time to lose my virginity. At the time, I thought the delay was just circumstantial: the boys too drunk, the rooms too crowded, the beds too full of vomit. In retrospect I think I was more sentimental than I wanted to admit. Like every other girl, I wanted my first to be special.

I'd already blown off Caleb as another idiot. I saw him in the bare-bulbed basement of a house party, recognized him from my history seminar, and approached him. The band was on the grunge–death metal spectrum. I hated the noise but appreciated the mood. We nodded and shuffled our feet, and whenever the band approached the chorus, Caleb would thrash around like he'd been electrocuted.

He laughed when I tried to kiss him between sets, before we'd even said a word to each other. He said, "What are you doing? Come smoke with me."

This marked the first time a man had not unquestioningly gone along with me. He was the only person who seemed like he knew what I was up to and found the performance entertaining, mockable and watchable like a campy movie. He thought I took myself too seriously, and he was one hundred percent correct.

I smoked several cigarettes with him, proud of myself for never coughing and for keeping pace with him though I didn't smoke and had no idea if I was inhaling correctly. I felt my pretense restored the balance of power, like I was misleading him about the kind of person I was. I often felt that the only way a person would engage with me was through a ruse or trap.

Later he fucked me in the off-campus house where he lived with dozens of roommates. His room was separated from his neighbor's by a tacked-up Rainbow Brite–themed fleece blanket. I bled on his sheets, a small stain in a near-perfect circle. When I woke up, he was still asleep, lying on his stomach and wrapped up poorly in the thin comforter so that one cheek of his ass was exposed. I admired the blot of blood for a moment in the sunlight angling in through the porthole window. I wormed a cigarette loose from a pack where it had fallen with his pants to the floor, lit it, and then pressed the cherry to the sheet until the telltale spot burned away.

I fled at seven in the morning. I'd lost my keys, so I sat on a park bench, waiting for it to be late enough that I could pester someone from my dorm to let me in. I watched all the healthy children with their parents on the Little League field, feeling proud and filthy and vaguely ill. I had an impulse to text May, the only living person who might be interested in my news, but by then we were no longer friends, and besides, it was not a story that made me look especially cool.

I worked hard to never see him again in a social setting but not hard enough. I was sitting on a plastic chair on the porch outside another house party, smoking because I'd acquired a taste for it. We often sat on porches and stoops, waiting for drunk drivers to smash into cars parked at the curb, which was one of the only forms of entertainment in the town. Caleb was leaning against the porch railing, tallboy in hand, maybe intentionally blocking my view of the street. Someone inside was playing a badly out-of-tune piano. Everyone but me was in a band then or about to start one.

There was an argument about a movie by some male director everyone thought was a genius. I was being contrarian and obstinate and annoying. I was saying that the director was gimmicky, a magician for little boys. I was correct but argued the point with more conviction than I felt. This was a tactic I shamelessly used to get boys to pay attention to me. Some were surprised by the novelty of a girl asserting themselves in the strident, half-informed way of men. Some thought this signified brilliance where there in fact was none, a narcissistic glint that passed for genuine shine.

Not Caleb. Caleb leaned down, one hand on either of the chair's armrests, boxing me in, and pressed forward until his face was scant inches from mine. My breath rippled his mustache. He was visibly drunk and visibly angry.

"The fuck," he said, "is your problem?"

I could see the perfect green ring around his fattened pupil, a forest growing from a black planet. I was afraid of him and knew it'd be death to show it.

Without blinking, I blew smoke back into his face, turned to another boy sitting on the porch, and said, "Put your friend here on a chain."

Caleb drew back and walked into the house. The porch went quiet, no one willing to risk touching the blown fuse of our conversation, but eventually a drunk did hit a car out front, and the remaining boys began cheering, and that restored a veneer of normal chaos.

Later I found Caleb brooding in the backyard under a tree, green empties rolling in the dirt beside him. I pulled a bottle from his fingers and took a sip and then held out a cigarette.

"Friends?" I asked. It was a dead-stupid approach, but I couldn't think of any better. I felt oddly historical, exchanging tobacco like colonizer and colonized.

He nodded and accepted the cigarette directly into his mouth like a quarter into a slot machine. Around the filter, he said, "Long as you don't destroy my mattress again, pyro."

The next morning, we rolled into that seminar together, something something policies in postwar Europe something, deeply hungover or possibly still drunk. I'd suggested ditching, but Caleb insisted on going. He seemed to think it'd be funny. Grubby and ill-used, we kept our hoodies pulled up and desks tucked into the corner. I had mascara smudges under my eyes and faint bruises on my hips. I'd loaded up my cafeteria coffee with cream and sugar, the way Mom used to make it.

The professor was even later than us. One pretty, well-rested-looking girl chatting with a friend said, apropos of our assigned reading, that if she'd been a German during World War II, she never would've been a Nazi.

"Why?" asked the friend. "Are you Jewish?"

"No," she said. "I'm just incapable of cruelty."

From across the room, Caleb laughed so loudly I jumped. Coffee spilled on my notebook, smearing the only words I'd written during the last lecture, *division of labor.*

"You definitely would've," he said. "You would've been Ilse Koch."

The pretty girl frowned. "I'm sorry, but like, who are you?" she asked, and then the professor showed up.

Caleb was a dirtbag on purpose, but I thought knowing it

made it fine. He trimmed his own mustache with uneven results and gave himself horrible stick-and-poke tattoos as a party trick and wrestled with his friends in the backyard. He often missed classes and never bought assigned books but read widely and randomly—the comedies of Terence, the entirety of *The Thousand and One Nights*, Ronald Reagan's autobiography—and would sometimes dictate amusing passages to me. He often went shirtless even in cold weather. He was drunk from sunup to sunup. Neither of us went home for summer or winter breaks. Like me, he hated his dad, whom he called his "old man," and his mother was dead, like mine. I thought we'd bond about this, but, as he put it, having a dead mother isn't an affirmative quality. It says nothing about you. Sooner or later, everyone's got a dead mom.

I told him more than once that I was going to kill my father, and he must've thought it was just late-night shit-talking, because every time, he tapped his drink against mine and said, "Hell yeah, me fuckin' too."

He supported himself not only as a work-study dining hall dishwasher but also as dishwasher in an overpriced Mediterranean restaurant that was popular with visiting parents. He called me bourgeois because my work-study job involved doing data entry for a sociology professor and joked about sending me to hard labor camp because my hands were too soft. I never told him I was paying for the bulk of my education out of the proceeds of my mother's life insurance and the sale of the house, instead pretending I too was deeply in debt. He got me a waitressing job at his restaurant one summer, but I was awful at it, dismissive and forgetful and quickly fired. I claimed I'd gotten another job at a bar he'd permanently been banned from after puking on the blue baize pool table but really just went to the library every day and read for six hours straight, coasting on my death money until the semester picked back up again.

Money wasn't our only problem. He had an ex who sang in

multiple basement bands. I met her once, smelled her stupid rose-petal joints and saw her stupid moppy hair, which was several colors at once, creamy pink and hay-thatch blond on top, brown and lizard-sick green on the stupid underdye. While she was speaking to me, she announced loudly that she had to pee and asked me to hold her beer. I did, but she never returned, stranding me with a lukewarm half-drunk can. I didn't like feeling I'd been bested.

"Don't take it personal. She does it all the time," said Caleb.

"It's a good way to get out of a conversation."

"You know, I thought that, but I think she really forgets who she was talking to before. She's mad genuine. She's like the most genuine person I've ever met."

"Yeah, okay," I said, doubtful. God, did I hate her. To torture myself, I sometimes pictured the album cover they'd have as a successful folk-punk outfit. I could never be in a band with Caleb; I had no talent.

"I'm not doing her justice," said Caleb. "You know why she broke up with me? 'Cause a bird built a nest on her windowsill, and the chirping woke us up at four a.m., so I moved it to the backyard. She thought the mom wouldn't touch the nest again. Like I'd contaminated it. I felt fucking terrible about it, too. She's so good at crying."

"Like, she looks pretty when she cries?"

"That and like, it suits her whole ethic."

It wasn't like I'd been planning on crying in front of him, but then I definitely couldn't, not with that kind of competition. I wasn't as pretty as her under the best of circumstances.

Caleb kept talking. "Did I tell you about the time she tried to free all the lobsters from the tank at Price Chopper?"

"You're better off without her," I said, pretending I didn't get her appeal, that I didn't envy her convictions, her wild stories. I leaned over Caleb to reach his side of the bed where our drinks stood in cold columns on the floor, the hairs of my unshaven armpit brushing his. "Most people are better off without each other.

You'd be better off without me. People are better off being by themselves, but they can't stand it."

Caleb laughed and nipped my arm. "Okay, Camus."

I punched him in the ribs with my free hand.

"It's so cute when you act all hard and edgy and dark or whatever. You're like three feet tall," he said, giggling.

I was fairly tall for a woman, especially in comparison to his ex, but I'd always be shorter than him. I punched him again, and he intercepted the drink in my other hand, gripping my wrist in such a way that it would surely bruise. He was sloppily rough in bed, pinning me down and smacking my cheeks or biting my breasts or yanking my hair. I'd fight back, writhing and throwing elbows to clock his chin, the rough stubble there leaving stinging red marks. I didn't want him to think I was a dilettante about pain. I think he hated women a little, resented the hold we collectively had over him, but I liked his brand of misogyny. It was artifactual, mostly safe behind glass like a museum display, and besides, it was rare to find someone as angry as I was. Other men have tried that kind of thing with me, feebly choking or pulling to imitate what they've seen in pornography like boys emulating action heroes, and I've found it tiresome.

I get how we sounded conceited. Like we thought our studied filth gave us a more direct line to truth than other people had. Every time I emerged from his bedroom, I felt like I was stumbling out of some cave of animal experience inaccessible to others. But mostly we were just having a good time. Lots of kids think they're different from, and better than, ordinary people, exempt from the basic rules of social pleasantness that bind everyone else. Being messy is a privilege of youth.

We fooled around on and off for years, never giving a name to what we were. We both catted around but always returned to each other. I didn't care who he fucked as long as it wasn't the ex, but that wasn't a real risk; she'd started calling him *toxic* and avoiding his parties. For a while after I graduated, we lived together, sharing a room in a detached three-story teeming with his friends and a potpourri of post-college hangers-on. Caleb kept pushing back his degree date, first to five years, then six. I was in law school already, straight after college, because I hated math but wanted to make money, my accounts having rapidly dwindled. I was trying to study in what was essentially a halfway house, still drinking but less and growing increasingly irritated with the never-done dishes, the basement shows that shook plaster dust off the walls in the slope-ceilinged attic where we slept, the browned apple core and used tampon abandoned in the shared shower, the cloud of black mold that grew next to the couch in the unlivable living room like an uninvited guest who wouldn't go home.

I was only ever halfway in that scene anyway, a tourist. Going to law school was like a dirty secret. No one in those circles believed you became a lawyer to fight the power, Dellinger et al. notwithstanding. Rich punks thought you became one to achieve suburban tameness, like their parents; poor punks thought you became one out of some perverse will to narc.

Thanks to his association with me, Caleb's punk bona fides were called into question. At first he said fuck 'em, what do they know, but it ate at him, and I could tell. We fought for real, without playfulness, first about school and eventually about everything, the bickering spreading like that black mold. I thought he was magnifying problems because of unhappinesses that had nothing to do with me. I thought everyone eventually grew up to want the kind of money that would enable them to escape their past. I thought I could bring him around to my point of view through reason alone, a classic lawyer mistake.

Our last argument was about how I wouldn't go to a protest. I don't remember what it was about; every month brought a new injustice, a new cause for show covers to be donated to, a new slogan to scribble on bathroom stalls. I'd been to a few with him before, plodding along beside him with my hands in my pockets, refusing to chant.

"I have an exam," I said, gesturing to the open contracts textbook in my lap, the notebooks and highlighters strewn next to me on our shared bed. This was true.

"Bullshit. You just don't want to go," he said. This was also true. He stood above me in his boots, ready to go. "You don't stand in solidarity with anything. You don't care about anyone but yourself anymore. You're a sellout."

"I can't sell out, I never promised anything."

He left, clomping down the stairs from our shared room, saying in a taunting singsong, "Soulless, soulless, you're absolutely soulless."

He got arrested that night. It was just disorderly conduct, criminal mischief, open container, four hours in a cell before leaving with a desk appearance ticket: nothing too ruinous or dramatic. Still, I sensed he'd done it on purpose, just to demonstrate how different we were. He went right back out partying after his release and came home thirty-six hours later with a yellowing bruise on his cheek. He acted normal, deflecting my questions with his usual drunken nonsense, jokes and feints. I let myself relax. He'd come back.

He disappeared for good shortly before his own much-delayed graduation. I refused to look hard for him at the time, unwilling to admit how attached I'd become. I didn't ask his friends, not wanting them to know I didn't know, and besides, I didn't much like them without him around as a filter. I'll admit I was intimidated by them. I restricted myself to a single, drunken text to confirm he was alive. It took him three days to respond. A month later, I was out of that house and living in a tidy apartment with three fellow 1Ls, all girls who'd been skiing before and had majored in international relations.

Later I heard he'd become a line cook at a restaurant so fancy half the staff had humanities degrees. That made sense to me. The speed and danger of a kitchen seemed to suit him. Faint ashen burns along the insides of his wrists, slices of knuckle lost to a mandoline, sips from a flask to steady hands that shook when he labeled prep containers. And all those years later, there he was.

9

Caleb came out of the kitchen to join me. The restaurant had become crowded, and his chef's whites drew stares from neighboring tables. I liked thinking that his absence from the kitchen was ruining everyone else's meal, that everything would go out cold and late because he was with me. It seemed selfish and romantic.

"Good?" he asked of the whole fish baked in herbed salt-crust and bottle of Montrachet I'd ordered.

"Very." Alcohol worsened the ache in my breasts. So did coffee or eating too much. I'd deliberately thrifted bras a size too small because I needed the compression.

"Have to ask. How'd you find me?"

This was a more polite phrasing of the question I knew he wanted to ask, which was *What the fuck are you doing here?* This is how I knew he'd done some growing up.

"I'm a sleuth." It only took light research. People shouldn't be surprised they're so findable anymore once you think to look for them. I continued, "I'm in town on business. Thought I'd see what became of you."

"It's been, what," he said, rolling his fingers on the table, "eighteen years?"

When he put it that way, it sounded more drastic than it felt. I could've had and raised a child during that time. Was that a fear that occurred to him now, that I was coming to deliver this news or ask for his help? Letting him think that seemed fun, like the plot of a ridiculous movie I'd never watch. We looked older and sadder, our structures listing like houses on sinking ground. I briefly wished I hadn't done this, hadn't sullied our memories together. Regret came with a force that seemed to destabilize the room, glasses vibrating and cutlery shaking. It passed.

"Seventeen," I said, "but who's counting."

He was still a long way from closing. I paid my bill, tipping an insane, viral-story amount of money, bringing my total bill above what I'd promised the maître d'. I went outside and walked around beneath trees that smelled like semen until he emerged. Waiting for him made me feel like a lovelorn sailor's wife, antique and obliquely erotic.

He walked me to his apartment. It was a long walk. All the trees on his street leaned north, lurching away from the shade of the buildings and toward the sun. The back half of a wooden piano with half its hammers missing waited at the curb for garbagemen to haul it away. The stairs leading to his apartment were exterior to the building, cramped and dark and made of peeling planks.

"You have so many plants," I said, fondling the stalk of a spider plant by his front door. Herbs hunched on windowsills. Through the ajar door of a coat closet I could see grow lights, probably for weed. A bicycle hung on a rack above the sofa threateningly. His space looked pleasant but generic, emblematic of the choices people of a certain generation made when they didn't have a lot of money to choose with. I was probably an asshole for thinking this, but it was too late; I'd already thought it.

"Chef's children," he said, handing me a can. The cold aluminum shocked my palm. I'd expected beer, but it was plain seltzer. I could imagine the predictable backstory to that choice.

"You live alone?" I asked.

"For now. My girlfriend wants me to go to counseling. She might come back if it, you know. Works."

"So you're going?"

"Yeah. She says I have a lot of repressed anger."

"I never thought it was that repressed." I was asserting an authority, a knowledge of him, that I no longer really had, and we both knew it, but for some reason I was still surprised when he didn't laugh.

"Why did you come here, Hester?"

It had been a long time since someone had spoken my name. It had a strange effect on me, like I'd forgotten myself and someone had to remind me. I tapped my fingernails on the unopened can.

"You disappeared," I said. "So I wondered."

"For eighteen years?"

"Seventeen."

I expected him to come to me again like he did on the porch, leaning in to demand to know what was wrong with me. It was a good question; I wanted the answer, too. Instead he kept his distance, sitting across from me on the windowsill with his hands in his pockets. He extracted one and fiddled with the blinds, peering out like he was looking for someone below.

"I know it was abrupt," he said. "We were kids, I didn't take it that seriously. I thought leaving would help."

"Help with what?"

"Being miserable."

I hadn't known he'd describe his time with me as miserable. I'd thought he was content to be malcontent, the only reasonable reaction to an imperfect world.

"Did it?"

"Yeah. For a while. For a while this was the right place for a wrong person. As opposed to before, which was wrong person, wrong place."

He hadn't asked me anything about myself, but I supposed the broad strokes were obvious: no wedding ring, nulliparous body, limitless bank account. Possibly he'd asked and heard about me through some grapevine, too.

I asked, "How long is a while?"

He looked at me instead of out the window but didn't answer. I put my unopened can down. I leaned forward where I sat on the sofa and hooked both of my arms back to begin to unzip my dress. I noticed belatedly that the person who last wore it had left ghostly streaks of antiperspirant up its lining.

Caleb came closer. I was able to observe his incredible scars up close, lightning marks and dark blotches against pale skin, a negative image of a constellation. His elegiac, well-used body. He held out his hand, and I bit his sinewy arm, and he swatted me away by hitting my temple with the side of his hand, and then we were back in it for real.

We wound up in his bed with the blankets pushed onto the floor and the top sheet knotted up by the headboard.

"You had me scared," he said, eyes fixed on the ceiling.

"Scared how?"

"I thought maybe you'd decided you didn't like how I was with you back then. And you were coming here to tell me."

"How were you back then?"

"Drunk. Rough. Messed up."

"You were worried I was going to say you abused me?"

I remembered the ex, her calling him *toxic*, the way no one thought much of it because that word was so vague and thrown around so loosely where exes were concerned.

He shrugged. "A little."

"Have other women said that?"

"Not exactly."

I shook my head and said, "I chose it."

"Still am sometimes. Messed up."

"Yeah, well, who isn't."

"That's dishonest. It's so easy to say everyone else is messed up the same. It's an excuse so you don't have to get better."

This sounded like a line from his sponsor or therapist or girlfriend, not a conclusion he'd reached himself. He sat up. I could count the notches on his spine, see the rippling of bones and fat in his ribs. I thought of those rabbits on the table. In one profile of that restaurant, I'd read that they cooked ten or fifteen to a pot.

"You shouldn't be here," he said.

"Why? Is your girlfriend coming back?"

He turned to face me.

"As a matter of fact," he began but then paused and turned away again. He muttered into his hair, which had fallen back over his face, nape-length and slick, "I don't know. I hope so."

"You've gone soft," I said, smacking him gently with a pillow.

He turned to look at me again with some notion in his eyes. It couldn't have been pity, I felt sure. I lay on my back, thinking about the pillow I'd just smacked him with, how it seemed unlike him to have pillowcases, not to mention pillows, at least ones that were clean of beer and sweat and spunk and spit. Probably the girlfriend's civilizing influence, or just the civilizing influence of time. I thought about my condo, white and clean and tomb-like, and the slatted heating vents that soundlessly kept it comfortable.

He hadn't stopped staring at me. "What?" I said.

"You haven't changed at all."

"Thanks."

It was no insult to stay the same, I thought, where looks were concerned or otherwise. Remaining focused was pure and honorable, particularly in the face of change. Adaptability and flexibility are overvalued qualities. A person needs rigidity and consistency to know who they are.

"Neither have you," I added belatedly.

He laughed. "You have no idea."

"No idea what?" I said, rising to rest on my elbows. "C'mon, tell me what befell you in these seventeen years."

"You really want to know?"

"Yes," I said, burrowing into the blankets in anticipation of a good story. I felt unserious, trying to keep afloat this rare post-coital high.

"Okay, are you ready?"

"Yesss," I said, burrowing even deeper.

"All right. When I first came down here, it was good. Parties and friends and okay money and cute girls."

"Boo," I said at the mention of cute girls.

"Shh," he said and reached back to the blankets to put a hand over my mouth until I bit his fingers away. "It didn't last. First the restaurant I worked at closed, then the friends moved to other cities or back home. I kept partying, but I couldn't afford the place without them, and so I wound up going couch-to-couch for a while. I had no fucking money, I mean none. I started taking liquor bottles from some of these places, or siphoning off vodka and replacing it with water, and I was getting nervous, especially as it got to be winter.

"Finally, I got this gig as an office park janitor. Not a nice office with plants in the lobby or whatever, just a ventilated box. They interviewed me in the parking lot of a Burger King, that's how sad this job was. Like, not even *inside* the Burger King. All I had to do was empty trash cans and run vacuums and mop bathrooms. It was paid under the table, this crummy no-union place. I tapered enough to function but still came to work with a pocket flask. I was not subtle, but they were accustomed to higher-order fuckups, and they let it slide. I was also dabbling in meth at the time, but not right then. Funnily enough, that was never really a problem for me.

"Anyway. First payday, I feel like a million bucks because I've lasted like two weeks. So of course, what do I do but go and spend most of it on a handle. As a result of this little mini bender, I get kicked out of the place where I'm crashing. I don't remember exactly what I did. At the time, I was pissed 'cause they knew me, they knew what they were getting into, they were fuckups too. But fine, whatever, I go without a fight, thinking it's good I only halfway burned that bridge.

"I get everything I've got, which isn't much, in a backpack, and my flask is full, and I've got a second bottle in my bag, and I kick around the highway until my shift starts. I go in and pick up my mop, and almost immediately I'm getting yelled at for knocking over some stupid office toys on someone's cubicle with the handle. Those plastic teeth that chatter when you wind them up, those wheel-drop novelty things, you know what I'm talking about. I can just see the loser who bought them, the guy who built his personality out of plastic shit made in China. I fucking hated that guy. As opposed to me, who built my whole personality around a potato vodka made in Kentucky.

"Anyway, I'm stumbling around without any way of covering up the alcohol smell or the sweat-diesel smell you get hanging around bus shelters, and I figure I'm gonna get fired, so. As it got later, I started gathering up every desk toy I could and taking them to this conference room where I hid under the table. The boss did his rounds, calling my name, and I could hear him muttering that he'd fire my drunk ass for leaving without notice. You don't often hear people talk about you like you're not around, which is a real shame, I think.

"He didn't look that hard and locked up behind him, so it was just me and these toys in this empty building, the dark and the emergency exit signs. I drink what I have in my backpack. I piss in the wastebasket when I need to. I've got these toys all laid out, a whole field of them like those army men I used to have as a kid, and I pass out feeling ready for war.

"I wake up to this guy in a suit standing above me screaming.

I run out of there so fast, you would not believe. Nothing left. It's so goddamn cold. I haul ass to that same Burger King for water, but I can't hold it down. I try to sleep at a bus station, and that's nice, like I'm not the only sad sack out there, until this cop comes and chases us out one by one. I'm over in the corner trying to sleep and thinking I can pass for a regular commuter, but of course I can't. Once I'm out, I really have nowhere to go. No shelters nearby, not even a dollar for the bus. I'm shivering and sweating, and I have that cottonmouth breath, that smell like you've already died. I pulled some random shit out of a Goodwill bin and curled up under a shrub, wondering whether I'd actually know if I was dying of cold or if I'd just drift off peacefully, and it finally occurred to me that though I didn't deserve to stop, I probably should. But I didn't. Not for a long time."

I waited for him to continue, feeling uncomfortable and stupid. Still on my back, I looked up at the ceiling, which resembled a lunar landscape, peeling and pocked.

"So how'd it end?" I asked.

"Medication, AA with my dad. Though I hate that religious shit. I think a lot about that night in the office. I still have one of those toys. The dipping bird, the one that won't stop drinking? Little on the nose, but."

I didn't know what to say. I touched his back, but the gesture felt false, so I let my hand fall back on the bed. In some other universe, I was Caleb's common-law wife, one of those red-faced couples you see arguing on sidewalks outside of fast-food places. Maybe that wouldn't have been so bad. Alcoholics at least have alcohol to live for.

"I wish you'd stayed," I said. "I would've let you ruin my whole life."

This was about as close to a declaration of love as I'd ever get. I didn't even mean anything particular to Caleb's calamitous circumstances; I was just accustomed to thinking that was what men did: ruin women's lives. I thought he'd understand that this was the highest compliment I could bestow, but instead he scoffed.

"We knew each other what, like. Four, five years?" he said. "You know how little time that is? That's nothing."

I understood then the strangeness of my being there, of having reappeared after all this time for a thin, bloodless vein of nostalgia. I nodded. "I know."

"Then why'd you come here?"

I wanted to tell him my plans, that I'd meant what I'd said all those years ago. I wanted him to come with me or beg me not to go. Another part of me wanted to tell him that, according to the best oncologist in the best city in the world, I was dying. I think he sensed I was nearing the end of something, and he didn't like that, didn't like that my life was sad enough that he was on the list of final visitations I'd make on my maudlin farewell tour. It was a burden to him.

I tried to nod again, but my head wouldn't move that way, some mechanical failure. "It was a dumb idea."

He said, "I think you and me, we need to be with happy people."

I felt this was an incredibly mean thing for him to say. He meant he could see himself with someone well-adjusted. Sunny. Not stupid, just simpler. Younger.

I believed people were responsible for their flaws. I believed that people could get better, and that they could get better faster if they accepted that responsibility. I also believed I was never going to be the kind of happy Caleb was talking about. It just wasn't in me. This was another reason to hate my father. He'd made it impossible to tell if I was like this by nature or nurture and seemed to wield undue power over my personality in his absence or presence.

My eyes felt full of molten copper. In all those years, I'd never thought to look up Caleb's ex. She was almost certainly fine, not an addict or would-be murderer, so I guess the joke was on us, the people who'd become exactly what everyone might've expected.

I blinked rapidly until the threat of tears retreated.

"Don't worry," I said. "I'm out of here tomorrow."

"Back to New York."

I'd either successfully masked my emotion or he was giving me the grace of pretending he hadn't noticed.

I shook my head no. "California."

He turned back to look at me and raised his eyebrows. "Yeah? It's beautiful there this time of year. That's where my girlfriend's from."

"I have to go to Death Valley, where it's ugly all year round."

My casual contempt seemed to irritate him. "Not if you like the desert," he said.

I felt reciprocal contempt. Hadn't he noticed how weird it was that I was going from Pittsburgh to Death Valley? Hadn't he noticed the changes in my body, the puckered-shiny scar on my left foot, a newer injury of mine he'd never seen? Couldn't he ask me a single good question? For all he knew I had a spiraling, strange addiction story of my own. I hated him and his Californian girlfriend, who probably cooked quinoa on Sundays and had expensive taste in weed.

"Do you remember that girl in our class? The one who said she never would've been a Nazi?" I asked.

"What?"

"You have to remember." The idea that he'd forget this was unacceptable to me.

"Oh, wait. Yes. Yeah. Wasn't she super Catholic?"

I didn't remember that part, but I said, "Yes."

"Yes. What the fuck made you think of her?"

Your girlfriend, I wanted to say. Instead I said, "I wonder sometimes if she was right, and we hated her because we were jealous."

"Jealous of what?"

"How certain she was."

He was still sitting up. He brought his knees up into the circle of his arms, thinking. "Maybe," he said. "But it was still a dumbass thing for her to say."

10

Long after Caleb fell asleep, I stayed up looking at images of untreated tumors on my phone, the way they marred and exploded the flesh, tender blooms in purpling pinks against white hospital cots. It didn't seem possible that could happen to me. It seemed likelier, and preferable, that I'd drop dead at some point, seemingly intact but consumed from within. I kept getting stuck on a sentence found on some website, *Sometimes there are no symptoms at all.* I repeatedly held up the phone and lifted the blanket to peek at my breasts, like they'd start crumpling and blackening before my eyes. I looked over at Caleb each time, half hoping he'd catch me in the act and ask what I was doing so I'd get to tell him, even though he'd probably just think I was making it up for his pity and attention. He never stirred.

I didn't want to do a sad, stilted morning after, so I got out of bed and dressed in the dark. The sun was rising just as I left. I took a bus back to the garage where I'd parked my car. I hadn't ridden one in years. I felt like a woman of the people until a man got on with all his fishing gear in a wire cart and a plastic bag full of something foul-smelling. No thanks. I got off and walked the rest of the way in my prescuffed shoes, thinking it was nice, at least, that I'd been well and proper fucked the night before.

From the car, I called the oncologist's office and got his

answering service. The bot told me to hang up and dial 911 if I was experiencing a medical emergency. I left a long, rambling message in which I called him a son of a whore and a sick, marathon-loving fuck and asked him how many miles he'd need to run to fill the void in his soul. One hundred thousand? A million? I told him I hoped he died of a heart attack during his next race and that it hurt, a lot. I told him I hoped all the poets he'd ever quoted kicked his shins in hell and then forced him to eat worms.

I hung up midsentence, nauseated. I rolled down the windows and took a deep breath even though I was still in the parking garage, and all I got was a lungful of sulfur and gasoline. Then I accidentally bit the inside of my mouth in the same place I had the day prior. It was all part of the process of making peace with my demise.

What would make me feel best, I decided, was to make progress toward my destination. With a full day of driving and one stop for gas, I could make it all the way to Chicago.

The radio picked right up where it left off. *The government wanted Wall Street to put the interests of the client first, they all fought it tooth and nail. They make more money selling you their products than they do protecting your interests. You're not like every Tom, Dick, and Harry out there, you don't want a big supermarket. You want boutique. If you're unique, think boutique.*

Life on the road had many chapters, episodic little towns and whatever went on in them, tawdry or wholesome. In between were gas stations that still had Bell phone booths and grain silos and tufted hair grass and bluestem in uneven gold waves. I wasn't from flyover country, but I'd grown up in a similarly unremarkable place. My parents had bought a plot deep in the woods and built a house. We were far from both of their families, their respective large broods that tended to clump together in snarls and knots. We stood out for being a small branch with no desire to expand, as far as I knew.

Dad was tall, the only good quality of his that he passed on to me. His hair was wild and erect, shot through with premature gray, and askew unless he combed it back and locked it into place with a cream that smelled of burned starch. I liked the prickle-slick feel of his cheeks when I sat on his lap, pulling his chin to open his mouth so I could admire the silver in his teeth. He had an odd face, asymmetrical but lively, like he'd been hastily sketched by a gifted apprentice.

He did some Dad things. He had a workbench in the garage. He built a backyard tree swing out of rope and a wooden slat that left splinters on the backs of my thighs. In the spring, he took a blowtorch to structured webs of gypsy moths, curling them away to black ash. He drew princesses for me on sticky notes that I pressed to one wall in my bedroom. I accumulated so many that the wall was hidden from floor to ceiling by paper waves that shuddered under the window fan in summer—never AC; we could not afford AC. I took this weird shrine down long before he left not as a declaration of war against him but because I thought I'd outgrown them.

I spent a lot of time outside. This was not elective. It was better to be out of sight and earshot of whatever was going on between my parents in that house, their world of inscrutable rules. We went months without mowing the lawn, and I lay out there for hours on my back watching the drift of dandelion plumes. We never used bug spray, unafraid of ticks and accepting that mosquitos would find us regardless. Mom's rules for me were simple: don't go in the road, don't eat wild things, come in before dark.

I went through a phase when I was small of adoring Dad, but even then, I didn't like being left alone with him. He was unpredictable, a thrower of remotes and a puncher of walls. Once I heard him tell my mother, "Hey, Irene, think fast," before chucking one of our dusty, rarely used champagne flutes at her head. He'd been going through a kitchen cabinet, which was organized haphazardly, so maybe he intended this as commentary on her housekeeping skills. Mom stood several feet away by the stove; despite their proximity, the fine, thin old glass missed her widely and shattered on the floor. He insisted he'd aimed badly on purpose, that it was only a joke.

Despite the obvious tension, I laughed. Good one, Daddy, funny, ha ha. When I went to help sweep up, Mom barked me off, saying I'd cut myself. Later that week, I stepped on a shard anyway; it was impossible to find them all.

Scenes like that drove me outside. I've heard people pin all the problems of younger generations on staying inside too much, so maybe it was ultimately to my benefit. What I did with all that unstructured time, I don't know. Our house was so rural that our neighbors and their children were literal miles away. I climbed crab apple trees and read books and told myself stories. Listened for solitary planes passing overhead on schedules I never figured out.

Dad came to look for me once. This was odd; usually he told Mom and I to leave him alone, as if we tormented him and kept him from his work. He found what I thought had been my concealed spot behind the shed with alarming ease.

"What is it you get up to out here?" he asked.

"Nothing," I said, drawing my stick through the dirt in patterns scrutable only to me, loose triangles to represent our family, mother father me, mother father me. I felt panicky, in trouble. There are many times as a child when you think death is nearer than it is. An effect of being so vulnerable, so tiny, so low to the ground in which we're buried.

"Nothing," he said. "That's hard to believe."

"You don't have to believe me." I intended this to sound brave but knew it was more like petulant. My words never came out sounding like I wanted them to in front of him. I did not have to impress Mom; I had her love. My father, though. He needed to be won over.

He crouched down. I watched him out of the corner of my eye, affecting absorption in my dirt art. He pulled a stem of a jewelweed plant over to me. He said, "Come here."

I hate reviewing memories like this, where I obeyed him. It's embarrassing to me. I felt embarrassed too when I found an album of photos of my birth while cleaning out our house to be sold. I'd never seen those pictures before, the two of them trading the camera, Mom fat and brown and bare-shouldered and Dad holding me, his hair and jeans fashionable for the time. It was like reviewing evidence of a war crime.

He touched his finger to one of the seedpods, which curled back explosively, delicate and fierce.

"You try," he said.

I reached forward. Before I could, he plucked one of the bright orange flowers and popped it into his mouth.

I gasped. "Don't eat wild things!"

Mouth still closed, he smiled at my wide eyes, my goody-two-shoes invocation of Mom. He stood from his crouch, put his hands in his pockets, tall as a tree over me.

I didn't know what would happen next. I looked back at the house, hoping to see Mom in a window or through the screen door of the back deck, watching and sanctioning this interaction. Like magic she did appear, calling us in to dinner.

Before we walked inside, he turned to me and opened his mouth, the flower still intact inside.

II

ROADSIDE ERRATA

11

I thought I'd make good time, but I took a wrong turn into the spindly tip of West Virginia and then delayed myself in a traffic jam because a poultry transport truck had tried to drive under a too-short bridge and gotten stuck, causing a daisy chain of smaller crashes and leaving a sprawl of white feathers on the pavement. Then I had to pull over twice to pee, such that by the time I made it through verdant, uneventful Ohio, all roadside trailer parks and POW/MIA flags and salt storage sheds and berry farms, and a good way into Indiana, tucked just under Michigan like a choker, the sun had already set. My brain felt fuzzed over, deprived of stimuli.

Following mute pictograms on signs rainbowed with reflective coating, I pulled into one final backwoods gas station. Its pumps glowed under their protective roof, neon green and fluorescent white, like a spaceship landed in the forest. I could smell pine, manure, gasoline, and the salt of the stale, lonely hot dogs turning on rollers in the convenience store window.

The attendant, stoned and unsurprised, watched me as I jogged in place, stretched my arms overhead. When I leaned back, I felt a tiny pressure under the flesh of my left breast, a tugging on my uppermost rib. Beryl making herself known. A squat family of five, two parents and three children all dressed in dark hoodies and soft pants, came in and browsed the aisles with me, cramming their pockets with plastic sleeves of powdered doughnuts. One of the children, probably no older than seven, backed up into me while I stood behind them in line, and the father immediately and loudly corrected him, saying, "What is wrong with you? Who taught you to be so rude? Say excuse me and apologize to the lady." I said, "He's fine," coldly. I felt my own upbringing entitled me to judge poor, messy families and their public overcorrections.

I bought coffee and a tough-skinned banana and a nutrition bar so aged that clouds of white fat bloomed over its chocolate surface. They had only one brand of beer in the refrigerators in the back. I was probably no more than five miles from a farm in any direction. I only had a few hours until Chicago and sleep. I went back to the car and tried to start it, but the engine rolled over and played dead. The cabin light came on too bright and then dimmed.

"Don't do this to me," I said to the steering wheel. I opened the battery panel and gave it a good whack. I got out and whacked the fuel tank for good measure. This was the extent of my automotive knowledge. I called the rental company's roadside assistance and sat on hold, eyeing the attendant behind the register. He was caressing a red cyst on his Adam's apple like he was going to pop it right there, unwashed hands and all. I felt like I was at a gallery, looking at a photograph not from my own life.

I was on hold for a long time. The moon got higher in the sky, pink and round as a compact mirror. I'd have to sleep in the lot, I thought, and call in the morning.

The attendant knocked on my window, startling me so much that I dropped the phone midcall and had to grope around for it on the floor. The car's buttons wouldn't work, so I opened the door slightly to speak to him.

"You been sitting here a long time," he said. He spoke very

slowly. His clear-rimmed glasses magnified his eyes, made them another source of light.

"Is there a repair shop around here?"

"Uh. Might have to wait until morning."

"How about a hotel?"

"Uh," he said, then trailed off.

"Uber? Airbnb? Cab?"

"Uhhh."

"Okay," I said with a tight smile. "Forget it."

"So what are you gonna do?"

"I just need to make a quick call," I said and shut the door. I Googled rapidly, feeling marooned and increasingly optionless as my battery percent drifted downward. I hadn't felt this stuck since I was a kid without a license.

The attendant had resumed his post inside. I went in and said, "I will pay you to drive me to a hotel."

"Can't. Can't drive."

"Seriously? You live out here, work at a gas station, and can't drive?"

"Got a DUI," he said, then amended, "Three DUIs."

"What are you, sixteen?"

"Twenty-two," he said, not sounding particularly thrilled about it. He added, "Gram and Gramps live just up the road. Give me two hundred dollars, and they'll put you up."

"No offense, but I'd rather sleep in my car."

He went back to fingering the welt on his neck and said, "Whatever."

I returned to my car only to find that I'd locked my keys inside. Not that long ago, it seemed, I'd been a moderately intelligent person, a competent lawyer, an immovable ice queen. In retrospect, it seems clear to me that my diagnosis had broken some supporting column in my brain, but at the time I chalked it up to the confusion of travel, the unfamiliarity of my circumstances. The city had made me sharp-edged and successful; it only made sense that leaving it would make me stupid again.

I went back inside yet again. I didn't care about money but didn't want him to know that, so I said, "Make it one-fifty."

"Deal."

He took me to his grandparents' house, walking in the sandy dirt next to the road, ducking under the down guys of utility poles. I followed the white of his shirt, turned a milky, opalescent blue in the moonlight. I wasn't afraid of him; he was shorter than me, wispy and slight. I didn't have to ponder my ability to take him in hand-to-hand combat for long. Their red clapboard house was maybe ten yards from the station. Two tractor tires in the front yard had been turned into garden planters full of showy flowers. The windows were dark but for a flickering light in a back room.

In that room were two old people watching TV, one of those true-crime docuseries where they interview former prosecutors and retired cops with too much free time. Mom used to watch those at night, alone and paranoid and alert, and I'd go to sleep with their maudlin theme music seeping through the thin walls. She often said she would've made a good detective. She was wrong, but I never corrected her; she so liked believing it.

Two ferrets were curled on the woman's lap. She patted them roughly, almost slapping them.

"Gram, Gramps," said the attendant. "This lady's car broke."

They looked at me and nodded placidly, as if the attendant brought home strays all the time, which I found eerie because that couldn't possibly be the case in such a remote location. The time for trusting strangers in America had long since passed, but there we were, trusting each other. The old man's head shook with an essential tremor.

The attendant brought me to a bedroom on the second floor.

There was a uric must from the ferrets, but the place was immaculately clean. Above the dresser hung an amateur portrait of Jesus in chalk tacked up with gold pushpins, his stigmata-ed hands raised in bloody benediction and surrounded by bodiless cherubim with wings for ears.

"Did you draw that?" I asked, counting out his bills. I knew his grandparents would see none of the money.

"My ma. This used to be her room," he said. He shuffled from foot to foot for a moment, looking unsteady, and then said, "Do you think I could get a hand job?"

I laughed. "A what?"

"You know, like, tug me off a little. It won't take long."

"I'm sure that's true," I said. "But no, we're not going to do that."

"Okay." He was almost laughably dejected. He walked away, leaving the bedroom door wide-open. I listened to his footsteps disappear down the rough carpeted hallway, then shut the door. The blankets on the bed had the feeling of not having been touched in a long time, stiff, cold wool with all its starch intact. I sneezed. Downstairs, the crime show continued. I could see the blue squares it cast on the lawn outside through the window panes, a quilt made of light.

I would never have let the attendant sleep in my apartment if he'd needed a bed there. This might seem specific to city living, but I never would've done it where I grew up, either. After Dad left, Mom became terrified of visitors. An old family friend once dropped by unannounced, and Mom clung to me, willing me to be silent, to not answer the door, though we were obviously home; her car was in the driveway. She never explained why, but I guess I know.

There's no word for this thing I want to describe, a thing that evokes hatred for the past, something that takes you back against your will. I'd once written a paper on memory and mythmaking in the liberal international order following World War II, and while drafting it at five on the morning it was due, jacked up on caffeine and malt liquor, with the birds starting to chirp in the tree outside Caleb's window, I'd looked up the word *nostalgia*, figuring that deconstructing its etymology would buy me at least a paragraph, and this is how I know it comes from the Greek words for *pain* and *return home*. People think of nostalgia as bittersweet, but its constituent elements are agnostic. It could as easily be all bitter, no sweet.

The internet signal was weak; my dad's site kept timing out. There was a bookshelf in the room, but it was full of board games, not books, boxes dusty and flattened at the corners. I had a hard time imagining when this had ever been the kind of family to play board games. The closet was a museum to one person's body and habits at a particular moment in time. Sweaters stitched with pom-poms hung next to silk dresses with padded shoulders, all reeking of mothballs and heirloom sweat. I wasn't sure what I was looking for, beyond some light entertainment, answers to the mysteries of who these strange people were who would so willingly take me in. On top of a shelf were boxes filled with shoes and a rusty metal case with the key jammed in the hole. I pried it open slowly, careful to avoid making a sound, and found inside not deeds and birth certificates or gold bullion but a gun.

I had that creeping sensation of feeling watched. I turned around and froze. One of the ferrets had writhed his way under the closed bedroom door and lay there staring at me, spine arched.

In the morning, I went downstairs to find the grandmother sweeping in the kitchen. The ferrets followed her broom around so that she had to shoo them away. The grandfather read a newspaper at a table with one uneven leg propped up with a telephone book. His hearing aid rested on a crumpled cloth napkin in front of him.

In the next room, the attendant sat on a plaid couch. He'd

crushed up some blue pills on a leather-bound Bible on the coffee table in front of him and had a dollar bill rolled at the ready. I sat down in the armchair opposite him, which, in the daylight, I noticed was velveteen and printed with a hideous institutional pattern. I felt strange watching him, too old to be his peer but too young to align with his grandparents.

"A Bible?" I asked, wondering if he'd picked it on purpose to be edgy.

"Oh, huh. How about that." He didn't offer any of the blue dust. He added, "Gramps got a bad hip. But he doesn't like taking these. Some macho thing."

"You know your grandparents are in the next room, right?"

He waved his hand dismissively. "They're deaf, dumb, and blind."

On the TV was another true-crime show, a story about a trucker who kidnapped prostitutes and runaways and held them in his sleeper compartment. Some he let go; others he murdered and put in storage barrels dumped in roadside forests. They only caught him when one of the girls escaped and ran naked and bloody and filthy into four lanes of traffic.

This was a little much, even for me.

"Anything else on besides murder?" I asked.

"Seems about all there is these days. Bad news," he said, before sniffing loudly and wiping his nose on the back of his hand. His eyes already looked gluey and vague.

"Noticed you have a gun upstairs."

He seemed unsurprised that I'd been snooping, maybe because he would've done the same in my position. "Who doesn't? BB in the credenza, too."

"Let me buy it off you. The handgun."

He sniffed again, not taking his eyes off the TV. They were interviewing one of the surviving victims, who had almost no eyebrows to speak of.

"What do you even want it for?"

I ignored him. "How much do you want for it?"

"It's not for sale. That was Ma's gun."

I'd thought it looked like a woman's gun, snub-nosed and small. "I see. What happened to her?"

"Suicide."

I winced. When I was sixteen, I'd found a journal of my mother's. I opened it from the back, skimming enough pages to know mostly it was empty, until I arrived at the beginning, where she'd written that she wanted to die and that, were it not for me, she would've. I'd shut the cover sharply when I read that, face hot. I didn't look for it again until I was clearing the house out after she died, but I never found it.

"That's hard," I said.

He shrugged and mumbled a few unintelligible words.

"I better call about the car," I said.

The rental company sent a tow to take the car not to a local garage but one in a larger town several miles away. I followed behind in the attendant's old truck; he sat in the passenger seat while I drove and his grandfather sat in the back, I assume so he could drive the truck home after. We passed a motorsports center, a boarded-up tobacco outlet, brick buildings with advertisements for no-longer-extant products painted on their sides, a Masonic temple. In the parking lot, glass glittered where it looked like someone had deliberately smashed a series of bottles against the ground.

There was some issue with the rental's transmission. I sat in one of three blue folding chairs while the mechanic behind a pink counter told me this. A wood-fronted air conditioner on fan mode blew his few wispy hairs flat against his skull. He had an aquarium murky to the point of opacity. He'd tacked up one of those wall calendars of nude women but hadn't turned the page to the correct month. Either he'd forgotten or just really liked

Miss January, whose brown nipples smiled benevolently down at us. The calendar legitimated him for me, so well did it conform to my idea of his profession. When he walked me outside with a slim-jim car opener to let me get my stuff out of the back, he said, "Here you go, sweetheart," and winked. I didn't like that I'd been reduced to accepting help from men, but it was what it was.

We drove to another rental outlet a few miles away, where I'd been told another car was waiting for me. I turned back to look at the grandfather and said, at immense volume, "It was very generous of you to help me."

I said this more as an observation of truth than an expression of gratitude. He nodded back at me slowly without smiling.

"He can't hear you. Left his aids at home," said the attendant, slurring a little, his eyes half-lidded. Without shifting his position at all, he yelled, "Right, old man?" loud enough to make me jump. His grandfather didn't react, just kept looking out the window at a scrap of litter blowing in the wind. The attendant laughed and slid further down in his seat.

"I left more money for you. On the nightstand in your mother's room," I said.

"Wow," said the attendant dreamily.

"You should use it to get out of there. That house is depressing. And those ferrets."

"That house is so nice. I love those ferrets, my life rules. You're a very mean lady. Hot but so mean. I wouldn't want a tuggie from a lady as mean as you anyway."

"All right," I said and got out of the car.

I guessed I was pretty cruel. Anyway, I'd taken the gun. I'd hidden it under my bulky sweatshirt, the barrel tucked into the center gore, nestled right next to Beryl.

12

Carrying on like this even when you get the outcome you want, for people who meddle or truck in this kind of thing, just shows that it never stops because if injustice was ever found to stop, then the whole outrage industry would collapse.

When they go low, we kick 'em.

I got out of Indiana three days after leaving the city. No one was on the road at that odd midafternoon hour but me and truckers. I felt part of a herd. Mid-century office parks came at regular intervals, huge signs on their rolling lawns advertising their emptiness: COME RENT US. The GPS took me past places with names like Potato Creek and Crumstown. Cattails grew up from ditches and trees overgrew power lines. I felt relieved to be back on the road, unusually thankful for the highway system, this dream of the nuclear age patched over and repaved. I couldn't understand that kind of forward-thinking vision. To say you knew what the future needed, that generations to come would appreciate the same conveniences, seemed hubristic in the extreme, and yet there I was, appreciating it.

On the shoulder up ahead, I saw a figure with a silhouette that looked familiar to me. "No way," I said aloud to myself. But as I slowed to pass him, I confirmed it was him: John the crustpunk, risen indeed. At some point he'd acquired a baseball cap, but otherwise he looked the same, wholly unwashed.

I pulled over. I was several yards ahead of him and got to watch his unhurried approach. He stopped at the passenger-side window and leaned in, preparing to do what I imagined would be his usual ride-thumbing spiel, and then he recognized me.

"This is a different car completely," he said.

"Other one broke. How'd you get out here so fast?"

"Hitched with the wrong trucker. High as a kite, wouldn't stop anywhere until Fort Wayne."

"So they didn't catch you?"

"No, I'm slippery like that. You?"

"Talked my way out of it. I'm slippery like that."

He grinned at me. I grinned back. His teeth were over-crowded, with a rogue one bullying its way out in front of the others. Dr. Remsen would not have approved, but the crookedness didn't seem like a problem that needed fixing. How strange to find him again like that. I'd never been the kind of person to believe in meaningful coincidences, but still, I sensed significance in his reappearance. I felt like an idiot, aglow with a kind of luck I hadn't known I wanted.

"Well," he said. "Where are you going now?"

"Same as before."

"Got time for a pit stop?"

Six months left, I thought, and so what? Six months can feel like forever or like no time at all. About two thousand miles remained to my destination, which equaled twenty-eight hours of travel, which meant no more than three days' worth of driving. Even allowing for my apparent rate of one mishap per day, that would extend it to a week, tops. Maybe two. I'd arrive too soon, like an early party guest, with too much life in me to want to die just yet. I could afford to run the clock a little longer.

"Get in," I said. "I got time for a few."

13

Following John's directions took us past a huge billboard that said HELL IS REAL. The board was black, and the letters were white, and the field it stood in was brown, and the sky was bright gray. It was one of those days when the sunlight got trapped in the clouds and had nothing to do but bounce around.

They're the greatest threat to capitalism. They're the greatest threat to your job. They're the greatest threat to democracy. They're the greatest threat to the American military. More than Islamoterrorists, more than communist China.

"Are you Republican?" John asked.

Despite studying politics, I'd only voted once. I chose a long-shot libertarian candidate with an incoherent smattering of policy ideas. I seem to remember them being very pro-vaping. I kept up with elections only to be conversant enough to avoid embarrassment in my work. My parents never discussed politics. I was surprised when I got to college and met classmates who canvassed or ran registration drives or hosted debate parties. Lack of political engagement is often derided as an expression of privilege, but in my experience, development of an active political consciousness was largely linked to disposable income.

"I'm not anything."

"You're listening to conservative radio," he said.

"So?"

"That suggests a degree of conservatism."

"It's what's available. I like background noise."

The voices on the radio were angry about things I couldn't imagine caring about. I wasn't a terrorist or school shooter or clinic bomber, taking diffuse revenge on strangers for phantasmagorical fears. Most murderers probably think they're the clear-headed exception, but I really did think I was different. *She's not like other girls; she's homicidal.* If I tugged at a loose thread in the fabric of civil society, who cared? I was hardly the first.

"Why not music?" he said.

"I don't like music."

"Nobody doesn't like music."

"Believe it or not."

"You just haven't found what's good."

"That's a stupid way to live. Invest a bunch of time in activities you hate on the off chance of striking gold."

"I mean. Isn't that what you do, though? Invest a bunch of time in living on the off chance."

I stared at him from behind my sunglasses. I couldn't tell if he was talking about a general *you* or me in particular.

"I just don't care about it," I said.

"What do you care about?"

"Nothing."

He narrowed his eyes. His expression reminded me of those punk friends of Caleb's who'd never liked me. Maybe they'd sensed a conservative in me, some fascistic streak I hadn't known I had.

"Okay," I conceded. "I care about some things. Just because I don't wear my principles on my sleeve like you doesn't mean I don't have them."

"So articulate them."

"You don't find out that kind of thing by asking someone. It comes out in what people do."

"That kinda sounds like an articulated principle to me."

"Jesus Christ, and you wonder why I have the radio on all the time."

"You're going to want to take a right."

I'd thought he was trying to argue for real, but it seemed he didn't find this conversation combative. I tended to take things too seriously, to see mortal threats where there were none. It had taken me a long time to understand when a judge was asking a friendly question. As with everything, I attribute this flaw to my upbringing.

For a change of topic, I asked, "Aren't you afraid of exposure at these places? Of getting radiation sickness and growing a third testicle?"

"I'm not drinking the water or eating the dirt, and I never linger too long. For the really bad ones, I have a respirator I got from a doomsday prepper."

"What?"

"This guy in Kentucky, he'd been prepping a long time but sold it all to pay for chemo."

"That's funny."

"Not really."

"Fine, sure. It's not funny at all. It is one hundred percent sad." I paused for a moment, then continued, "He told you he had cancer?"

"I mean, he was obviously sick. But yeah. He told me all about it. People tell me lots of things, their life stories."

For some reason, I was jealous of this quality of John's, though I hated strangers and had no patience for stories. Beggars rarely even asked me for spare change, probably because I looked like what I was: a stony, unfeeling bitch. At least I was as described on the tin.

"Must be something about the way you look," I said.

We arrived at John's destination, an ammunition factory

inactive since the Vietnam War. John had me park in the empty lot of a church with a marquee that read BELIEVE ON THE LORD JESUS CHRIST. A tree on its front lawn had an acid-wash jean jacket caught in its branches. A chain-link fence skirted the back of the lot. Through a gap in the curtain of ivy, I could see a set of rail tracks leading deeper into the forest, choked with weeds and wildflowers. John squatted down a few feet from me, further prying apart the wires where someone had already been with a bolt cutter.

"How did you know to come right here?" I asked.

"Message from God," he said before he slipped through.

I assumed that was his idea of a joke. I bent down at the waist to look through the gap. At first I couldn't see him, as if he'd crossed some portal to another dimension. He must have been standing, because he abruptly leaned down, his face suddenly filling the fence from an unexpected angle. I let out a startled yelp.

"You don't have to come," he said.

"I know that," I said. Then I crawled through after him.

The tracks were crowded in on both sides by shaggy vegetation and woody vines. Grass and moss and pine saplings had sprouted between the ties, which had gone spongy with rot and a wet carpet of dead leaves. I ripped a dandelion stalk up from the earth and squashed it between my fingers to produce that fine, milky sap I remembered from childhood. The path was long and quiet except for excitable birds.

We came to a one-time way station, or weigh station, I've never been quite sure. On the platform was a massive scale, big enough to drive an E-Type onto. I stepped on it. The rusted plate didn't shift under my weight, nor did the needle budge, which I enjoyed because it made me feel I did not exist.

John, meanwhile, was pulling himself up onto a rusted fire escape ladder. Whether he knew where it led or feared its collapse was unclear; he proceeded, as always, with a confidence so total and unearned, it seemed spiritual. I followed him onto a roof of gravel and corrugated tin. Flakes of rust freckled my palms. The top offered a view of a wide field surrounded by concrete structures, some so decayed I couldn't tell what they'd once been. Water towers and huge silos with blown-out windows stood sentry. In the middle was a set of stairs that ended in midair, leading nowhere.

John shielded his eyes against the sun with his hand, scanning the horizon.

"Imagine thirty thousand people down there," he said. "That's how many workers were here at the height of the war."

"Imagine thirty thousand ticks down there."

Those abandoned spaces had a humbling, sacred quality, cathedral-like in their quietness and emptiness and high-ceilinged massiveness and the way birds nested in their rafters. Even a faithless wretch like me could tell, or at least I could tell that this was how John thought of visiting them: as a kind of worship. I never regret my actions, and I do not apologize as a matter of principle, but I felt oddly shamed for having spoken, and for having spoken so inanely.

John snapped a few pictures and then climbed back down. I followed. In a former laboratory beyond the way station, signs read NITROGEN SAMPLES ONLY and CLEAN MERCURY THIS SINK ONLY. The door of a defunct elevator was partly ajar, and I peered down into the dizzying dark. We had to push aside rows of abandoned carts to reach the next room, startling birds whose sudden flapping wings startled us in turn. Insects had gotten trapped in ridged plastic sheeting, their carcasses piling up to varying heights in each groove like a bar chart. Graffiti colored the walls to the point that they seemed made of ink.

In a hangar-size space, two massive funnels or hoppers hung like stalactites from the ceiling, descending into holes carved out of the floor. John called them electrostatic precipitators.

"Basically a giant air filtration system," he said.

"How do you even know that?"

"I read a book."

"On electrostatic precipitators?"

"On air pollution."

"Why?"

"For my own edification."

I wondered if he'd ever been in school, had at one point led a more quotidian life. He could've been a more mature, solemn member of Caleb's college crew. He stepped into the next room, another long hangar with a ceiling supported by tall arches. The floor was pocked with puddles and curling tension wires. Broken panels of the ceiling let light through in chunks, casting spotlights on machines gone an oxidized green. Someone had turned a circular communal sink into a witch's altar with a sprayed-on pentacle. We stood looking down at it.

I heard a distant, tinny sound come up the drain.

"What is that?" I whispered, standing stiffly.

"Music," John said in his normal speaking voice.

I frowned, uncomprehending. My first thought was, stupidly, ghosts.

"Kids, probably," said John, as if I'd spoken out loud. "It's a good skate spot," he added. This made me picture an adolescent John on a skateboard, tooling around his comfortable suburb; more clues and misdirections.

In a hall downstairs, kids were indeed sweeping debris aside with their feet to make a space to skateboard. The music came from a phone resting in an empty plastic fast-food cup. They couldn't've been older than fifteen, with backward caps flattening their hair and darkening their heavy-lidded eyes. One wearing the witless expression of the recently robotripped sat with his back to the wall, unmoving.

I was glad John was there. He looked like a possible version of what these kids might become when they grew up. I thought they'd be suspicious of his camera, but they were the post-smartphone generation and instead seemed to take it as proof that he wasn't a cop. They shook his hand, told him to take a few pictures of their tricks and crude, inscrutable gestures and to help himself to a puff of their spliff. They were friendly, curious, little birds drawn by crumbs.

I kept my distance. I reflexively thought of them as I had when I was their peer: sneering at them for being try-hards, avoiding them out of fear. Now that I was old enough to be their teacher or mother, though, that default posture no longer worked. I could step out of myself to see the pickling in progress, how my habits of thought were unintentionally preserved.

John returned. "The light in here's amazing," he said. "These windows."

"Can I see?" I asked, gesturing to his camera.

"It's not digital, you're not gonna—"

"Just, c'mon." I coaxed it out of his hands and, when I had control, took a picture of him.

"What're you wasting film for? Quit it."

One of the kids noticed and, thinking I'd take more, tried to photobomb by flipping us the double bird, but it was too late; I only wanted to get the one. I'm not sure why. Like I thought the camera would capture some dimension to John that otherwise would've passed unseen.

On the way back to Chicago, we passed that same billboard coming from the opposite side. It said JESUS IS REAL, white background, black font.

14

In Chicago I drove for hours in search of a room, from neo-Googie palaces to run-down motor lodges. There was some convention or festival or sports event, something I paid no attention to, and every place was booked.

I pulled in front of the most expensive hotel in the city.

"What are you doing?" said John.

"C'mon, leave your bag."

John didn't look up at the marquee bulbs under the entrance's canopy, didn't admire the fountain out front or the obsessively trimmed and hydrated hedges, into which more money had been poured than an average American public school. John barely passed for normal elsewhere; in this context, he looked like an outright vagrant.

"Wait here," I said, depositing him next to a planter brimming with roses induced to bloom year-round.

I went to the lobby bathroom and changed into that same still-unwashed dress, a minor but necessary improvement. I used one of their fluffy monogrammed hand towels to rub away a stray white mark on the side. The bathroom had an essential oil diffuser, the kind with a bundle of rattan reeds, and I pulled one out and floated it around my temples and wrists. I told the concierge I'd stayed there years earlier with the firm, which was true; they'd rented out a block of rooms for a monthslong trial, converting a few into offices. I showed him my fancy credit card. I was collegial, overly familiar. I asked him if they had any cancellations and could accommodate a last-minute request.

The only free room was one with a queen bed.

I went outside and fetched John, whom the bellboys were eyeing with suspicion. He was about three minutes from getting escorted off the premises.

I said, "There's a room. One bed but there's probably a chaise longue or a sofa."

"I'm not sleeping here."

"Why?"

John demurred. "I'm all right."

"Do you have, like, religious objections to sharing a room with a woman? I'm not going to seduce you."

He took off his dingy baseball cap and ran a hand through his hair, limp from lack of washing. He shook his head no.

"Is it the hotel? Too fancy? I'm paying for it. You don't have to worry about that."

"It's more of an ethical problem."

"An ethical problem with what? Four-hundred-thread-count sheets? Room service? At least try the good things in life before you reject them."

"It's just not for me."

"Sleep in the car, at least."

"I'll manage. I like to spread out." He fixed his hat back into place.

"Fine," I said. "But come to dinner. I hate to eat alone."

I don't know why I said that. I'd eaten alone for years.

The hotel's restaurant was reputedly excellent, better than Caleb's, though it wasn't fair to compare the two, Chicago being almost a real city. The hotel had a chef it treated like an artist in residence and an entrance with a self-serious chandelier and a koi pond with a waterfall feature in the center of the dining floor that children were discouraged from making wishes in. In fact, children were discouraged entirely.

The hostess didn't so much offer John a blazer and tie as conscript him into them. He looked like a lost kid, seeking some responsible party in this playground of the very rich. He smelled like a sneaker. A woman in purple lipstick and thick powder wrinkled her nose as John walked by. I decided on a fake narrative for us: John was an unwashed tech genius newly fat on VC funding; I was an oil heiress introducing him to civil society.

The place had a trendy, sustainable menu with "global" flavors. Instead I ordered a bottle of burgundy and a steak. When the waiter turned to John, I could see he was about to say he'd have nothing, so I said, "Make that two, please."

"Just one," said John. "Nothing for me."

The waiter raised his eyebrows.

"Two," I said.

"I wish you hadn't done that," said John when the waiter left.

"Done what?" I said, draping my napkin over my lap.

"I don't eat meat."

"What's worse, eating meat or wasting food?"

"I see what you're doing."

"What's that?"

The wine arrived. We paused so I could taste it and approve the bottle. The first time I'd participated in this ritual was during law school, when a professor I was dating took me out to dinner at a restaurant not so nice as this. He'd seemed to like that I didn't know why this was done. It wasn't enough to be young; I also needed to be naive, dependent on his guidance. Thinking that someone wanting to fuck you in any way constitutes flattery is a youthful mistake.

"You're laughing at me," John said when the waiter had poured us two glasses and walked off. I drank mine quickly, almost like a shot—an ignorant, sorority-sister way to consume wine so expensive—and then settled in to savor John's. When I drank at all, I drank like a lawyer: too much, but never enough for there to be consequences.

"I'm buying you dinner," I said. "What's so bad about that?"

"You're a rich person toying with me for fun."

Rarely did anyone call me rich to my face. In addition to actually being rich, if not by Russian-oligarch standards, then at least by my own, I worked hard to cultivate the impression that I was, so I wasn't sure why it rankled so much when he said this.

"Live a little. Life's too short to spend accounting for every sin."

"This is living? I feel like I'm in a mausoleum."

He was right. The rigid symmetry, the candles, the silent waiters, the white flowers floating in glass bowls, my black dress: it all felt funereal.

"Do you want a salad?" I said, opening the menu again. "We can order you salad."

"Why are you going to California?"

"What?"

"You said you were going to California. Why?"

"To see my father."

"Why?"

"Do I need a reason? He's my father."

"There's always a reason. Why are you driving instead of flying?"

"I like to drive."

"Is your Dad rich?"

"No."

"So how can you afford this place?"

"I made money in my line of work."

"Which is?"

"None of your business."

"You used past tense. Are you not working anymore?"

"No."

"Why?"

"I quit."

"Why?"

"Because I could."

"When was the last time you saw your father?"

"Twenty-five years ago. No. Longer."

"He knows you're coming?"

"No."

"What are you going to do when you get there?"

"I don't know."

"I find that hard to believe."

"Then don't believe it."

Our steaks arrived. They were cut into thick slabs and balanced atop stacks of sliced and fried potato rounds. Artful globs of sauce circled the plates. The presentation was so absurd, I felt embarrassed for the cutlery.

John stood, dropped his cloth napkin onto the table, and left. The woman in the purple lipstick watched him go. She turned unsubtly to look at me, and I gave her a big cartoon smile. She wore a topaz ring, the gem the size of a postage stamp and throwing an interrogatory light. My cheeks were flushed like I'd been slapped.

I ate my steak. Then, dumbly, like a shark, I ate John's. My breasts hurt, particularly the left.

15

Back in my room, I took out all the candy stored in the mini fridge, indifferent to the criminal price markup but still hearing my mother's nagging about it in my head. I set all the packages around me in a circle on the bedspread, propped myself up on the plentiful pillows, and looked up my dad's site while methodically unwrapping and chewing every bar.

There was no update since I'd last checked, which had only been a few days before, though it felt much longer. His writing was mostly abstract and impersonal, stilted and poetic:

> *arranged pigments*
> *and light*
> *its the only way to smirk-less-ly*
> *capture g-d*

Only occasionally were there full sentences: *To think most of my work will end up in a landfill.* Of course it was going to end up in a landfill, I thought; almost everything does.

The last image was a selfie taken with the wife against the sunset, the angle poor so that their faces were half out of the frame. That's what he called her: the Wife. Teasing, lightly ironic, the same way you'd refer to furniture with a little personality: the Chippendale, the Wedgwood.

It was hard to believe a person gormless enough to not only take but also share such an image had once been capable of life-ruining cruelty. I wondered if it was possible that he was better with the new wife. If their personalities were more compatible, or if she had led him to the light of a gentler God. Maybe the irredeemable flaws I'd seen were just circumstantial, a temporary derangement, a bad reaction. What would killing him accomplish? Nothing, mostly.

Then again, neither would letting him live.

I clicked through his portfolio. There were many large canvases of women's bodies, all his circle-perfecting efforts applied to colorful anuses and vulvas and buttocks and navels and nipples and breasts. In college Caleb had shown me an interview with an artist popular at the time. The artist had faced criticism for drawing scantily clad women with exaggerated proportions; when asked, he said, "Yeah, I like breasts, so what?"

Part of my visceral reaction to Dad's work comes from the same place as any child's embarrassment about their parents, a basic *Ew, Dad*. Part of it comes from the void between how he beautified the world in his art and how unbeautifully he treated us in reality. But I also believe that his sickness, his selfishness, his cruelty unconsciously manifested in every line and color and brushstroke. I lack the language to say more.

I'd gone over once to the penthouse of a partner at the old firm only to be confronted with one of Dad's paintings. It was hung in a narrow hallway leading to a bathroom. The graphic, geometric nudity was probably too risqué to display in a more public-facing part of the home. According to the placard in the frame, Dad had called it "Bathers," probably invoking some dead Frenchman. Years ago I'd read the catalog copy accompanying one of his shows, which had described his work as "buoyant" and "reveling in the contradictions of consciousness."

No one was looking, so I splashed wine on the frame on purpose, but it didn't matter; it was protected by glass.

I was halfway through my candy bars. I ordered champagne from room service and turned on the TV. Any noise would do. For a while during the divorce, I slept in my mother's bed, though I was too old for that kind of thing. She had a big, soft, depressed body that was bad for her but that I loved. We'd fall asleep to the tiny TV atop her dresser. I remember waking up once in the night halfway through a black-and-white movie where a log cabin was about to topple over the edge of a cliff. It was years before I saw that movie again with Caleb and realized it wasn't an image of my mind's creation.

"You can tell me anything," Mom had once said in that bed. "You know that, right?"

"Yes," I'd said. And I did know. But I told her very little. I wanted to protect her from the darkness of my depths. On some level, I think she knew the darkness anyway. That it terrified her exactly because it was her own—that death wish in her diary, that big blue void of sorrow under her outward placidity.

The champagne arrived. On the screen was a political rally, an arena full of red, white, and blue balloons. I'd forgotten it was an election year. By now, all that remained for me was a Baby Ruth. I moved the champagne bottle to the sink and plunged my left hand inside the ice that remained. I left it there until I couldn't feel, my skin turned opaque pink. I stared at the white wall, dimmed to a blue milk shade in the TV dark.

16

In the morning I went out early. It was a weekday, and the streets were teeming with workers, suits and briefcases and paper coffee cups and the brisk clack of good shoes on pavement. I was not dressed so differently from all these important-seeming business people who navigated without looking up from their phones, but enjoyed being privately out of lockstep with them, running on my own schedule. I've always liked having a secret.

I was trying to see May again, that old teenage friend of mine. I wasn't even sure what I would say when I did. My goodbyes were always oblique. I wanted to see her in a way I couldn't on the internet: the run in her tights or the smudge in her eyeliner or the stray gray hair she forgot to pluck. Why did I do what I did? Because soon I'd be unable to do anything else.

When I'd last been in this city, working that trial, I'd texted her at the old number I still had saved and gotten a message delivery failure notification. It didn't matter; I'd been so busy with work that I'd barely left the hotel, feeling bunkered down in a windowless conference room on the tenth floor.

I felt shier than I had with Caleb. With him, I could at least offer sex as a prize for putting up with me. I had nothing but personality to offer May.

She'd become a shrink. I'd made an appointment with her

office using a mélange of retired details: my mother's name, the address of the house where I'd lived with Caleb, the phone number of the courthouse in the county where I grew up. Her office was in a building that appeared to be constructed of many interlocking glass boxes stacked to perilous height. The glass was reflective, which was disorienting, making passersby acutely aware of their bodies moving through space. I wondered if May had chosen to rent this office deliberately as a psychological trick on her patients. The atrium had one of those trendy living walls. The plants in it were a vivid green that proved fake; they were plasticky to the touch, synthetic.

Her office was full of small sculptures of narrow, distorted, abstracted human figures in heavy bronze. There were no magazines, only books. I could see faint vacuum lines in the ecru carpet. Sound-absorbing panels hung on the walls; she was on a low floor, but I could not hear the city outside, only the occasional typing of her receptionist, the blurred ringing of a telephone on low volume. This was a significant upgrade from the last psychiatrist's office I'd been in, with that riggable gumball machine and the tacked-up posters that said things like *Denial is a river in Egypt.*

May's decor was intended to soothe, but I found myself sitting erect, my hands gripping the wooden arms of my seat. Funny, I thought, that we'd both left our small town, had both become sophisticated and adult in these large anonymous places.

May opened the door to her office. I had a moment to observe her as she said goodbye to her prior client. She had a sensible bob and a pearl-gray suit, a silky cream button-up shirt, a gold wedding band. She was trim and wore makeup subtle enough to look like no makeup at all. I saw none of the flaws I'd hoped to see. She looked properly middle-aged, which startled me, because it meant I did, too.

She turned to me with a hand extended and said, "Irene?" Her hand, when I shook it, was well moisturized, bony, and cold.

Oddly, I liked being referred to by my mother's name. Like I'd found a loophole to resurrect the dead.

May's tight smile loosened, and her brow furrowed slightly as she took in my unadorned face. She was trying to place me while maintaining her professionalism. "Please, come in," she said, standing aside and gesturing to her open door. I went in and sat on a hard, narrow sofa opposite her chair, which was low-slung, wide, and a forbidding shade of matte black. A golden box of tissues rested in the center of a wooden coffee table like a little altar to sadness.

I noticed belatedly that she was not wearing any shoes, just sheer black anklets. I was reminded of sitting in my doctor's office at the time of my diagnosis, how I'd tucked my bare feet out of his view. May's tiny toes in that oversize, powerful chair were funny to me, so I laughed.

"What?" she said in a polite tone, smiling along with me.

"Nothing," I said, and then amended, "Your feet."

"Oh, yes, my receptionist should have explained. I find being shoeless helps keep us comfortable, relaxed, grounded. You're welcome to remove yours, if you like."

"No thanks."

"I'm sorry," she said, folding her legs up beneath her body. She had extracted a slim notepad and a shiny pen from some unseen cache. "But you look very familiar to me. Have we met before?"

"Oh, I get that a lot. I just have one of those faces."

"Hmm," she said. "Well, welcome. What brings you to my office?"

"I've been having trouble sleeping," I said. "And when I do manage to fall asleep, I keep having these dreams about killing my father. It's very disturbing."

She tilted her head slightly. I was tempted to fidget, to shake my leg or inspect my fingernails, but I forced myself to sit still. It seemed it had been a long time since either of us exhaled.

"Oh," she finally said. "You."

"I didn't think it would take you this long. I've been told I haven't changed a bit."

"This is strange," she said. "But hello."

"I couldn't figure how else to see you."

"Most people who want to reconnect would do something less intense. Send a message over social media, for instance."

"I'm not most people." I didn't elaborate that I had no online presence, aside from a few dummy accounts I'd made strictly for research purposes. The only traces I left were related to law school or work. It sounded like she'd never tried to find more about me, never been disappointed by the absence.

"You could have provided your real name."

"I've always liked the element of surprise."

"Well. It is nice to see you," she said. "But this isn't an appropriate venue for this conversation. This slot could have gone to a real patient in need."

"Maybe I am a real patient in need," I said.

She looked at me quizzically.

"I'm just passing through," I continued. "Had to stop for the night, and I thought, who do I know who lives in this city? I knew you'd gone to school here, I figured you might've stayed, so I looked you up. I thought you might get a kick out of it. I mean, after all these years."

This invented explanation and my manner of expressing it seemed to mollify her. Her shoulders dropped by a centimeter. A plain gold bracelet she wore had ridden up her slim forearm and she pushed it back down. "You always had an odd sense of humor," she said. "Where are you traveling to?"

"California."

"What's in California?"

"I've always wanted to go," I said, then added, "I'm driving there with my partner. Sort of a road trip. Making it up as we go along, stopping where we like. Very liberating. Have you ever traveled that way? I recommend it."

I thought the mention of a partner would make me seem saner, suggest to her that I had something resembling a life.

I continued, "Seems like you've done pretty well for yourself."

"I have, thank you for noticing."

"And your family," I said, nodding at a picture mounted on the wall behind her desk, below a few framed degrees. It showed a smiling man sitting on the bench of an upright piano, a baby in his lap leaning forward to reach the keys. There were deep coffee-colored circles under the man's eyes, and the baby had a small strawberry mark on its scalp.

I hadn't expected May to have a kid. I never expected anyone to, though every other lawyer my age at both the firm and the company did. Even Robert—one of the firm's partners, an aging bachelor nearly as unlovable as me, who picked up and discarded waitresses half his age just to rile the office feminists—had an adult son from his first marriage. I felt arrested, paused in a frame while the rest of the movie kept playing. Not that everyone should have children. Of all people, I definitely shouldn't. Despite my promiscuity, I've never had so much as a pregnancy scare.

May turned to follow my gaze, then turned back smiling, probably at whatever happy memory the photograph called up for her. "That's an old one," she said. "She'll be seven in a month."

A long minute passed of us smiling at each other idiotically. I could almost hear the ice between us cracking, the face of the glacier shearing away.

"I won't take up any more of your time," I said. "Just wanted to say hello is all. Do bill me for the appointment."

I stood and moved to the door. I'd just put my hand on the knob when she said, "Wait."

She stood and moved closer to me. She used to wear these fat-soled combat boots that helped her reach my eyes; now, barefoot,

I was taller than her and could see the vulnerable white at the part of her hair, a thinning patch there.

"Would you like to come to dinner?" she said. "My husband and I just bought a house, and we've been redecorating it, and frankly, I'd love to show it off."

This last line had a practiced quality that made me think she'd said it before to many potential guests. Her social grace impressed me. We'd both been spiky and unapproachable in our youth. I couldn't remember us ever inviting each other anywhere so formally. I seem to recall us becoming friends almost accidentally, when we used the same broken emergency exit to sneak out of gym class.

"Leaving today," I said, wincing in an oh-that's-too-bad way. She was probably only asking to avoid hurt feelings, or to make herself seem generous or polite or, what was the phrase she'd used? Comfortable, relaxed. Grounded.

"I thought you were making it up as you went along, stopping where you liked?"

I pretended to chew my lip, to be thinking it over. She said, "C'mon," in a voice that sounded more like the version of her I remembered, that maladjusted kid. I knew, before I opened my mouth, that I would lie and say yes, and that is exactly what I did, only it wasn't a lie. I stayed.

17

I grew up in a poor town up the Hudson that rubbed elbows with a rich one. An invisible line divided it; luck and redistricting put us on the rich side by a hair. Though I had more in common socially with the trashy girls who wore pajama pants to school and filched their mothers' Parliaments, I got to ride the bus with six other broke kids to classes filled with children whose mothers or nannies dropped them off in BMWs.

One of my great-great-grandfathers had gone to Yale for his JD and became deputy mayor of some small city in New York State before his descendants married poorly and frittered his inheritance away. Or so I was told; I've never tried to verify this. Mom seemed to hope I'd get back to his general level of success. She told me often that I deserved better, that I was better. Molly S. down the road had a father who made lawn sculptures out of bent motorcycle license plates, but Mom insisted that wasn't real art, like my father's. As with many loving parents, she let me be her blind spot, the one thing about which she was cruel and unreasonable and unfair. In this way, nothing much ever changes.

In this nicer school, my only friend was May. She had bright violet hair. She'd ordered permanent dye from the internet and had it delivered to my house so her mother wouldn't find out until it was too late. She colored it with me after class in the handicapped bathroom, then walked home with a shower cap on. Her mother threatened to shave it all off—dyed hair was not common in that time or place—but May knew she'd never.

We were known around school as the Dykes—the hair, the big boots, the moodiness—but I didn't want to fuck her; I wanted to be her. She expanded the range of what I thought possible, the ways I could be angry and how I could make that anger look good. I admired her precociously consistent style because I had none myself. Our friendship began accidentally, but before then I'd seen her around and decided from looking at her that I'd like to know her. I'd previously thought friendships were built more on proximity and time than affinity.

May was adopted; her parents, like mine, were divorced. Her father lived in Manhattan, a long train ride away. He was important, May told me, though she needn't have; I associated this quality with anyone who lived in the city. By virtue of living there, you held a certain interest. She often said she was going to leave to go live with him.

This was our only disagreement: fathers. She thought I overstated the nature of Dad's problems. Immigrant kids get beat all the time, it's no big deal, she sometimes said, though she had not personally been beaten. I never told her my entire history, but even if I had, I think for her my angst still would've fallen under the general heading of "white people shit." I wasn't offended by this. I just thought she was wrong.

"What are you so happy about?" I asked her once.

"I'm seeing Daddy tomorrow."

"Glad a slot opened up in his schedule for you."

"Just because your dad doesn't love you doesn't mean no one else's does," she said serenely. "He lives in a big apartment with views of the park."

"I know," I said. "You've told me like a million times."

She ignored me. "Huge windows."

"Sounds nice."

"It is *so* nice."

"If it's so nice, how come your parents split?"

"Irreconcilable differences," she said, relishing the sophistication of the phrase. All I knew about her parents' relationship was that her father was much older and was a professor of art history at a school May wanted to attend.

"Listen," she added, grabbing my forearm with startling urgency. "Come with me."

"Me?"

"You'll stop talking shit about him once you meet him."

"Right," I said, skeptical.

We cut school. We were seventeen, seniors. I'd walked out on the occasional period but had never missed a whole day like that before, though I pretended otherwise. It didn't strike me as odd until later that she was skipping to see her father, which implied that this plan wasn't sanctioned by her mother.

We biked an hour to the closest train station two towns over and arrived simultaneously sweating and freezing. I seem to recall it being shortly before Christmas; someone had wrapped the platform's light poles in evergreen garlands that were already shedding orange needles. Half a deer carcass lay on the tracks with its hind legs shorn away, its graying guts spilled out all over the gravel between the rails. It had been there awhile, with black flies pouring from the cup of its eye. It had no odor. We stood on the yellow stripe at the edge of the platform and looked down.

"What happened to the other half?" asked May.

"Carried off by the train, I guess."

"Cool. Come on, let's go to the waiting room. It's cold," she said, tugging at my sleeve.

We lived so far away that the ride took hours. May fell asleep on my shoulder, leaving a warm patch of drool on my sleeve. I liked being awake while she slept; it made me feel useful. I watched the landscape transform through the window from forest to marsh to hamlet to suburb to exurb to city, a seamless and untraceable progression. At the station we emerged from dark tunnels and presses of people up into the light and bustle of the street, and I had to shove my red, dry hands into my pockets.

We had time to kill before meeting May's father. She dragged me to a museum. Every gallery seemed a monument to time and its waste. If Dad had been born in any of the eras we looked at, he would've painted endless iterations of whatever God he worshiped instead of secular nudity, and it would have been just as hollow, I was sure. His was a timeless idiocy.

Funnily enough, I was actually pretty good at drawing, or so a teacher had told me back before art classes became elective. I doodled for May's entertainment, sharks carrying briefcases and fat women with lopsided eyes all over her math notebooks.

We stopped in front of *Ugolino and His Sons*, and I let May explain it to me: Ugolino's treason, his eternal punishment in damnation, his temptation to eat his own offspring—all very dramatic.

I yawned performatively. "Boring."

May looked at me with a disdain more sincere than I'd expected. "You're such a tool," she said.

"Snob."

"Philistine."

We went to a café afterward. May ordered a black coffee, and I immediately regretted not doing the same because it both sounded and looked cool, like ordering a cup of death. We sat at one of the café's inconveniently small tables, designed to discourage loitering. It seemed an awkward time of day to meet someone; too late for lunch, too early for dinner. Had he really made her come all that way only to get coffee?

"What time did he say?" I asked.

"It's okay. We're early."

I picked up an abandoned magazine from a neighboring table and read the horoscopes aloud, keeping us amused with futures full of promising nonsense. May wasn't paying attention. She kept looking out the big plate glass window. I gave up trying to divert her and silently read the articles, scanning but not absorbing their words.

"Do you want to call him?" I asked.

"No."

"Maybe something happened."

She crumpled up her napkin, then unfolded it and carefully pressed it out flat. She'd barely touched her drink.

"He does this a lot, doesn't he. Forgets about you," I said, not even trying to keep the joy of being right out of my voice.

"He's busy."

"He's not busy. He doesn't care."

"You just want every family to be as messed up as your own."

I let the remark pass.

"Whatever. Let's go home," she said.

"Wait, sit down," I said, grabbing her sleeve and tugging until she fell back into her chair. "Let's go find him."

"I don't know," she said, chewing her cheek. I couldn't understand her reluctance.

"He lives around here, doesn't he? What if he's in trouble? What if he had a heart attack or a stroke and he's waiting for you to rescue him?"

I didn't think this was likely, and I didn't care if I scared her. I just wanted to satisfy my curiosity. I wanted to meet this man, this doctor of art.

"Doubt it," she said, but I could tell she was wobbling.

"You won't know till you know, you know?"

Outside it seemed to have gotten colder. The streets of the Upper East Side were wide empty canyons. We passed blondes in quilted Barbours and men in boat shoes walking teacup dogs in tartan fleeces; an old woman in seasonally inappropriate kitten heels, her feet blue with cold; a man on a bench taking bites of a baguette before spitting out the bolus for pigeons to eat. Doormen paced the curb, hunting cabs as if for sport. This was the neighborhood where I bought my condo so many years later.

I followed May for a few blocks before I realized we were walking in the wrong direction.

"You said he lived on the park?" I asked.

May ignored me. We walked a long way, passing storefronts for clothing designers with unpronounceable names. There were no shoppers, only security guards protecting the merchandise and mannequins inside. I felt we'd entered an alien place. The hostile race living here would launch us back into the thinning air of the galaxy where, exposed and lacking protective suits, we'd promptly die.

"There," said May, pointing to a gray brick building across the street. We jaywalked across the avenue under a rare gasp of open sky. I noticed a nearby community garden, which might have been the park May had somewhat misleadingly referred to. Affixed to the exterior wall of the building was a column of brass plaques bearing the nameplates of the various professionals who worked inside, with bells for residents above. Although not quite as nice as May had implied, it was still an elegant building. I momentarily resented her parents' evident wealth.

May rang the bell. A moment passed before there was a crackling, buzzing response. I felt an unpleasant crimp of anxiety but chalked it up to the coffee I'd had.

"Daddy? It's me," May said into the intercom.

Static rendered the reply unintelligible.

"May. Your daughter."

Another moment of waiting and then there was a high-key, piercing ring, and May pushed open the door. We made it through the foyer, and then May was leading me up a set of marble steps with a tacked-down carpet runner until we reached a white-painted hall, each door with a peephole and gold-plated apartment number. We stopped, and May rang again. I heard creaking floorboards on the other side of the door before it opened a crack and stopped on its chain. The way I was positioned prevented me from seeing inside. I couldn't hear whoever answered, their voice was pitched so low.

"It's me, Daddy," May said again. She didn't mention me, and it was unclear if her father saw me before he let us in, which is an important distinction in retrospect.

The door opened, and May stepped inside ahead of me. I noticed the darkness first, then the smell, then the mess. Tremendous stacks of books, records, newspapers, magazines, paintings, and binders teetered on either side of a narrow pathway. Half-crushed cardboard boxes labeled with Sharpie scrawls or logos of dead companies or words like PERISHABLE and GOD LOVES YOU threatened to avalanche down. Piano keys lurked under the mound, the only visible part of the instrument. Wires and cables snaked and coiled with no clear origin, end, or purpose. My eyes adjusted to faint daylight, though no window could be seen.

I followed May down this path into a slight clearing, a carved-out area with a couch that had only one seat available, the other being piled high with bundles of undistinguished junk, knotted plastic bags, a copy of a *New York Post* from February 1994 announcing that Jackie Kennedy had cancer. There was an open bag of cat food but no cat in sight. An old banker's desk lamp offered warm light. A few feet away was a small kitchen with a tiny stove, the counter space crowded with dishes and pans in various states of uncleanness.

Her father looked even older than I'd expected, with stooped posture that only made him seem more overwhelmed by the space. I could believe he was a professor based on his dignified doddering and moth-eaten sweater.

"Sit, sit," he told us. "Coffee?"

May took the chair. I sat on a stack of old *Artforum*s that had become so compressed over time, it didn't slide beneath my weight. We hadn't answered him, but he busied himself with a French press. He turned and handed May her coffee, black, on a teacup with a proper saucer. He knew how she liked it, or else she liked it because that was how he'd always made it.

I watched a roach skitter across a cabinet door. I stood and said, "Just need some air."

I went and sat at the base of the steps, making my body as small as possible in case another resident came. None did. It was drafty and cold down there. I waited a long time. I'd been convinced I was impossible to surprise, cynical enough to handle anything, but reality had outdone me.

When May finally reappeared and sat next to me, I said, "Had you been here before?"

"A long time ago," she said, her voice clipped and dulled. "He's worse."

"He's really a professor?"

"Retired."

"I shouldn't have made you come."

"Hess," she said. "Please shut up."

We didn't speak on the miles-long walk back to the station. May stayed a few indifferent steps ahead of me the whole time. I wanted to suggest the subway but was afraid of her silence and anyway deserved whatever punishment she felt fitting. She stopped at a traffic light behind a clump of tourists and in front of a flower shop. With her colorful hair, she looked like another bulb in the buckets, a dyed tulip or carnation. The neon sign of the shop cast a red glow over her. I hated art but understood then why an artist might want to keep that tiny change in light. Render it possessable and preserved, this last moment we were friends.

On the train home, the seats were full of businessmen on their return journey, laptops and cell phones and paper bag–swaddled beers purchased in the station all cracked. We had to stand in the vestibule by the doors, swaying unsteadily. My feet had blistered and my shoes were full of blood. I wished a terrorist would board the train so I'd be able to sacrifice myself saving someone better than me. So I'd die a noble death.

That didn't happen. I waited until a high-speed train blasted by us, that gut-punch sensation. Half-covered by the brief roar, my hand cupped from my mouth to her studded ear, I told May I was going to kill my father.

The train whooshed out of earshot. She pulled back from me, her eyes first wide and then slitted, narrow.

"That's not funny."

"I'm not trying to be."

"That's worse. You need help."

"Forget it," I said, and then added, "You're right."

She rested her head against the door, watching the landscape whizz by outside, trees and roads and fenced-in yards that backed up to the tracks. It looked like she was nodding, but it was only the movement of the train. I couldn't decide if I wanted to catch her eye or not. I'd look at her, and then the moment it seemed likely she'd look back, I'd dart my eyes away again, pretending to be engrossed in whatever lay at the other end of the corridor, thinking that if I needed help, I couldn't imagine where to find it.

Several seats away, one of the older beer-drinking men, ears coddled by foam-coated headphones, saw me and winked.

18

It was barely noon when I left May's office and went back to the hotel. I found John outside, largely hidden from view by an engaged column several feet from the entrance. On him, the sun just looked like more filth, like he was caked in a rime of light. That he stood instead of sitting on one of the nearby stone benches felt correct. He was so austere and opposed to comfort that I was surprised he hadn't broken the ceramic vase displayed in the niche behind him and knelt in the shards.

I'll admit I was happy he came back.

"Sleep well?" I asked maliciously, but John just nodded. I continued, "I have dinner plans tonight and I'd like you to come." I had to produce someone who could plausibly pass as my "partner" for May's benefit.

"Is it going to be like last night?"

"No."

"Then what will it be like?"

"I'm not sure," I said. He seemed to accept this as true.

I sent my clothes to be laundered, hanging around my hotel room in a bathrobe. I let John use the shower while I browsed satellite maps of the county where, from my research, I'd figured out my father lived. John emerged from the bathroom shirtless with his hair and beard flat-wet and a towel draped over the back of his neck. His chest was concave, his sternum pronounced. I tried to imagine fucking him because I imagine fucking almost everyone, less out of lasciviousness and more as an interpersonal shorthand. I found I couldn't do it, couldn't relate myself to him in that way, though sex had been part of my rationale for picking him up. I wondered if he was gay or asexual. I could've asked, but it was none of my business. I concluded that if I did fuck him, it would be hot, like convincing a monk you were worth abandoning his ideals over, but only in that specific way.

We rode the El and then walked to May's, John's hair growing as it dried in the spring air to halo his face. *We.* I thought of the word *partner* and laughed. Maybe it would have been accurate to call him my friend. Was he? I felt like a visitor to an alternate universe, one where I lived the life I could've had were I not quite such a hopeless case.

May lived in a half-baked neighborhood, not having reached a high enough property valuation to gentrify all the way through. The streets were lively, crowded with both junkies and healthy twenty-somethings who looked like they went camping with friends often and had orthodontia as children. Now and then we'd pass a Polish beer counter manned by a grandmother with whiskered cheeks. The side streets were full of townhomes and subdivided former Victorian manses. May lived in one of the latter. She was an actual person with a family, full sets of dishware, full sets of friends.

Even in relatively clean condition, John looked like what he was, which was a street person. May shook his hand with alarm, like he'd just cut himself badly but was insisting nothing was wrong. I'd already crossed the threshold by then, pushing in ahead of him; if she'd wanted to change her mind, it was too late.

The piano from the picture in her office was right there in her living room. Her husband seemed dependable, as far as husbands went, with a soft beard and belly and those persistent rings under his eyes. He was a professional musician. I briefly entertained seducing him, then banished the thought. I barely saw him anyway; he took care of putting their kid to bed to let May socialize.

She'd picked up food rather than cooking. This seemed calculated to suggest that she wasn't a try-hard, that she didn't need to impress us and just did whatever was simplest. Correct or not, such minor decisions can constitute your whole impression of a person. During the meal, her daughter came down to say good night, not satisfied with the first good night she'd received before we arrived. She wore a princess dress the color of mint sherbet, the shiny fabric faded in patches. May put her hands around her daughter's face and pushed her cheeks in. The daughter squealed in delighted recognition of the ritual before May leaned down for a kiss.

"This is my old, old friend Hester," May said to her daughter. "Say good night to Hester."

I'd thought I was doing a passable rendition of normalcy, but the girl looked at me suspiciously, unable to place her mother and me together. I felt like an untrustworthy chaperone on a field trip nowhere good. Children are more perceptive than most adults know. Or maybe adults just become more forgiving of flaws, their expectations lowered by experience, which is a synonym for disappointment.

May's husband swooped in and hoisted her up in his arms. "All right, Harpo, bedtime," he said and whisked her upstairs, the folds of her skirt crinkling in his arms. I was reminded of how, when I was very little, I used to feign sleep after long drives so my father would have to carry me inside.

"That dress is filthy," said May. "She either has to sleep in it or with it. Dry-clean only. Worst purchase of my life."

"Is that normal?" I asked.

"Yes, very. You didn't have a comfort object?"

"I don't remember."

There was no one I could ask for that information. Even if I'd had a good relationship with my father, I don't think he noticed other people that way, especially not children. Not that it mattered. I preferred to pretend I was never small and vulnerable.

"How's your father?" I asked, since I was thinking of mine.

Her eyebrows folded like she was troubled I'd ask, like my asking so soon after asking about her daughter implied unwellness by association.

"He passed."

"That's sad."

"It was a long time ago. Out here we could've just gotten a dumpster and parked it in the driveway, but in Manhattan it's a whole different story. We had to hire this discreet removal service so as not to upset the neighbors or bring the sale price down."

For a moment I was confused, thinking she was talking about getting rid of the body, and then I remembered the junk inside the apartment and how much worse it had probably gotten with time.

"I can't imagine how that works," I said.

"Covered opaque plastic bins and people in unmarked jumpsuits, done in increments over several weeks."

She scratched her forehead, trying to scrape away the memory, then took a generous sip of wine. She hadn't gone to the school where her father had taught; she'd gone to Chicago, far from home. I'd wondered how much that day in the city had influenced her choice. She was worse off than me, I thought, because she'd never stopped loving her dad. Not everything bears comparison, but I wouldn't have traded places with her. I was in some perverse sense glad Dad had hurt me. The line he'd crossed was clearer, easier to find in the dark.

"What about yours?" she asked.

Though she asked with nothing but evident polite interest, I sensed she relished bringing it up. A revenge in proportion to my crime.

"I'm going to see him, actually. He lives out west now."

"So that's why you're going," she said. "Reconciliation."

She might have forgotten what I told her that day on the train, my remark to her in her office. Or else she hadn't taken me seriously. I don't know why I ever expected anyone to take me seriously. Even—maybe especially—people close to me.

"Something like that," I said. I'd slid far back in my seat, idly fidgeting with the blunt butter knife next to my plate, rotating it this way and that to watch the way it glinted under the staggered chandelier. It was preferable to meeting her eyes.

"I knew you didn't just 'want to go to California,'" she said in the same mocking imitation of my voice she'd done when we were kids, that easy familiarity.

"We'll see how it goes."

"Who initiated, you or him?"

I lied, "He sent a letter."

"An apology letter?"

I hid my wince by coughing into my cloth napkin. "In a manner of speaking."

"Gives me hope for humanity that you can be that old and have a change of heart like that."

I wondered if there was an element of professional interest in this for her, some thread of therapeutic value. I was my own case study. "Who knows what'll happen," I demurred.

May nodded and said, "Smart not to set the bar too high." Then she turned to John. "And what about you?"

John, who'd been chewing meditatively this whole time, swallowed and then smiled. He had a slow, stately manner of eating. I hadn't asked him a single thing about his family. He seemed more like a fungus to me, a product of fragmentation or budding. Thinking of him having people was like walking down the opposite side of an old street, seeing all the buildings from a wholly new angle.

"What about me?"

"Well, anything," said May. "Your family, I guess, since that seems to be the topic."

"Dad's a pastor, Mom stays home. They're getting old, but I have four brothers and two sisters, so they've got plenty of help."

"Seven? I can barely manage one," said May.

"Easier in the woods. Just let them roam outside. Someone dies or gets lost, you still got the other six."

May laughed hard. This was more volume and charm than I'd expected of John. It vexed me to think May had an ability to draw him out that I lacked.

"How'd you two meet?" May asked, gesturing between us with her fork.

"Online," I said, too quickly and hoping May didn't ask for specifics. John cut me a brief, confused look, but May was looking at her plate, and it probably went unseen.

"Us too," she said, referring to her husband. "But we always lie and say we met in college. We went to the same one, just at different times. What do you do, John?"

"He's a photographer," I said.

"Really?" May laughed. "You know she hates art, right?"

"Do you?" said John, who seemed to be taking my lie in stride.

"Remember the museum?" May asked. "You were such a brat about it."

I pictured myself slouching through the galleries in my big black coat, grousing about how stupid everything was, and yes, ha ha, it was true, I could see it, I'd been a brat, subject to swings of mood and fits of grandiosity like any other adolescent. *Why had I come here?* I thought. The whole evening was as exquisitely funny and painful as a minor blow to the head.

"I used to hate it," I said, feeling I'd either had too much wine or not enough. "But I'm beginning to see the light."

There was a lull. May said, "Do you two want to spend the

night? We have a spare room. A guest room. We just redecorated and haven't really had guests in it yet."

John said, before I could intervene, "We'd love to."

"We've already paid for the hotel," I said.

"So what?" said John. I almost expected him to add a derisive *honey* or *babe.*

"No, no. We'd have to pick up our things. But thank you."

"No pressure," said May, throwing up her hands in resignation. "Really, I just wanted you to ooh and aah at the window treatments I picked."

She smiled at me. I tried my level best to smile back.

After Mom died, school became intolerable. A guidance counselor tried to get me into group therapy for teens by telling me a cheerleader I wasn't friends with also went because her little sister had died of leukemia. A Spanish teacher pulled me out of class and hugged me in the hallway. May had gradually stopped hanging out with me after that disastrous day in the city, but she walked me home once and spent some time puttering around my mother's kitchen, drinking water straight from the tap because I'd already begun packing up everything to sell. I knew she only did it out of pity and a sense of duty, to maintain this image of herself as a good person. She kept asking if I'd be okay, and I kept telling her I'll be fine, it's fine, go home.

I don't know why I thought that was such a problem. To want to think of yourself as a good person.

John and I followed her to the guest room just for her to show us. She told us, with mellow but genuine enthusiasm, about which era the vintage items in the room were from, how they'd been acquired, other household improvements they'd made, about the challenges of working with contractors, as I nodded and hmmed and wondered what sixteen-year-old May would've thought of all this, of her evolution into a propertied woman who cared about curtains, and whether that was really a reasonable metric, what your old self would've thought of your current and future selves.

Before we left, I went upstairs to the bathroom. A few family photographs crowded one end of the hallway, and I realized they were leaving room for more, for their planned future happiness. I could hear May's husband, still reading a story at this late hour, voice variably pitched to imitate different characters. A story whose individual words were obscure yet still familiar.

I applied more lipstick. A little voice said, "Daddy, I'm not sleepy." I left the sink faucet on to drown out all sound.

19

We rode the train back in silence. It wasn't until we were on the elevator back up to the room that John asked, "Why'd you lie?"

"About what?"

John looked at me like I'd asked directions to the moon. "About us being together," he said.

The question irritated me though he had every right to ask it. People lied all the time; there hardly needed to be a particular or remarkable reason.

"I didn't want her to worry."

"Why would she worry?"

Speaking slowly because I was thinking hard, I said, "Picking up a drifter is not consistent with what I would've done when she knew me. It's the action of a different person entirely."

The elevator doors opened onto our floor with a gentle ding. An entire bachelor party stood in the hall waiting their turn, all wearing novelty sunglasses shaped like beer steins and T-shirts that said *Ricky's Getting Hitched*.

"So? When was the last time you saw her? People change," John said as we pressed by the group.

"Not me, I never change," I said, fiddling with my room key card. "Plus, it'd invite questions."

"What's wrong with questions?"

"I don't have designs on you, I didn't intend to suggest that. I appreciate that you went along with it, I do, and now I'd appreciate it if you stopped asking questions."

We'd made it into the room. I went over to close the curtains just for something to do. John leaned on the dresser next to the television, watching me. He asked, "Did your father really write you a letter?"

"Do you want a free ride or not?"

He nodded.

"Then stop with the questions."

"You're," he said, pausing to search for the right words. "Really tense. And controlling."

"And you're a really big dumb hippie," I said. "You know what? Forget it, get lost. This was a stupid idea."

His eyebrows raised in mild surprise. "For good? No more free ride?"

"Easy come, easy go," I said, lifting his canvas bag—which was heavier than I'd prepared for—and holding it out to him. He hesitated to take it like he thought I'd slam it onto his head. He waited so long my arm started to quake. I didn't know him at all. I wondered if this was the point when he'd pull a knife on me, revealing himself to be a meth head after my cash, someone my instincts had misled me about, but he took one strap and hoisted it onto his shoulder and said, "Thanks anyway," and I said, "For what," and then he was gone.

20

Right around the time Mom got pregnant with me, Dad quit his day job selling insurance to focus on his art. It was my understanding that until that point finances were tight but no worse. They'd taken out loans to build our house with the help of an architect friend of my dad's and a general contractor. Land was cheap then and materials, too.

Later there was a falling-out with the architect friend; I never understood why. Dad felt he had enough expertise to do some of the remaining jobs himself: build a deck, install a sliding door in the sunroom. The deck was only ever half-finished, the remainder covered in a blue tarp weighed down with cinder blocks. Dad tinkered without real progress, cultivating the impression that it was less a problem with him and more something intractably complicated with the house, which people were generally not inclined to question, because who knew a man's house better than the man?

In this way, our property became an eyesore. Neither the interior nor exterior was ever complete: the basement unfinished, the wall-to-wall carpet untacked, the shelves never installed in the bathroom closet. That closet became a cache for all manner of odds and ends: a broken-handled broom, an ironing board with a scorch mark, an upturned hamper on which rested folded towels. Why we even bothered folding the towels, I'm not sure. There was space enough in the center for a child to stand, not even a bare bulb but only the cracks around the jambs for light. I'd focus so hard on shutting out noise from outside that I thought I could hear my hair and nails growing.

A better spot when I got a little older was the roof. To the left of my bedroom window was the front door. Above it, a portico extended just far enough for me to climb onto its edge and then up to the peak. From there, one foot on the bathroom windowsill and hands on the drip edge, I could hoist myself on the roof proper. I could be up there for hours. I had a stash of acorns, and whenever Dad appeared outside, I'd pelt them at him and then hide behind the crumbling mortar of the chimney because I wanted to avoid punishment and because I wanted him to think that nature was against him, down to the birds and squirrels. That he was judged or watched by a greater power, since he didn't seem to care about my judging or watching.

I wanted Mom to come with me, to teach her my tricks, but she was too old, too stiff and heavy for escape. She was not even forty then.

She tried to encourage me to be normal by signing me up for activities, such as they were in our nothing town. She'd attempt to get errands done while I was at my piano lesson or softball practice, but I wouldn't let her. I'd make her wait until inevitably I'd run out of the field or rec center or teacher's house, having found some unforgivable flaw in the instructors or peers or activity itself. I didn't give her a moment's peace until the divorce was finalized. Only then did I become civilized: doing homework, running punishing distances on the track team. Making one singular friend.

The day the papers came through I made her take me out to a diner named after a dead Indian chief.

"I want one of everything," I said, perusing the menu.

"You can order one of one thing," Mom said.

"This is a special occasion. We're celebrating," I countered.

Mom smiled sadly. "I don't feel very much like celebrating."

I felt giddy and free; ding-dong, the witch is dead. To me the divorce was an unequivocal good.

"You will," I said. "Once you've eaten."

When the waitress came, I ordered a full stack with cinnamon and peach slices and walnuts swirled into the batter and a side of bacon crisped almost to black and a gooey fried egg flecked with griddle grease and smothered by a slice of melty cheddar and peppery hashbrowns studded with rings of sausage and airy towers of buttered toast and a tiny ceramic mug of fresh pulpy orange juice. I didn't think we'd come anywhere near to eating all that food, but once I started speaking, I couldn't stop. I went on for so long and gave such exhaustive instructions that the waitress laughed when I was done and said, "You're sure that's all, hon?"

Mom only got coffee, and even that she seemed uninterested in, not bothering to cream or sugar it like normal. Typically when she felt blue, she had an appetite, a quality Dad had also noticed and openly mocked. I couldn't believe the table supported the weight of so many plates. A white-haired woman in a teal turtleneck and gold clip-on earrings eating a modest bowl of oatmeal turned to look at us with obvious disdain for my mother's parenting.

"Don't you want any, Mom?"

Her eyes seemed fixed on something at the far end of the diner. Chewing loudly, I turned to look, but there was nothing there.

She muttered something I couldn't hear.

"What?" I asked. "Mom, what did you say?"

She finally turned to look at me. She looked like she was settling back into her body, her shoulders relaxing and her head drooping forward. These faraway episodes would happen occasionally in the ensuing years. I later wondered if they were early symptoms of her illness.

She said, "You're a happy kid, Hester. Things have been hard, but you're okay."

I slowed my chewing. I hadn't really thought about it. She sounded strange and bitter. I'd thought she liked having a daughter who was wild and fearless and fierce, but it occurred to me then that she wished I were a softer, weepier, more delicate child. One she could've comforted and cradled. One more like her and less like Dad. There was a coarse, cynical quality to my cheer that frightened her because it reminded her of him.

"I'm okay right now," I said, mouth still full.

"Good," she said. "That's good. Promise me you'll keep it that way, okay? Promise me you'll try to be happy. Can you promise me that?"

I swallowed. "Uh," I said. "I guess?"

"Good," she said again.

She picked up her fork and dug in.

21

After John left, I went to the hotel gym and ran on the treadmill until my legs felt disconnected from my body and my left foot, the bad one from my old injury, ached. No one else was there. The walls to either side of me were mirrors; if I looked to the left or the right, I saw my reflection into infinity. I didn't like full mirrors; there was too much of my father in them. I preferred to see myself in glimpses: a single eye, my lipsticked mouth alone. The TV showed me an unseasonal monsoon in Florida, flooding in the north, wildfires in the southwest, a tornado outbreak in the southeast.

Back in my room, I showered. The countertop and the tissue box resting on it and the tub and the toilet all looked carved from the same plate of marble. As I toweled off, I examined my chest and found what looked like a dimple or a shadow, a shy pocket in the flesh on the left side. The lighting in the bathroom was so soft I could have imagined it. I pushed my fingers on it to stretch the skin taut, and then pressed down hard, and then harder still, hard enough I thought I'd bruise. *Beryl*, I thought hatefully. I threw away my entire cosmetics bag, including all my mother's lipsticks, then picked up the hair dryer from its rack on the wall and dropped it onto the hard marble floor so that its plastic casing cracked. I turned off all the lights and wrapped myself in a robe so I wouldn't have to see anything anymore.

I turned the channel to a show about a detective with a secret heroin habit. The volume was loud enough that I didn't hear the rain start. I wasn't watching the screen but instead the interplay of shadows across the wall next to my bed, the way the light dimmed or brightened depending on whether the protagonist was in trouble or not. Rain landed on the window, the drops casting another layer of faint, quaking shadows. This was how I understood the weather.

I pulled the sheets up over my head, my breath suffusing the crisp space with suffocating warmth, stale saliva, and phantom toothpaste. *Go to sleep*, I willed myself, but an hour later the rain hadn't let up and neither had the wakefulness. I got my phone and looked at my father's site, hunting specifically for images of the new wife, more specifically for ones where I could see her wrinkles. I wasn't going to kill her, even if she was there when I arrived. I'd just have to do it too quickly for her to react, to panic or scream or otherwise complicate my math. Two shots, bang-bang, done, to ruin two lives already in a state of serious disrepair.

Another hour passed. I'd gone so far back in his archive that the wife had not even appeared yet. I huffed into the darkness and threw back the covers like they were to blame. I put on a coat and went down to the crypt-like lobby and had the night valet bring me my coffin-like car. I told myself I was not looking for John; I was just going out for a night ride to cool my nerves. It had been an upsetting day.

I didn't know where to begin looking. Traffic lights flashed for no one on empty streets. Bodies were lumped in bus shelters and doorways with newspaper blankets and makeshift cardboard mattresses, none of them John. God had probably told him a good place to sleep, warm and dry and tucked out of public view. I doubted he'd be near the road unless he'd already started trying to hitchhike again.

In the end, he was by the water, of all places, heading north toward who knows what. The wind shook the surface of the lake like hunting a dead man's pockets for change. John was recognizable from behind, his sealskin backpack turned almost black with wet and his pant legs rolled up to show his hairy calves, taut and trussed and free of tattoos. He wore a poncho that made him look polygonal, inhumanly shaped.

I rolled up, slowed to walking speed, and lowered the passenger window.

"Hey," I called.

There was a joke there somewhere, me trying to pick him up the way a john picks up a hooker, and the fact that his name was John, but these are the kinds of thoughts you have only when you've thought about something several times. Consider anything long enough and it becomes a joke, the way a word repeated dissolves to nonsense on the tongue.

He turned, his hood raised and eyes shadowed, accumulated water pouring off him at gutter speed.

"Get in the car," I said.

He came to the window and rested his hands on the ledge. The seat was already getting soaked; I could feel droplets spraying all up my arm. The dark was high and rich and velvet-black and his knuckles were bone-white and jutting, and it all gave me this sensation of collecting a ghost.

"You've been walking this whole time?" I asked.

He didn't acknowledge me. "Couple months ago, this was all flooded. If we'd been here then, the water would've been up to my ankles where I stand now. Higher lake levels, worse storms. Warmer winters, less evaporation off the lake."

It was hard to hear his little sermon over the roaring rain. He turned his head and looked north like he saw an approaching threat, but there was nothing, no pedestrians, no cars, not even a streetlamp. I started to worry we looked conspicuous, lingering long enough for a cop to come and ask what was going on here, and then a long chain of events would ensue that would culminate in the discovery of the gun in the glove box and that'd be it, the end of it all.

"The car. Please," I said again.

"You feel all that doom in the air?" he asked, still staring off into space. "Creeping up behind us?"

I had no idea what he was talking about. Presumably, his kind of doom looked different from mine. But something about the dark and the rain and the lake made me feel it, made me feel that I'd felt it forever. I nodded. "I feel it, I do," I said.

Finally he looked back at me. I could tell even in the dark that our eyes were meeting and his were feral. My adrenaline spiked like we were about to fight or fuck, but then he stood tall and opened the car door and got inside in a crinkle of fabric and metal, and that was it; the moment was over.

22

In the morning, I ordered half a cantaloupe from room service. I took it and the now-warm champagne to the balcony. Sitting at a little table, I scooped the seeds out with a spoon and flung them over the railing, ate two plain bites, then poured the champagne into the gaping wound of fruit and began mashing it together into a sweet, carbonated soup. I'd never done this before; the feeling simply came to me. Then I called the oncologist. To my surprise, he answered.

He said, "Did you leave me a very long message?"

"Describe it."

"Unpleasant with a dash of incoherence."

"Hm," I said. "Doesn't sound like me."

"It's all right. I understand this is a difficult time for you. Believe it or not, I've taken worse abuse in my day."

"Oh, I can believe it," I said, twirling my utensil in my fingers. "I know you feed a cold and starve a fever, but what about a tumor?"

"Evidence suggests starve," he said distractedly. I could hear the clack of his keyboard, the whirring fan of his computer. He added, "I have your file here, and it looks like we're missing some information from you."

"I'm traveling. I quit my job. My insurance is kaput at the end of the month."

Silence on the other end of the line. I began scraping the spoon again and again into my poor abused breakfast, digging a canal from the alcoholic lake to the rind.

"This can't be delayed or deferred. I thought I was clear on that score."

"You were. I understood you perfectly."

"I don't think you did. 'To know and not to act is not to know.'"

He sounded weary and competent, which I hadn't expected. I'd expected exasperation or conceitedness or an abrupt end to the call. Stories below me, the city's river shone blue. The wind blew shards of gold foil from the champagne bottle away like so much false confetti.

"Bashō again?" I asked.

"Wang Yangming."

"One day I'll get it right. Listen. How long do I have before I start feeling bad?"

"You have no pain? Swelling? Bouts of breathlessness? Loss of consciousness?"

"Nothing," I said. "Maybe a little tenderness in the left."

"I can't answer your question. It's between you and your body now, Hester," he said. "You can always change your mind."

I hung up. I stabbed my spoon vertically into the cantaloupe and left it in the sun for the birds to get drunk off and went through the sliding glass door back into my room. John had slept there last night. I'd awoken to him asleep on the floor, having pulled several pillows and the top sheet down with him to form a kind of nest. He was still there now, swathed in white and lumpen, recognizable only by the eupneic movement of his back.

I'd only had three glasses of wine the night before but had this nagging sense that an important piece was missing from the evening.

I prodded him gently in the ribs with my toe. "Up," I said.

23

Mom died in late April when all the flowers were blooming, lilacs and daffodils, with great indifferent fanfare. I'd just turned eighteen, school almost but not quite over. I dodged my extended family, aunts and uncles and cousins, none of whom I knew well. I didn't want to be pitied or assisted or reminded of anything. I wanted to believe I had no family at all, like I'd sprung from the earth fully formed. I didn't intend to deprive them of the opportunity to mourn her, exactly, but planning a funeral felt beyond my skill set at the time.

A week after she passed I drove her old car to the crematorium to pick up her ashes. The crematorium was in a converted colonial home on a road that had been bucolic until around the time of my birth, when it started to become a busy thoroughfare. I waited a long time to pull left into the parking lot, imagining slamming my car deliberately into every passing vehicle. Commuters, babies in car seats, retirees running errands. I was in a pretty apocalyptic frame of mind then, hating everyone untouched by my brand of suffering.

The linoleum in the lobby had been buffed to such a high sheen, I could see my own reflection in it. I don't remember the receptionist's face. In my memory, she's been replaced by Magda because that's what my mind supplies when I think *receptionist.*

The receptionist had a decorative desktop fountain, water electrically pumped in a bubbling loop over fake river stones. She produced a catalog of receptacles. At the back, on a page labeled *novelty*, was a bronze box with a lid in the shape of a car leaping over a hill. The headlights were fake diamonds. It cost more than a thousand dollars, not including shipping, which, for such a heavy item, was exorbitant. It was unusual in its tastelessness, but I was, after all, eighteen years old and grieving and could not be judged. It was the most expensive purchase I'd made to that point.

"I'll take that one," I said. "That's a Jaguar, right?"

It obviously wasn't, but I wanted badly to believe. The receptionist looked confused until she remembered her sales training and said, "Mm-hmm, that's right."

I got one of their installment plans. Money was imaginary to me at that point anyway. Five weeks later, it showed up at my door and was so tacky, so much more hideously shiny than pictured, yet also so unreturnable, that I had no option but to pretend I was proud of the choice.

This became the first entry in my long history of having no regrets. Once I lived on my own, I even displayed it on shelves or mantels. Years later, the super came over and asked about it. He said, "Now what is this?" and made these little vroom-vroom sounds like he was a child and it his toy. I said, "Those are my mother's ashes," and he put them down, horrified. Moldovans or Serbs or whatever he was have great respect for the dead.

Anyway. At the funeral home, the receptionist had me lean forward over her desk to fill out the paperwork, this odd receipt of my mother's remains. She asked for my relationship to the deceased, and when I said, "Mother," her face crumpled under the weight of artificial pity. I jerked back, so revolted I was almost propelled. My elbow hit the fountain and sent it crashing to the floor. The water floated above the tile as if on oil, and the stones skittered several feet over the polished surface, and the false basin of the fountain cracked in two. The two of us looked at the mess, me standing and her sitting, neither of us doing anything about it. Then the receptionist let out a long, tired-sounding sigh, as if this or similar misfortunes befell the fountain often, and the disfiguring pity passed from her like a high cloud. I grabbed the cardboard box of ashes, Mom's temporary home, and walked out.

The attorney who read Mom's will, forbearing and mildly depressive in the way of many small-town professionals, told me she'd left me her share of the house and the proceeds of her life insurance. It was a small windfall, an adulterated piece of good luck, following as it did on the heels of bad. I enlisted the attorney's help in selling the house, in contacting my father to get permission. My father evidently agreed so long as he got his piece. If he'd asked the lawyer if he could speak to me, I would've refused.

I liked the attorney. Because of my circumstances, he charged me significantly reduced fees, but not nothing, which would've been an insult of charity. Mom had used him in the divorce. I used to harbor fantasies that they'd fall in love, because the attorney was patient and well-to-do and his eyes crinkled when he smiled. That, though by then she'd long ago lost her looks, he'd recognize the same qualities I admired in her. Her quiet dignity. But it wasn't going to happen. The attorney was married and had a daughter my age. She went to private school and so had never been subject to the local gossip that was our town's only export.

I invested no money or time in fixing the house for sale. I accepted the first lowball offer from a buyer who I was fairly certain would tear it down and build from scratch on the land. If you look online, though, you'll see it's still standing, albeit with a new coat of paint and a fully finished deck.

At signing, the attorney stood in the living room, which looked so much larger without furniture in it. His arms were folded behind his back while he inspected the dust on the built-in shelves as if some history was legible in it. I liked him but hated him, too;

his generosity, his knowing what had happened to me. If he knew how I felt, he didn't take it personally. He even wrote one of my recommendation letters for law school.

He said, "You're not sad to see it go? Your childhood home."

He had his own childhood home for which he felt nostalgic. Maybe still lived in it, had never left. Common in our town.

"I'd burn this place down if I could," I said.

24

We're gonna talk about some of the consequences of sleep deprivation and what your body goes through when it's not getting enough sleep. So a very big deal if you're concerned about your longevity. If you think pulling an all-nighter is going to help you ace the test, the people who pulled the all-nighter, their ability to absorb new memories, new information? Down by forty percent. They have actually done research showing that men who get four to five hours of sleep a night instead of the seven or eight hours recommended, they have the testosterone of a man ten years older. Men who only got five hours a night actually had smaller testicles. Can you believe that?

After Chicago, I let John dictate our course for a while. I figured I could lose a week or two. Maybe more. I could even burn a month and still make it to my father's before July, when the heat would become unbearable, with a daily average of nearly 120 degrees. I thought seeing ruination up close would surely strengthen my resolve to leave this wretched and injured world. I was dawdling, grasping at flimsy pretexts, but I didn't see it that way at the time. At the time I thought I was just doing what I'd always done, which was whatever I wanted.

John's itinerary took us to landscapes ruined by barium and benzene, mercury brine pits and manganese. The number of Superfund sites in each state ranged from one to over one hundred. John was opting for a representative sample rather than completeness. My only limiting principle was that I wouldn't go backward; what he'd missed, he'd have to return to on his own time. I had to maintain that illusion of momentum. We went up to Wisconsin, then over to Minnesota, then down into Iowa, and then back into Illinois, spending a day or two in each. To entertain myself on these long drives, I sometimes stared out the window and built the world in inverted colors. The sun blue instead of yellow, the leaves on the trees red instead of green, the clouds black. A child's game, it passed the time.

John mostly appeared asleep or engrossed in his notes, only looking up at critical junctures to give directions. He seemed to intuit when these junctures would arrive, or maybe he could tell by subtle changes in my driving, a tension in my body when I was beginning to wonder where to go next. Another driver once cut me off without signaling, and I cursed them more loudly than I'd intended, "Oh, you fucking *cunt*." John looked up, watching my driving impassively.

"Do you regret picking me up?" he asked.

"I don't regret decisions I make."

"Ever?"

"Never. It's a personal policy," I said.

Without ever discussing it, I began booking motel rooms with two beds. Four feet apart seemed the correct level of closeness. He always fell asleep immediately, without fuss. The proceeds of a clean conscience. Except for his floor-nests and the boxers he handwashed in the sink and hung over the shower curtain rail to air-dry, he was unobtrusive. His world was his body and his pack. Making several unfounded assumptions, I diagnosed his self-containment as a reaction to growing up with the domestic sprawl of six siblings. I envied him his family. I'd often thought my life would've been better with a witness around. Someone to redline my version of the past and tell me I was an asshole.

By mid-May, we were in Missouri. We went straight past the spot where Buddy Holly's plane crashed and on to a former gas plant that buried barrels of coal tar before it went defunct and developers built an apartment complex on it. You could pay $1,200 to live in a place that still needed the air quality of its crawl space tested annually. A sign on its exterior said it was THE PINK PALACE and that parking was available. Each apartment had a balcony looking across the street at a quick mart with a mascot of a chicken's head on the body of a generously endowed woman. We didn't even get out of the car.

There'd been a major flood in the area earlier in the year, and many houses had exposed plywood bones and walls two-toned below the high-water mark. We drove looking for any place untouched by the flood. Atop a hill we found a diner with a concrete brachiosaurus in the parking lot.

For once America offered some promise, Sal Paradise's vision of endless apple pie. My plan seemed far off just then. I wanted to bring it up so we could laugh about it. *Isn't that crazy?* I'd say. Sometimes I pictured the future as a cartoon. I'd pull the trigger, and all that would come out of the gun was an unfurling flag that said *bang*. Dad would let out a girlish scream, vanquished in bloodless fright. I'd throw myself off a cliff but screech to a stop just before I hit the ground.

Sitting in a booth, I upended the syrup pot over my platter of pancakes and strawberries.

"You eat like a little kid," said John. His hands cradled his glass of water. I goaded him into ordering a BLT but hold the B, confusing our poor harried waitress.

I sucked syrup off my thumb. In Manhattan I'd been careful about my diet, lots of exotic green leaves dressed in unusual vinegars as part of my complex about being thin and attractive and rich. I was less consistent on the road, driving for hours on the strength of nothing but gas station apples wrapped in superfluous plastic and the occasional cigarette, then scarfing two large cartons of drive-through fries just before bed.

"You eat like a little bird," I said. "You're like. Ecorexic."

The bulk of John's diet seemed to consist of various dry goods purchased at bulk stores and kept in knotted bandanas in his bottomless bag: raw, phallic-looking cashews; dried apple slices; raw roadside farm-stand corn gnawed off the cob; and peaches whose flesh he worried off the pit with his teeth. To emphasize my point, I bit off a huge, chokeable piece of sausage.

"Thing about sausage is how it's made," John began.

"Uh-oh," I said, steeling myself for a lecture.

"Starts with pigs or beef. Pig farming is a little better than beef farming. Let's say that's a pork link. Production makes up most of the greenhouse emissions. Sow feed growth and manure management and transport and fuel and electricity and reproduction. It's mostly making methane and nitrous oxide, which contribute 21 times and 310 times the impact of carbon dioxide, respectively. Processing the meat in factories, pulling it apart and grinding it, also produces emissions, and then the inevitable retail or wholesale packaging, and then storage and transport, which also produces emissions, and then the actual consumption of it, the refrigeration, the cooking, the methane from food waste sitting in a landfill. All told for a four-ounce serving of pork, it's 2.5 pounds of carbon dioxide equivalents. Your average American eats 50 pounds of pork in a year, say. That's 375 pounds per American per year, multiplied out by 300-some-odd million Americans and you get like 120 billion pounds of those equivalents per year, not counting pollution from waste."

He stopped. I could feel his leg jumping around under the table, a nervous tic. I knew production and destruction went on around me all the time, and what was I supposed to do about it? It was baked into every decision I made, invisible and prepackaged. Everything was terrible long before I got here, an inheritance that couldn't realistically be refused.

"Neat trick," I said, wiping my mouth with the heel of my hand. "Like being able to recite poetry."

John went on, intonation dull as the diner's flatware, "Americans emit 5.1 billion tons total every year."

"Drop in the bucket," I said, waving my hand. I jutted my chin slightly in the direction of my mug and told him, "Do coffee next."

"It's all bad. Deforestation and soil erosion, hundreds of liters of water per plant, fertilizer runoff and cherry pulp eutrophying rivers. Transportation, packaging, pods, disposable cups. Everything has a cost, a consequence. Everything."

"How about murder?"

He raised his eyebrows.

"Just curious."

He said, "Depends. Let's say it's by gun. You have the production of the weapon, the fact that manufacturers work with or yield byproducts like asbestos, lead, arsenic, mercury, nitroglycerin, cadmium, perchlorates, chromium"—he rattled all these off on his fingers—"that can get into creeks and soil or the air if incinerated. Transport and storage of the gun and its ammunition also have some impact, which buying used might mitigate. There's the firing of the gun and how many times it must be fired for the act to be complete. Emission levels also depend on the type of gun and ammunition used: leaded, unleaded. The steel is eternal and will not break down. If you want to take a very wide view of it, you might include the electronics used to track the gun's registration and process its sale, how e-waste doesn't biodegrade, the energy required for the data to live in a server. And then there's the corpse."

"The corpse," I echoed.

"A rotting body produces methane and other gases. The nitrogen will be so potent at first, it'll kill surrounding plant life, but after a year, it'll nourish the soil, make it fertile for trees or grass, which pull carbon, although if the grass is mown or the trees cut, those benefits are moot. If the body is found, it all changes, you have to know how and for how long the body is transported, refrigerated, and disposed of. So. Too many unknowns to say."

"You should count what would've been consumed had the victim kept living."

"That'd also depend. The age and life expectancy of the person, how much they consumed or were expected to consume. Killing the CEO of a petrochemical company who drives a Hummer on their daily forty-minute commute to their suburban McMansion, sprawling lawn and automated sprinklers and all, would have a much bigger offset than, oh, I don't know, an old Laotian beggar."

"So would killing the CEO be justifiable to you?"

"You can't go around killing people for being jerks. Don't think you need me to tell you that."

"I mean. You can."

"Take that line of thinking and a lot of people would have to die. Me and our waitress and everyone in this diner and you. Maybe especially you."

I wondered if I ought to confess to him the exact kind of lawyering I'd done, which companies I'd defended from what claims. Instead I nodded at the waitress and said, "What'd Doreen ever do to anybody?"

"Her name's not Doreen."

"Okay," I said, extracting a fennel seed stuck between my molars with my tongue. "I can buy we're all assholes. What's the solution?"

"Devolution. But we're not going to get there deliberately. It's too late. It'll become unavoidable, eventually. I hope."

"You hope?"

"It's better than the other option."

"Which is?"

"Extinction."

"You know Saudi Arabia has no natural drinking water? Just desalination plants. Millions thriving in one of the most hostile places on earth."

"What's your point? Desalination is terrible for the environment."

"It's an example of perseverance and the triumph of technology over adverse circumstances."

"Yeah, great, what are they going to do when they run out of oil?"

I shrugged. "Desperation is the mother of invention."

"Desperation is the mother of migration crises."

"Do you think you're maybe more inclined to believe retribution is coming because of your religious upbringing? Like it biases you in favor of the apocalypse."

"Maybe. Do you think you're more inclined to believe things are more or less fine because of your anthropocentric godlessness?"

A sip of coffee went down the wrong pipe. I coughed, recovered, and then said, "I've got bigger fish to fry."

"This is the biggest fish. The fish to end all fish. There are no other fish."

"You must enjoy that sense of superiority, having your pet cause be the only one that matters."

Some kids a few booths down from us had put twenty dollars into the jukebox and chosen the same Elvis song on repeat and were giggling hysterically about it. My Moldovan super had loved Elvis. He used to put him on while he went around painting vacant condos. It was one of the few facts about him I'd known. I wondered if the super knew about the dying world. If he'd retire in a few years and go home to find the birds he used to hunt had all died and the rivers where he used to fish had all emptied. If he considered his life in America a worthwhile trade-off and whether having me around to fuck had changed that calculus for him at all.

John said, sounding immensely tired, “What I’m doing won’t change much. But it makes me feel better.”

Light bled through the slatted blinds, covering him with an otherworldly glow. He looked part human, part migraine aura. The skin next to his eyes was tanned and crinkled and dappled with sunspots. I felt sorry for him then, this kid who took everything so seriously, who earnestly logged his consumerist sins. This kid who didn’t know that, last night, while he slept, I’d gone to the bathroom and dry-fired the gun at my temple, like for practice.

I forked my last pancake off my plate and helicoptered it onto his.

25

Immediately after law school, I began working at a large, multiservice white-shoe firm. I craved the accompanying money and prestige, a rubber stamp validating my intelligence and self-control. Some people genuinely love the subject matter they master and have careers they intrinsically enjoy, but not me. I became an expert to cope.

The firm's services covered many aspects of corporate law—transactions, contract disputes, taxes, environmental and land use, permitting, compliance, disaster recovery—in a wide array of industries. I'd never liked the messy intimacy of criminal or family law and avoided these even during pro bono practice, of which the firm required fifty billable hours annually. I didn't think much about the ethics of working for a place like that. Every party has a right to protect itself, and that's all I did: defend that right.

As a junior associate, I worked for a time on a case to limit liability for a client the government had ordered to pay for sediment cleanup costs, a bill totaling in the billions, a bill that my firm softened to mere millions. I mainly assisted with document review, sifting through corporate memos and core sediment samples dating back many years before my birth. I reviewed these in the abstracted comfort of an air-conditioned office against a list of keywords chosen to identify potentially privileged information, words like *incident*, *unfortunate*, *situation*, and *difficulty*.

Robert, one of the firm's partners, was the lead attorney on the case. He used to tell all the associates, but especially the women, about his membership to Manhattan's only firing range. People probably would've been into this had it come from anyone else. Plenty of attorneys at the firm—the men, mostly—had handled guns in the patrician way of the well-to-do, the cosmopolitan hunting of grouse or pheasant on their grandfathers' estates. One particularly wealthy associate had shot wildebeest in South Africa and would show you gruesome pictures of it on his phone when he'd had a little cocaine.

But Robert was old and strange, on the outs with the other partners over his refusal to retire. While most staff were on the left side of centrism, Robert was a right-winger, a litigator who believed every generation after the Greatest was a worse iteration of insipid, narcissistic decline; who thought Clarence Thomas was wrongly derided; who ascribed to "family values" writ large despite being an inveterate skirt-chaser. He was a mistake they'd made along the way. He'd invite women or effete men to join him at the range, a joke he'd grown tired of but persisted in making, a veteran comedian wedded to his shtick.

Once, at a firm dinner, when I was still considered new, I said, "I'll go with you."

Robert looked at me with unfocused eyes. He drank too much at these dinners. Everyone did.

"Wise choice," he said. I was afraid he was going to call me *young lady* or something else terrible, but he just walked off in the direction of the bar.

One of the other female associates told me, martini in her hand and disdain in her throat, "You don't have to suck up to him, you know."

I didn't try to defend myself. Being genuinely curious seemed worse.

I met him at the range, since we'd reached an unspoken agreement that it would've been too strange to leave the office together. It wasn't far. It didn't announce itself; it was just an anonymous doorway hidden by scaffolding, tucked between a bakery and an upscale home goods store. One thing I liked about New York was that it was always capable of surprising me.

Robert was there in a Henley and boot-cut jeans. It felt wrong to see him so casually attired, especially since I was still in my firm clothes, a tidy blouse and gold earrings. This was a working-class basement range, with exposed pipes and a taxidermied goose on the counter. A poster showed a heavily armed, chesty blonde in a khaki-and-camo bikini kneeling on a piney mountain boulder. EXPERIENCE THE REBIRTH OF AMERICAN HERITAGE, it said.

People there weren't just comfortable about being American; they liked it, cared about it, cultivated it. I suppose there are worse things—like patricide—but I found all the rah-rah, I-bleed-red-white-and-blue patriotism overweening. Embarrassment was the price I had to pay to make myself more compatible with revenge. To be among these people now.

"I should've told you how to dress," Robert said.

"I don't mind," I said, upsettingly turned on by the idea.

Misunderstanding me, he said, "No. You shouldn't ruin fine things. Besides, you'll get burned. You don't have something you can change into?"

Having owned few fine things up to that point, I was both flattered he thought my clothes fit the definition and defensive at his tacit accusation. How was I supposed to know the care fine things required? I optimistically carried workout clothes in my purse back then, as if the firm ever left us enough time to exercise, this being, actually, the first time I'd left the office before sundown, aside from medical appointments, in many months. My work building had a twenty-four-hour gym on the ground floor, and sometimes I'd run there at two in the morning, shower, and then catnap on one of the locker room benches until it was time to go back to work again.

I went to the restroom to change. I masturbated quickly, propped up against the stall. I thought it would make me steadier, more confident when handling the gun. It only took a few seconds. The trashiness of the place, the men staring at me walking by in my heels, Robert's scorn. His hands closing over mine to aim. Boom, flash, done.

Every other lane was separated by walls and occupied by jocular men who knew what they were doing. A family sat in a viewing area outside the range, middle-aged parents and two sons with regrettable haircuts sharing a bag of pretzels. I felt I was an obvious stranger. I was given ear protection that limited my ability to sense what others were up to. Like blinders for a horse, they calmed me.

Robert handed me a rifle from his collection with instructions to keep it pointed downrange. My fear was that I wouldn't be able to resist the temptation to fire wildly in any direction, like the intrusive urges I occasionally had to say or do horribly inappropriate things: power-slap the old lady ahead of me in line at the pharmacy or pour scalding coffee over my own head during a conference call.

"Nervous?" Robert asked in my ear. I wondered if he guessed what I'd been up to. When I told him no, he said, "You should be."

On cue, I felt a jagged pull of panic in my gut, the way your organs slosh upward when driving over a hill. "I lied. I'm terrified. You really enjoy this?"

"It's not for everyone. Try it and see."

Robert pointed out the bolt, chamber, magazine, forestock. He explained how a bullet and cartridge work and how to choose the right kind for the gun. He told me to support its weight with my bones, not my muscles. He said I should form triangles with my elbows, but I couldn't see my own stance, so I just let him maneuver me like a shop mannequin until I stood to his satisfaction. I didn't know what he meant. All I knew was the gun was heavy and inelegant. A crude object for morons with unsubtle ends.

"Stop leaning back," he said, pulling my shoulders forward. "Rest your cheek here on the comb to get the sights. Like so."

"It's going to punch me in the eye."

"Scope kiss," he said with a grin. "Not if you do it right."

"That's less than comforting."

"It won't be a problem. Move with the rifle instead of letting the rifle move back. Keep a good distance between your eye and the scope. Firm grip. And both eyes open, no squinting. You got your eye protection anyway, so you're okay."

It felt like an hour before I pulled the trigger. When I did, the gun kicked back into my shoulder hard enough to bruise. For weeks after that lesson, I watched the bruise blossom into a galactic blue before wilting to a diffuse yellow. I shifted back a bit but didn't lose my footing or yelp in pain or shoot anyone or myself.

"Ow," I said belatedly. I didn't even look at what happened to the paper target.

"Fun?" Robert asked in the half shout he had to use to be heard over anything. His veneers were white and smooth, incongruous with his wrinkled skin, like his face had been collaged together from advertisements for very different products.

I nodded. "Yes."

"Hold it tighter to your shoulder next time," he said. "No more bruising."

He stayed with me so I got to watch him use his own gun. There was something unnatural about a man so old handling a weapon so powerful, a force he wasn't meant to have.

"There are all these rules," he explained as he packed up after.

"You can't just carry it, you have to put it in a separate case from the ammo in the trunk of your car."

"Sounds fussy."

"You can never be too careful."

He was one of about five men in America who meant it when they said they were serious about safety. I almost asked about the subway before remembering Robert was the kind of wealthy that didn't take the subway. This was in my pre-Jaguar days.

"Why guns?" I asked. "Why not cars or boats? You know. Things that can be used for something besides death."

He snapped shut the closures on his rifle case loud enough to make me wince.

"What makes you think I'm not into cars and boats?"

26

Arkansas is a state that's easy to forget unless you're in it. On the map, I could draw an almost-straight line from our location to my father's house, less than two thousand miles away; if I'd changed my mind, I could've been there the next day.

A full week remained in May. I couldn't sleep. Sometimes I hit the efficiency button on the TV, leaving the display off while the comforting chatter about events befalling other people continued. When I did nod off, I was plagued by fitful dreams full of unremembered violence. I'd awake abruptly, with the blankets and sheets trashed and my body in strange positions, overheated and confused.

The dimple on my left breast had deepened and darkened, the skin there red and warm and rough. Once, my nipple wept a foul brown liquid. Beryl making herself known. I wished I hadn't given her a name. I preferred to remain strangers with my own condition. I bought rolls of medical gauze and wrapped my chest each morning, then wore that beneath my sports bra. I brought my entire bag with me into the bathroom to change in the morning, keeping it from John's view. Beyond that and the deep insomniac circles under my eyes, I thought I still looked like myself, if not beautiful, then at least well preserved.

The worse my breast looked, the more I kept trying to visualize the end. It had to be perfect. I didn't want to lord it over Dad; didn't want to be too proud. I wanted to be efficient, almost bureaucratic. A quick enough dispatch that he couldn't resist but slow enough for him to recognize me, to comprehend what was happening. Then, without fanfare, I'd turn on myself.

This is what I thought about on our long drives. Every day I idled with John, I was creating risks of dying in other ways: a car wreck, a lightning strike, an act of God. I told myself to hold steady. That I'd know when it was time. That I'd waited this long and could wait a little longer.

John wanted to see a ghost town. Decades before, birds in the area had begun falling dead from their nests, horses had become emaciated, alopecic, rashed; children were plagued by headaches, cramps, and seizures. What the residents initially thought was a curse from God proved to be the result of a waste subcontractor mixing a now-banned disinfectant with motor oil and using it as dust suppressant on farms and stables. The town had to be abandoned wholesale, hand-built homes and four churches buried beneath an earthen mound covering five acres.

It had since been converted to a park. It no longer officially met the criteria for John's list, not being a Superfund site, but still we went. It was in a flood plain off a river, so low the houses in the surrounding area were built up on stilts. The landscape seemed underachieving, never aspiring to the heights of mountains.

The river was wide and low and probably deeper than it looked, a royal shade of green from a distance but churlish brown up close. A rainbow sheen of biofilm floated on its surface, changeable as a mood ring. An impassable truss bridge ran to the opposite bank, its roadbed removed and the struts capped with ochre rust. Two older men stood knee-deep in the water, tossing white-bellied, gasp-mouthed carp with a normal number of gills and fins back into the depths. A family passed us on foot, arranged by height from tallest to shortest like in a bad sitcom.

We stumbled across pockets of nonindigenous flowers, lilies and hydrangeas, leftover from the yards of the people who'd lived there once. Flowers I hadn't thought could thrive without human intervention. We made it far from people to a field of yellow rocket, stalking a deer that munched on pond weeds in a shallow, slow-flowing offshoot of the river. John tried to align a shot with his camera just so while I preemptively consulted my ankles for ticks.

"Do you think they felt bad?"

"Who?" asked John.

"The pesticide company, the subcontractor."

"They might not've known better. And if they did, they were only making things people wanted. Or needed. If not them, someone else would've."

"Ever spoken to anyone who used to run these?"

"I don't even know how I'd find one."

"Easy. Court cases, public records. FOIL requests."

"I'm not interested in blame."

"Who said anything about blame?"

"Those sound like things you do when you're looking for justice."

I said, slowly, like I was speaking to a small child refusing to climb down from a great height, "What are you looking for if not justice?"

"As long as people are in a system that rewards profit-seeking behavior, this kind of thing is going to happen. There's not a lot of choice."

"You made a choice."

"The way I live isn't a standard I'd hold other people to."

"That's very Christlike of you."

"I'm just saying the problems are systemic."

"Blaming the system is the same as blaming nobody, and blaming nobody is useless. You have to be specific," I said, beginning to get irritated.

"Who said anything about blame?" he echoed back to me.

There came a loud crack. Something whizzed by and struck a tree mere feet away. A chip of bark and wood-meat ricocheted upward. I didn't comprehend what was happening until the second shot. The deer, which had moved on from the water to nudge mournfully through the grass, reared its head back and dropped to the ground with its hooves at an awkward angle, a movement no animal would voluntarily make.

There came an inhuman whoop from beyond a stand of trees. The forest had an odd effect on sound; I turned my head in the direction I thought it came from, only to see a man come crashing through the undergrowth into the grove from an unanticipated angle. The man was in Walmart camo and an eye patch, a tuft of hair perched atop his skull like a pet rodent. He held a rifle. He went directly to the deer.

"Hey," yelled John.

The man looked up.

John yelled again, "You nearly hit us, man."

The man looked like a person who thought about how he moved in order to spare himself the effort. It was no easy thing, to be so large. I wondered if he didn't scare off the animals he tried to hunt. His rifle was slung over his shoulder on a strap. He came closer to us and squinted dopily where John pointed to the scar in the tree's trunk.

"Aw shit, folks. I am so, so sorry."

I hadn't anticipated gentleness. There'd never been many backcountry hunters where I grew up. My father had kept a BB gun, a childhood gift from his father, in a long wooden box in our attic, which was full of pink fiberglass insulation that I used to think was spun sugar. That was as close as we came.

"It's not season. What are you doing?" said John.

He spoke at a controlled volume but was obviously furious, his hands shaking. He was correct to be mad. The man was reckless.

He'd done and would continue to do similarly reckless things. This was valid cause to hate him. He could've hit me and ruined my whole plan, but oddly I didn't feel upset. It had to do with his haplessness. Clearly, what we were dealing with was an idiot who couldn't help himself. My fury was reserved for Dad; I could spare little for strangers.

The man doffed his cap and scratched his scalp, where the hair was whorled and matted with sweat. "I usually just pay the fines," he said.

"You're going to kill someone out here."

"I won't, won't do it again," he said, fumbling the lie.

"I should report you."

A small, cruel part of John was maybe enjoying this private masculine exchange. I felt removed from the scene. I realized then that to a certain extent, nothing that had happened to me since my diagnosis felt quite real to me, and this was how I'd been able to tolerate the rot in my breast. I was watching myself walk into traffic, my traffic-self panicked but my watching-self impassive, on mute.

The man said, "C'mon, now. I don't mean to hurt anyone. Let me process her, and I'll send you folks home with a quarter."

"Nah, man, we got no use for that."

"Let me make it up to you somehow. I feel rotten, I do. Come back to mine for a beer or two, you'll see I'm good people."

I wondered what made him so servile, so eager to prove he wasn't bad. If he was always like this or if it was the sternness of John's voice that extracted it from him.

John seemed on the verge of saying no again. The man turned to me and broke the fourth wall of the nature documentary by saying, "Ma'am?"

I said, "I wouldn't mind a beer."

John gave me a withering look. In reply, I said what sounded to me like a fitting Arkansan idiom: "Let bygones be bygones."

"Just let me dress her," said the man, thumbing back to the doe. "Can't have her go bone sour. Won't take more than ten minutes. Got some beers if you want to get a head start."

"You've been drinking?" asked John.

"Of course not," said the man, too quickly and with too much outrage. There was something perverse but comforting about the fact that someone like this could hunt and kill. It confirmed for me that killing was easy, the dumb man's move, and that it wouldn't be difficult for me.

"Can I watch?" I asked. "I've never seen it before."

I meant field dressing, though I didn't have the term for it at the time. "Sure," he said. "Long as you're not squeamish."

"I'm not."

"Hell, then, you can help," he said. "Easier with two people than one."

We walked over to where the deer lay, leaving John where he stood, frowning.

"Want some Vick's?" the man asked.

"What?"

"For the smell. Hit her in the neck, so she shouldn't stink too bad, but."

"No." I wanted the raw, unadulterated experience, however horrific. I don't know why. It's not like I planned to taxidermy my dad, though the idea appealed. I saw myself wearing a bush jacket in a safari villa, smoking a cigar lit from a roaring hearth, my dad's head mounted above the mantel.

The man's name was Frank. The doe's eyes were still open, glossy and vacant as candy. Frank was right that it had been struck in its neck, the white beneath its jaw exposed and tinged red. For a moment, I hated Frank for what he'd done, for being a person who enjoyed this elective primitivism. I saw a whole gallery of him gloating over every animal he'd ever crushed with the overwhelming advantages of modernity, advantages he'd done nothing to earn beyond being born at a time that enabled him to use them. It would've somehow been more respectable to kill the deer with cruder tools, with rocks and hands, to meet it closer to its own terms, even though this made no sense and would only prolong the suffering, escalate the brutality. The odds, then, at least would not have been so drastically skewed.

I looked back. John, in protest, was keeping his distance. Frank positioned himself behind the deer. He carried a knife with an arched handle and a fat, snout-shaped blade, silver as a fish scale. It was an attractive object. I couldn't take my eyes off it.

"Your buddy's got kinda a stick up his ass, no?" Frank said.

"He's right. You'll kill someone if you keep it up."

"And I am sorry about that. Lesson learned," Frank said, faux chastened. "Hold her legs, would you?"

I shuddered at the phrase but did as I was told. The deer was turned on its back, belly up to the sky, with matted fur dotted with dirt and bits of leaf and a few fat-bodied ticks and early flies. It had a musk, like hair not allowed to dry fully after rain.

A memory came back to me then of being alone in my father's studio, looking through his crates of reference books and nested newspaper clippings. I tried to read the words on the backs, but so much had been shorn away, I could never tell how the stories ended. I found a stash of pornography. It wasn't at all well hidden. There was an especially glossy spread of naked girls on all fours seen from behind, arranged in a skin-tone gradient from pale to dark, all in the same blond wig, all with panties around their knees and their intimate anatomy on display. I hoped never to be so fleshy or so pink.

He caught me snooping that time. I was eight, maybe nine. My mother wasn't home. Or was she? I recall the panic of being discovered, the heavy inevitability of his approaching footsteps, but not my punishment. It's funny, for a person obsessed with the past, you'd think I'd remember it better.

One time I wouldn't eat my dinner and he grabbed the back of my neck and pushed my face into the plate, I remember that.

Frank set to work at the far end of the deer. Then he came up to its neck, nearer where I stood, and slipped the knife down its sternum. Heat still rose from her body. He made it look effortless, no harder than cutting cold butter. The long slices turned to deft flicks over the belly, peeling away the thick white lining beneath the hair and hide. Entrails bloomed into view, livid and slick, the pale stomach, bulbous and festooned with thick white veins. The air reeked of iron. Frank sawed away near the ridge of pelvic bone. I confess the grinding sound made me lightheaded. I clung to the deer's legs for support.

Throughout it all, Frank didn't stop talking. He'd produced two cans of beer from the oversize pockets of his cargo pants, one for me and one for him, and occasionally stopped his work to sip at his. I was so focused that my drink sat unopened in the dirt and I hardly heard what he said. Something about a divorce, about sole custody, about early retirement, about spending his time doing what he really loved, hunting and trading cryptocurrency. He seemed like a bumper sticker person. I tried to guess the kinds he'd have on his truck, because it would almost certainly be a truck. DON'T TREAD ON ME and TAXED ENOUGH ALREADY and I LOVE MY WIFE.

He was standing back up by the front legs now. He slit the trachea and trimmed away a membrane around the diaphragm and then, in one firm motion, holding it by the broken windpipe, yanked out the entirety of the woven innards.

We were standing on a slight slope. The organs seemed to slither of their own volition, away and down to rest against a rock. It looked like a macabre bunch of plush balloons. Frank dug around, pulling out the heart and deep mulberry liver and the topaz jewels of the kidneys. Blood pooled in the cavity of the doe's rib cage, and Frank's fingers were smeared red, but it was still a tidier operation than I'd expected. The smell in the warmth of the day was indescribable, not rancid but still overpoweringly animal, a deep blue stench. Breathing through my mouth seemed worse than through my nose, and so I took it all in.

"You good?" Frank asked. His hands had left red imprints like children's artwork on his beer, which must have been warm; the can wore no condensation.

"Yeah. Yes," I said, blinking myself out of a trance.

"You're tough," he said. "My ex wouldn't even let me keep a carcass strung up in the garage. Had to take it straight to a processor. She had nightmares the deer were in our bedroom watching her sleep. She was a nervous person."

I could see it, a woman in a long cotton nightgown, sitting up in the startled blue of night to face the black-eyed ghost at the end of the bed, legions of eyes outside, pressed against the window panes. Probably Frank's wife was nothing like the Victorian wisp I imagined. If Frank and I fucked, he'd try to protect me from his weight, and I'd invite its airless press, its agonizing crush. He seemed my age exactly.

"You and your boyfriend should come over," Frank continued. "This is a good forty pounds of protein here. Ever had meat this fresh?"

"No."

"He is your boyfriend, right?"

I realized I was still holding the deer's legs, the solidity of bone and hoof. I let them go.

"It's complicated."

Frank grinned. "Oh, I know all about complicated."

This must have been a reference to the ex. I wondered when he was going to do something about the blood on his hands, under his fingernails. In law school, we'd read an old piece of jurisprudence involving a hunter and a fox, straight out of Aesop, and a pursuit on an empty beach. The setting is irrelevant; it's just that the image of a fox on the shore helped me recall the facts. As the first hunter closed in on it, another hunter shot the quarry. The court ruled in favor of the interloper. Pursuit didn't constitute possession; damage did. Harm something and it's yours to keep.

I asked Frank, "What happened to your eye?"

He flipped the patch up, revealing a normal, healthy, heavy-lidded eye, set far from its partner. "My left's dominant, thinks it's running the show. Messes my aim."

"Oh."

"Well. I gotta get her back before the flies get to her. But y'all are welcome. Plenty beer 'n' deer to go around."

I was curious. Having withstood this one test, I wanted to see if I could withstand another, to take this doe and consume it, make it part of myself. I decided I already knew the answer.

"We have to keep moving," I said.

"Suit yourself." He offered a hand to shake and said, "Thanks for the company. S'more fun with folks around."

I looked down at his unwashed red hand, and he retracted it with a laugh. "Where're my manners?" he said, but by then I was already walking back to John.

There was no truck in the parking lot. Presumably Frank kept his vehicle somewhere less visible so as not to give himself away. John still wanted to report him, so I let him borrow my phone and *67 it. He paced around outside while I sat behind the wheel, thinking.

Maybe I had a hoard of memories I was motivated to forget. I didn't really want to know. I had other reasons to want Dad dead. I wasn't going to invest time contemplating events that might not have even happened. Whatever he did couldn't've been as awful as what some endure.

Besides, some matters are too sacrosanct to broach. Like letting the sun shine on a painting, the light sapping away the pigment to dust.

27

Six students were killed Thursday morning and sixteen others wounded when a seventeen-year-old boy opened fire during a pep rally at Mesquite High School. One student described a chaotic scene, with teens scaling fences and running in the street to evade gunfire. The suspect was wounded and taken into custody after a standoff with authorities.

Oklahoma was a blur of similar-looking roads through similar-looking landscapes leading to similar-looking motels. The dates radio DJs or TV news anchors said were fabulist confections. Everywhere I looked, I saw faint reminders of my destination, which made me feel like I was accomplishing something despite my obvious drift, my slantwise approach. Gas stations reminded me of my father. So did old telephone poles with thousands of staples stuck to them and very hunched trees.

The heat seemed imported from August. It was, I was told, still only May, yet I was sweating within seconds of leaving the car and blistering when we sat back into its sun-heated seats. The sky was insultingly blue, a mean joke. I didn't see how I'd last a second in Death Valley.

We passed an anti-fracking billboard; then, fifty yards later, a pro-fracking one. I drank water out of a plastic gallon jug that weighed down my lap, and John sucked at his canteen, and I kept the air conditioning at full blast. I expected some resistance from John on that, but he was quiet. It seemed too hot to speak.

In the rearview, I saw a cherry top, red light twirling drunkenly. The siren blipped a moment after.

"Fuck," I said.

"Out-of-state plates," said John.

"Nothing I can do about that."

I pulled over to the shoulder, which wasn't so much a shoulder as a place where asphalt lapsed into dirt and dry grass. Branches of stunted trees curled gray and dry. On the other side of a wire fence was a black-windowed, broken-boarded shack. In the tall tan grass outside were rusted tractor guts, an unhitched utility trailer, and prickly pear cacti clustered like warts. An old windmill stood with a filthy plastic drum on a raised platform beside it. Over the crest of a low hill was a wind farm, turbines erect and orderly, one for each pillbox cloud above.

The cop took his time. I could see him in his car, aviators on, impassively doing nothing, just waiting for us to get antsy. I wasn't intimidated. One of the five police officers in my town lived two miles from our house. In grade school I'd gone to his daughter's birthday party, where he got red-eyed from canned beer and then yelled at the birthday girl for hogging the onion dip. He'd been there the night my father was taken away and had patted my hair in an abortive gesture of sympathy.

"What's your take on wind farms? Energy savers? Ruthless bird murderers?" I asked John.

"Maybe this is a bad time to tell you I got a warrant."

Of course he had a warrant, living like he did.

"Bench?"

He shook his head. "Arrest."

"What? What'd you do?"

"Long story."

"It's okay. I'm a lawyer."

I felt stupid immediately after saying it, like I was claiming ownership of a special power with limitless potential to get us out of trouble. Knuckles rapped on my window. I rolled it down. The heat on the other side of the glass approximated an inner circle of hell.

"Morning," said the officer. His skin was soft and folded like the crotch of a baseball glove, and his white mustache rippled like grass in the breeze. His uniform was impressively free of sweat stains. "Y'all know how fast you were driving?"

"No, sir."

"It's okay," he said. "Hell, I was from Indiana, I'd want to drive fast as I could to get away too."

I was briefly confused until I remembered Indiana was where the plates on my rental were registered. I smiled, all lips and no teeth, to be polite.

"One thing you gotta know about Oklahoma is that you slow for cattle," he said, nodding up the road.

One gut-shrunk, nubble-skinned cow with sagging udders was crossing the road about fifty yards ahead. I didn't know what he wanted me to say about this. I was aware of John beside me, sitting woodenly with his hands visible on his knees.

"Thanks for the tip," I said.

"How you two meet?"

"Us? In a bar."

"Y'all fuck?"

I swear I heard him ask this. I said, "Come again?"

"Your boyfriend," he said, moving right along. "He deaf-mute?"

I turned to John, who barely shifted his head in my direction, like he thought he was camouflaging into the seat and movement would spoil the illusion.

I said, "He's the strong, silent type."

The cop leaned back. The black fingerless gloves he wore

reflected the sun at their seams. Hoping he was satisfied, I gave him a smile with all my teeth this time, trying to look both winsome and uninteresting.

"License and registration," the cop said.

I took my wallet from the center console. "Registration's in the glove box," I said, and John reached for the latch.

I closed my eyes, willing the gun to stay hidden. I tried to remember how the glove box was configured: manual, registration, gun, fast-food napkins, tire pressure gauge, wheel lock, Tylenol, pack of gum with chewed-up wads filling the foil-punch voids. It was possible neither John nor the cop would see it. But it was also possible it would be visible from their respective angles, and I didn't know what I'd do then. Speed away in this ill-suited car, cop shooting at my rear tires, get put on a wanted list, and then what? Life as a fugitive, dyeing my hair and putting aliases down in motel logs and dragging John along, and we'd die in a firefight while my father carried on untouched.

I heard the pop of the glove box, and then the paper was in my hand. As I turned to pass it over, the cop's radio staticked awake. He chattered into the mouthpiece at a low pitch, almost cooing, like he didn't want to be overheard. Then he turned and, without a word, got back in his car and drove off, waving like we were old friends as he passed on the left.

We sat watching him diminish down the road. Ditches on either side were thickly knotted with white and lavender wildflowers crisping to brown in the sun. I was desperate to be gone but afraid that as soon as I started the car, he'd circle back; I wanted him out of view first.

"Lucky break," I said, finally turning the key and feeling the car shudder awake. "About that warrant."

"Why do you have a gun in your glove box?"

I could still see the seemingly ownerless cow walking freely to nowhere. Something slumped and already dead lay on the road ahead, and I ran it over again.

"You first."

"I've been known to dabble in ecotage."

"What?"

"Monkey-wrenching."

"I don't know what that is."

"Mischief and destruction of property with an environmentalist bent. Tree spiking, pouring sand into gas tanks at construction sites. I haven't been doing it since we joined up."

"Why do it at all?"

"Be a fly in the ointment. It's harmless, mostly."

"Why not just plant trees, do something actively good?"

"I also plant trees."

"They're just going to buy another machine and keep going."

"I try to be thoughtful about it."

I wasn't sure what he meant by that, and that wasn't quite the point I'd been making, but I let it drop. "So they figured out who you were?"

"I don't know how. Surveillance video, and I was caught a couple times when I was younger. That's probably all they need."

"Doubt they'd extradite you over a misdemeanor."

"Felony. Government property. National park leased out for natural gas pipeline expansion in Kentucky."

"I thought they only did that out west."

"It can happen anywhere. Some states don't have any leases, but. Always a possibility."

We listened for a while to the sound of tires on the road. John was increasingly a liability. I debated dropping him at the next gas station, kicking him unceremoniously out of my car and life, but when we passed a rusty Gulf pump, I didn't even slow down.

"Are you really a lawyer?" he asked.

"Yeah. I really was."

"You get disbarred?"

"I took an early retirement," I said, wondering why disgrace was his first guess.

"Why?"

"I got tired of it."

"Why?"

"What do you mean, why? I just got tired. People get old, they get tired."

"How old are you?"

"Don't ask that," I said, and then, a few moments later, "Forty."

"Forty's not old."

"What is it, then, young?"

"No."

"Exactly. It's a nothing age."

"One of my sisters is a nurse. She told me they got this classification system for old people. It starts at sixty-five, so you're not even old by those standards. You are clinically sub-old."

"Whatever. I just didn't want to do it anymore."

"I don't know why you lie."

"What do you think I'm lying about?"

"Lots of things."

"I'm not."

"You don't remember what you told me, that night with the rain?"

I honestly didn't, only the vague sense I had of a piece of the night missing, some information my brain hadn't retained.

"No."

"You told me you were dying."

"That was it?"

"Of cancer."

"Nothing else?"

"What else would there be?"

"Nothing."

"Are you going to kill yourself?"

I had a sudden urge for a cigarette even though—and this was almost surely my imagination at work—my breasts hurt more with every inhale. I reached into the center console and pulled one out and lit it and dumped the match into an old soda cup.

"I'm not."

Two easy words, but I worried about how naturally that lie came to me, like maybe it was true. Maybe I wasn't really going to do it.

"Why do you have a gun?"

"Self-defense."

"You're so concerned about self-defense, why're you picking up hitchhikers?"

"You're different," I said with a wave of my hand. "I trust you."

I said this without forethought. It was just a feeling that had been hanging around in my mind, waiting for me to round the corner on it. He was who he said he was; no one would be able to keep up the performance this long if it were just an act. I couldn't say exactly why, but that one spontaneous action was all I felt I'd done right in some time.

"Thanks. I guess. You don't strike me as a person who just goes around trusting people, so."

"Okay."

"And I'm glad you're not going to kill yourself."

"What's it to you?"

"Crime against creation."

I stared at him, remembering that moment he'd ducked into the fence. *Message from God.* If I were in the habit of being honest with myself, I'd admit I wanted him to say something simpler, like *It would make me sad.*

"Can't believe you're religious."

"What's so unbelievable about it?"

It was a good question, and one I didn't have an answer for. I wasn't accustomed to talking about this. Nobody asked what you believed so nakedly. You could only have earnest conversations about these things with children and drunks, and we were neither.

"I'm not actually sure."

"Your folks believers?"

What my parents believed was a mystery to me. Mom had received kindness from the local congregation in her dying days. I couldn't tolerate it, the pity that smothers a sick household. The pity had no relation to the outcome; she would've died regardless, but I felt it was the harbinger of the end. After all, with all those people watching and expecting, it would've been awfully anticlimactic not to die. Never once during her illness did I hear her pray. The last thing she'd asked for was that same promise from me, and then a glass of water.

As for Dad, I doubt he was a believer, despite his recent colorable conversion.

"No."

"America's mostly Christian. It shouldn't be some big surprise."

"But it's becoming less so."

He nodded. "We're turning away from God 'cause it's easier to deny his existence than admit we're failing as his stewards."

I nearly stroked out trying not to roll my eyes.

He kept going. "We don't want to avert disaster. We know it's coming and know we deserve it. In seminary school once, this kid was like, 'Man, when is shit really gonna hit the fan?' Like with climate change. He was wondering when it would rob him of his plans, his future. His comfort. As opposed to just reading about poorer people getting robbed of it on the news. He talked about it like it couldn't be stopped or helped. Like it was predestined."

"That's, um," I said, grasping for words. "I think we're turning away from him because he doesn't exist, but."

"God's just a word pointing to the indescribable."

"You've lost me there. I am a very literal-minded person."

"I don't think a big dude lives in the sky is what I'm saying."

"Some do."

"Sure."

"You went to seminary school?"

"Thought I had a vocation, but I dropped out. They didn't like what they called my doom-mongering up there. Said it was anti-Christian," he said, pronouncing those last words like they hurt.

"You would've been a good preacher," I said to cheer him up. "I get a sermon from you every other day. You really wax rhapsodic."

"I possess a lot of random knowledge."

"And a nice camera."

"It was always something I messed around with."

"This is your first project like this?"

"Yeah."

"What are you going to do with it?"

"Do with it?"

"I don't know. Whatever it is professionals do that makes them professional."

I thought of my empty condo in New York that I'd never see again and the interior decorator I'd hired to make it look inhabited. How she would've framed and displayed one of John's photographs. Robert, that older partner at the firm, had recommended her, I assume because they were fucking; I don't think Robert knew or cared enough to recommend her on the merits. When she'd liked the way an object looked or the way a piece of furniture was arranged, she used *keen* as an adjective, as in *Isn't that georgette keen*. All her assistants were gay twenty-five-year-old men with extraordinary frowns.

That life felt so separate from me now. I wondered, had I not gotten sick, how long I would've kept at it, moving through the calendar on Magda-managed cruise control, procrastinating on my fate because I was stupid-sure I had time to spare.

"Naw. I'm not after that kind of thing," John said, affecting an aw-shucks country-boy drawl.

Up ahead, we saw what must have drawn the cop away. It was an accident, a silver tanker turned on its side across the highway divider, black sheen of oil on the pavement like a silken shroud.

28

The same day I'd retrieved Mom's ashes, I found an old child support check in the glove compartment. My mother kept them there, where I was less likely to see them, because she knew I hated her acceptance of his money. I didn't mind the deception. She needed that money because of me, and I appreciated her awareness of how much that nagged at me.

This was how I found his address, blotted by an old stain of coffee or blood but still legible in his stylized, all-lowercase scrawl. He still lived in state then, just a few counties over. I drove there, stopping twice to ask directions. I'd promised Mom to pursue happiness, but technically killing Dad would make me happy. I had no plan, map, or weapon. I wasn't sure he knew Mom had died, if he'd seen the obituary in the paper or the courts had told him.

Maybe he'd be outside pruning the bushes and I'd mow him down with my car. Maybe he'd let me inside, ready to play the prodigal father, and when he turned his back, I'd strangle him with a curtain tie. I enjoyed thinking about these possibilities. If I couldn't bring Mom back, I could at least do this.

He lived in a colony of rentable suburban units spreading malignantly over a big hill that had been razed of all natural features, no trees or shrubs or even field grass, just recently disturbed earth and smooth imported turf. It was a frictionless place.

The development was a wheel of road with several spokes, each lined with identical duplexes or condos. It was difficult to find him because the main wheel was the street name, with each spoke unnamed, and all the unit numbers were affixed so low on the exterior walls that they were blocked by parked cars, so that you had to get out and walk to see them. Adding to the confusion was the fact that the units at the end were actually apartment clusters accessed via shared outdoor stairs. I tried to gauge where he'd be based on his house number and the number of units in each unchanging row, but some irregularity in the system meant it wasn't where it should've been. Clearly the development expected no one to drive there who didn't live there, in a neighborhood as artificial and hermetically sealed as a film set. This place with its dream-logic appeared prominently in nightmares later in my life.

I stalked up and down each row. I tried to look both unhurried and purposeful, like a mailman. That place almost definitely had an overzealous neighborhood watch.

I stopped the car and got out. Each building was constructed such that its front windows abutted the sidewalk connecting them all. They were separated only by a foot-wide strip of black mulch where I assumed holly or pansies would one day grow. For now, though, you could see directly into the living rooms of each occupant unless they had their curtains drawn.

A purse dog rested its paws against a sill and yapped at me. Its owner, an old woman, did seated calisthenics in front of the news, her upper arms flapping like clothes drying on a line. The anchors were telling some story about a kidnapped child who'd escaped his captors and returned to his parents, and I remember thinking, if that kid lived here, he wouldn't have found his way home.

It was by then getting dark. In the crepuscular light, two teenagers played roller hockey between two rows of parked cars. One had turned the fenced-in communal dumpster into the goal while

My keys jangled in my palm. I was in bad condition to drive but had no other option.

"Hey," one of the boys called, the one who'd hit his friend. "You know Mr. S.?"

I was at my driver's-side door. I felt I had to proceed very slowly and carefully or else the key would not go into the lock. My hands were so steady they were almost immovable.

I turned and let them see my big, blackened smile and I said, "Yeah. I do."

the other took slap shots. They were the only people I'd seen outdoors, though it was a warm spring day. The kids stopped to watch me. They were just a few years younger than me, but we may as well have been different species. I asked them where I could find number eleven, and one of them pointed wordlessly.

"Fantastic," I said.

I went to the doorbell and rang it. Then I knocked. I was polite and patient. I didn't make a scene. Mom had hated public scenes. Suffering in private, she tolerated.

A person was inside. That was obvious, even in the absence of noise or movement or changed light beneath a door or lifted curtain. I don't know how I could tell. Some change of the carbon register in the air, maybe. A covetous sense that you might have to yawn soon to keep another body from stealing your air. By then I'd started to believe I really was as harmless as a mailman, and the fact that he didn't open the door for me became further evidence of his guilt. Like that he felt compelled to hide even from the benignity of the postal service.

Someone screamed. I glanced over my shoulder. The kid hitting shots had smacked the puck into the goalie's crotch. The goalie was lying on the asphalt, tucked up into himself. The hitter was laughing and hooting, arms raised triumphantly.

I knocked again, then leaned to the side and looked through the vertical blinds, which struck me as cheap, provisional, motel-like. I saw him. He was only a silhouette, but a silhouette was all I needed. We stood immobile. I could tell he saw me, too.

I slapped my hand, palm flat out, to the window, hard enough that the blinds swayed. He startled, then turned and disappeared down an unlit carpeted hallway.

There was no quick way to reach the back of his house. I had no choice but to jog to the end of the row and curve around back into the wide, green alley between the spokes. There were no numbers on the rear side of the row, nor were there rear doors. I guessed which house was his based on its rough position and the fact that the window to his bathroom was wide-open.

I turned to see where he'd gone. Beyond the end of the row was nothing but a downward slope that rolled up again into the next hill, the next distant development, behind a clump of trees. It took a moment for me to spot him, the running man. My father. He wore the black long-sleeve thermal he always painted in and a pair of jeans and had left in such a hurry that he was barefoot. His hair looked almost blue in the bending light.

He was running. Running from me. This giant, this grown-up.

If I were a different person, that might've been victory enough: seeing that he feared me. Or it might've seemed farcical; that was the first and only time I'd seen him run, and he had an ungainly gait for such a large man, windmilling and slapstick. But I am the person I am, and what I felt was humiliated. I couldn't believe I shared genetic material with him.

I turned back to the bathroom window and hoisted myself over the ledge. I wanted to see the life he'd made for himself without us. In the mirrored cabinet above the sink, I found a potpourri of pills in white-capped, cloudy-orange bottles. One I recognized as a mood stabilizer. The others must have been left over from procedures or accidents about which I knew nothing. I ate three blue diamonds that I'd heard induced euphoria as a side effect and pocketed a whole container of white squares that promoted wakefulness. I took those pills all through law school, long after they expired.

The blue diamonds made the rooms blur together, or maybe it was the rooms' sameness. It was a place where he'd barely begun to live, though it had been years since the divorce; he must've recently moved again. Most of his art supplies and all his pornography were missing, presumably still in all the unpacked cardboard boxes. His closets and cabinets contained little. A single sweater

on a hanger, a glass jar of store-bought sauce in the kitc
thought about shitting on his carpet, but my shit was too go
that place, would be wasted on its beigeness. I didn't want l
have even the worst parts of me.

On his bachelor's dining table—small and square, de
to seat only two—was an open sketch pad, a glass of black
ink, and a mug of clear, unspoiled water. The paper was blan
must've been about to start when I arrived.

The black in the cup was intoxicating. I sat in the only c
get a better look at it. I've heard since of a pigment made
bon nanotubes that's so black it eats nearly all light. So blac
when you paint it on crinkled foil, it looks featureless, that
disappear into it. That color hadn't been invented yet, but
imagination, it was that exact viscosity.

I knocked the glass over with one finger. Slowly anc
cately, almost like I didn't want it to spill. The black went
where, flooding the white sheet and dripping over its sn
clean edge onto the table and from there to the carpet. L
oil slick, ageless dead matter, over a beach. I rested my hea
to the puddle and watched it expand and then licked on
line across the paper, leaving a horizontal smear across the
The taste was flat, bitter, and foul.

I left through the front door. The lake of fetid ink was
how still growing. In my fragmentary reflection in a mirror
door, I saw that my mouth was stained perfectly and com
to match my blasted pupils. It took days for the hue to fully
from every line of my lips, every papilla on my tongue, every
and cusp of my teeth. In those nightmares I later had, the in
spilling impossibly, wicking into the furniture and creeping
walls to edge onto the ceiling. The blackness I swallowed i
swallowed me.

The boys had abandoned their game but were still outsic
ting on the trunk of a nearby car, their backs to my father's

29

On a cold winter morning, Megan woke up to go get an abortion. A mother of three young children, she just didn't see how she could care for one more. But when she got to the clinic, she saw the mobile Women's Life Care Center across the street. Offering free ultrasounds from their "miracle machine"—

Texas took two weeks total, an eight-hundred-mile barrier to the west. The state was a big sheet of paper inexpertly coloring itself in with oil and dust. Everything large and jagged and awkward, not in proportion to itself or any natural law. We were on a highway twenty-six lanes wide. A man pushed a shopping cart filled with watermelons outside a drive-through liquor store. A girl on a bicycle with iridescent streamers on the handles crossed the street at a light in front of us, her T-shirt announcing in swooping cursive, *Boys ruined my life.*

The first place we stopped was an old military training site that had been converted into grazing pastures. John began explaining how to tell unrecovered scrap metal from old mortars and projectiles left behind from training exercises. I thought this was only a problem for countries that had endured air bombardments but evidently not. Taken together, he said, the amount of unexploded ordnance on American soil could cover an area about the size of Florida, like an unseen spare state.

John said, "Where I grew up you could still find Civil War shells. Our neighbor was really into reenactments. He found this cannonball landmine that he tried to detonate in his driveway. Chunk of shrapnel came through our living room window, nearly took my brother's eye out."

"Did he survive? The neighbor."

"No. But you could say he died doing what he loved."

The field was a patchy green speckled with invasive Dalmatian toadflax with flowers so brightly yellow they looked neon. In the distance, a sheep bleated and shook its bell. I was starting to get a sunburn; I could feel the skin pinkening along the part in my hair.

"It's pretty here now, at least," I said.

"You say that because you can't see how nice it was before."

"All the war games, you mean."

John nodded.

"Well, neither can you," I said.

"I don't have to see something to be bothered by it. You know we're all a little bit plastic now? I can't see microplastics, but that bothers me."

I pictured the surgeon to whom my oncologist had referred me slicing open Beryl to find her full of confetti, or those tiny Styrofoam balls they put in packaging. Packing peanuts and candy wrappers and glitter and other things that don't go away.

I found I was suddenly dizzy and had to sit down. There was nowhere to sit in the middle of that field, so I tried to squat, slowly, and as I did, the world blacked out, and John with it.

I came to looking up at a pear-shaped cloud. Dry grass tickled my scalp and the backs of my bare knees, and I was coated in a film of sweat. I felt a strange sensation behind my ear, and when I touched it, I came back with a tiny ant that ran in a fascinated hurry down my arm.

A shadow eclipsed my view of the cloud and the sun behind it. A hand came to my face and held my mouth open, and into it poured a lukewarm iron-tasting rinse of water.

I coughed and spat into the dust. "What happened?"

"You passed out," John said.

I sat up. "Seriously?"

The question was rhetorical, but John said, "Yes."

I tried to roll onto my knees, but John rested a hand on my shoulder, preventing me from going faster. Keeping me slow.

"Hey," he said.

"I'm fine," I said, though my hands were shaking and my legs felt like they belonged to someone else. "Just need water."

He passed me the canteen.

"When did you last eat?" John asked as I took a long sip.

That wasn't the problem. Beryl was the problem. I didn't want John to worry, though, so I told him I wasn't sure, which was true; my thoughts were unsorted.

"Okay. Up. I'll drive," he said, hoisting me by the arms.

I liked that he took care of me. I liked that he drove. It had been a long time since anyone did things like that for me without an exchange of money, or since I had done them for anyone else. A memory of my mother vomiting yellow bile into a saucepan I'd brought her; too revolted to clean it later, I'd simply thrown it away.

John looked elegant and patient driving, from my slumped vantage in the passenger seat, canteen held steady between my thighs. By the time we found a grocery store, I was feeling mostly recovered.

John said, "Let me go in. What do you want?"

"I've got it," I said, excited to be in the cold aisles of a store mostly empty at midday.

I bought green apples, two packages labeled *nutrition squares*, a jug of water, more cigarettes, and a boxed cake with vanilla buttercream icing. I was drawn to its coquettish pink rosettes and lime-green vines under the cellophane cutout window on its front. The light in the store was dim because the windows were coated with film and on top of that crowded with neon posters advertising that week's discounts. A bar of fluorescent lights haloed the vegetables, dewy bunches of ruby radishes and curling parsley. I spent a long time milling the air-conditioned rows, feeling oddly safe.

As a favor to John, I declined the plastic bag the cashier offered. It took me a while to configure the items I was carrying in my arms in such a way that I wouldn't drop them and could still open a door. In the end it was impossible. I sat at the tiny ledge under the front windows, where people left brochures and postcards advertising realty or babysitting services for the shopping public. I opened the cake, not minding any stares I drew as I ate it with my fingers. I thought I tasted a hint of cornmeal in the batter. I wiped my lips and folded up my box of half-eaten cake, feeling much improved. I gathered up what I'd bought in my arms and went out to the parking lot.

When I left the store, I was briefly confused. Several seconds elapsed where I couldn't understand what I was looking at, these bodies intertwined and posed like a Renaissance painting, if men back then had worn wifebeaters and cargo shorts and tattoos fading from black to dull green. I couldn't even tell John was involved at first. I'd had him pegged as a pacifist, but if he'd ever been, he wasn't now, swinging and ducking wildly.

Not knowing what else to do, I said, "Hey!"

I dropped what was in my hands to the curb, bruising apples that rolled away under parked cars, and ran to them. I didn't know what I thought I was doing. I think I thought if I wedged myself between them, it would create space enough for them to come to their senses. Instead I immediately took a hit to the side of the head and stumbled back, dazed, thinking for a moment I'd vomit frosting all over the pavement and pass out again.

"Gun!" yelled John.

At first I took this to mean that one of the men had a gun. Then I remembered that I had a gun, that I was a gun owner, that this was exactly the scenario most gun owners imagined when they purchased one. I went to the car and leaned into the open door to unclamp the glove box. My hand paused over the latch, hesitating because using this gun here might mean an inability to use it later.

The store owner or manager, an old Vietnamese man holding a broom, came out and started hitting the involved parties about the head with it. The broom and the screeching pitch of his voice seemed to embarrass everyone involved. The three men got into the truck they'd come in, spitting "Fuckin' pussy" out the window as they backed out of the lot and sped off.

I made my way slowly back over to John, stopping to pick up the groceries I'd dropped, the smashed remains of the cake. He was sitting on the curb, head in his hands. The store owner was there, looking like he'd been waiting a long time to put the broom to good use and was disappointed its time in the spotlight had ended so quickly.

I nodded at him and said, "Sir."

"Fuck off my property," he said, using the broom handle to point to the NO LOITERING sign.

Now it was my turn to hoist John up.

I took him back to the motel, laid him on the bed, and brought him a roll of toilet paper. He wore a quickly blackening line across the bridge of his nose, a cut on his lip, scrapes on his knuckles, blood in his beard. He crammed knotted tissues up each nostril until they turned from white to cheerful red. I sat on the bed opposite, waiting for my eyes to adjust to the dark from the brightness of the sun outside.

"What happened?" I said.

"One of them tossed a beer can. I picked it up and put it in the bin. Guess he didn't like that."

"Did you say anything?"

"No."

"You're sure?"

"It just kinda escalated."

"Your eye," I said. "Hold on."

I took a hand towel down to the ice machine at the end of the hall and came back with cubes wrapped up like a bindle, a runaway in an old cartoon. I knelt on the bed next to John, pressed the cold against his face. The room smelled faintly of an electrical fire, like someone had shorted one of the lamps once. I wondered if this was the first violence he'd encountered. If he'd ever had to fend off thieves after his camera or his good boots, if he'd gotten into fisticuffs like this with his older brothers.

"Keep fighting the good fight," I said.

"They started it."

"What are you, six?"

"What's the point of having a gun for self-defense if you're not going to use it for self-defense?"

"I'm not murdering anybody over some litter."

"You didn't know it was just about litter, and it wouldn't've been murder."

"Brandishing's a crime."

"Not in this state. Not for self-defense."

"I can't go around flashing it at every scrap you get into."

He looked at me sideways, disbelieving, but said nothing more. I was mildly troubled by my uselessness in that fight. I'd practiced grappling with that personal trainer, but at my first opportunity

My keys jangled in my palm. I was in bad condition to drive but had no other option.

"Hey," one of the boys called, the one who'd hit his friend. "You know Mr. S.?"

I was at my driver's-side door. I felt I had to proceed very slowly and carefully or else the key would not go into the lock. My hands were so steady they were almost immovable.

I turned and let them see my big, blackened smile and I said, "Yeah. I do."

on a hanger, a glass jar of store-bought sauce in the kitchen. I thought about shitting on his carpet, but my shit was too good for that place, would be wasted on its beigeness. I didn't want him to have even the worst parts of me.

On his bachelor's dining table—small and square, designed to seat only two—was an open sketch pad, a glass of black India ink, and a mug of clear, unspoiled water. The paper was blank. He must've been about to start when I arrived.

The black in the cup was intoxicating. I sat in the only chair to get a better look at it. I've heard since of a pigment made of carbon nanotubes that's so black it eats nearly all light. So black that when you paint it on crinkled foil, it looks featureless, that lasers disappear into it. That color hadn't been invented yet, but in my imagination, it was that exact viscosity.

I knocked the glass over with one finger. Slowly and delicately, almost like I didn't want it to spill. The black went everywhere, flooding the white sheet and dripping over its smooth, clean edge onto the table and from there to the carpet. Like an oil slick, ageless dead matter, over a beach. I rested my head next to the puddle and watched it expand and then licked one long line across the paper, leaving a horizontal smear across the page. The taste was flat, bitter, and foul.

I left through the front door. The lake of fetid ink was somehow still growing. In my fragmentary reflection in a mirror by the door, I saw that my mouth was stained perfectly and completely to match my blasted pupils. It took days for the hue to fully recede from every line of my lips, every papilla on my tongue, every groove and cusp of my teeth. In those nightmares I later had, the ink kept spilling impossibly, wicking into the furniture and creeping up the walls to edge onto the ceiling. The blackness I swallowed in turn swallowed me.

The boys had abandoned their game but were still outside, sitting on the trunk of a nearby car, their backs to my father's house.

on the rear side of the row, nor were there rear doors. I guessed which house was his based on its rough position and the fact that the window to his bathroom was wide-open.

I turned to see where he'd gone. Beyond the end of the row was nothing but a downward slope that rolled up again into the next hill, the next distant development, behind a clump of trees. It took a moment for me to spot him, the running man. My father. He wore the black long-sleeve thermal he always painted in and a pair of jeans and had left in such a hurry that he was barefoot. His hair looked almost blue in the bending light.

He was running. Running from me. This giant, this grown-up.

If I were a different person, that might've been victory enough: seeing that he feared me. Or it might've seemed farcical; that was the first and only time I'd seen him run, and he had an ungainly gait for such a large man, windmilling and slapstick. But I am the person I am, and what I felt was humiliated. I couldn't believe I shared genetic material with him.

I turned back to the bathroom window and hoisted myself over the ledge. I wanted to see the life he'd made for himself without us. In the mirrored cabinet above the sink, I found a potpourri of pills in white-capped, cloudy-orange bottles. One I recognized as a mood stabilizer. The others must have been left over from procedures or accidents about which I knew nothing. I ate three blue diamonds that I'd heard induced euphoria as a side effect and pocketed a whole container of white squares that promoted wakefulness. I took those pills all through law school, long after they expired.

The blue diamonds made the rooms blur together, or maybe it was the rooms' sameness. It was a place where he'd barely begun to live, though it had been years since the divorce; he must've recently moved again. Most of his art supplies and all his pornography were missing, presumably still in all the unpacked cardboard boxes. His closets and cabinets contained little. A single sweater the other took slap shots. They were the only people I'd seen outdoors, though it was a warm spring day. The kids stopped to watch me. They were just a few years younger than me, but we may as well have been different species. I asked them where I could find number eleven, and one of them pointed wordlessly.

"Fantastic," I said.

I went to the doorbell and rang it. Then I knocked. I was polite and patient. I didn't make a scene. Mom had hated public scenes. Suffering in private, she tolerated.

A person was inside. That was obvious, even in the absence of noise or movement or changed light beneath a door or lifted curtain. I don't know how I could tell. Some change of the carbon register in the air, maybe. A covetous sense that you might have to yawn soon to keep another body from stealing your air. By then I'd started to believe I really was as harmless as a mailman, and the fact that he didn't open the door for me became further evidence of his guilt. Like that he felt compelled to hide even from the benignity of the postal service.

Someone screamed. I glanced over my shoulder. The kid hitting shots had smacked the puck into the goalie's crotch. The goalie was lying on the asphalt, tucked up into himself. The hitter was laughing and hooting, arms raised triumphantly.

I knocked again, then leaned to the side and looked through the vertical blinds, which struck me as cheap, provisional, motel-like. I saw him. He was only a silhouette, but a silhouette was all I needed. We stood immobile. I could tell he saw me, too.

I slapped my hand, palm flat out, to the window, hard enough that the blinds swayed. He startled, then turned and disappeared down an unlit carpeted hallway.

There was no quick way to reach the back of his house. I had no choice but to jog to the end of the row and curve around back into the wide, green alley between the spokes. There were no numbers to use those skills, I'd been graceless, inept. I was a civilian, basically, with a civilian's bumbling instincts.

I'd have the gun, I thought, consoling myself. I would die, and that would give me an audacity that would compensate for my limitations.

The map was open on the bed next to me where he'd left it that morning. We were supposed to go to a former industrial complex whose operations included bauxite refining, cryolite processing, coal tar distilling, and gypsum lagooning. The community had relocated decades ago. Houses were disassembled, seeping toxic tar pits capped with clay, and Little League teams moved to new fields. You could still see the faint outline of a dirt diamond in the grass. Crabs, finfish, and oysters in the nearby bay were drunk on mercury and selenium, all their spines strangely shaped.

"Your nose isn't broken, is it?" I asked.

"It's not."

"Are you sure? We can find a doctor."

"No doctor."

It was hard to believe I'd fainted earlier. I felt fantastic, probably an effect of white sugar and fading adrenaline. Maybe the blow to the head had knocked a few misaligned synapses back into place. John rested on his back on the bedspread, legs bent at the knee and hanging over the edge, face upturned toward the ceiling. His eyes were closed, one of them already swollen egg-size and shut up blue.

"They really did a number on you," I said.

"I got in a few good hits."

"I bet."

"We should go."

"What?"

"To the site. Once the bleeding stops."

"That's enough excitement for one day, no?"

"I'm fine."

"I don't care. Go without me on foot if you want. I'm tired."

He stayed put. I picked up the remote and turned on the TV. The picture was screwy, double-haloed and with inverted colors, slowly crawling up the screen only to jumpily shake its way back down. We had no books but the motel Bible and John's atlas. An ice cream truck off in the distance played its looping tintinnabulation. John hobbled up from the bed and limped his way to the bathroom. I could hear his little grunts and mutters of pain, the way he banged the faucet open and shut.

"There's aspirin in my bag in there," I called to him, sounding banal and domestic. I got no response.

I slid John's atlas to the side and lay back with my head against the board. The image was dizzy-making, but I could still tell it was a game show, maybe *Family Feud*, and I fell asleep to the sound of an audience that roared and clapped.

I woke up before John. The TV was still on. I went to the bathroom to sleepily reapply my gauze. When I came out, I got a better look at John. His eye looked like a magic plastic bubble, shiny and puffed. He'd fallen asleep with the atlas unfolded over his legs, all fifty United States keeping him warm. Looking at it, I felt oddly bad for America. For being, like any idea or object or word, unable to resist those who tried to define it.

I wiggled the map away from him, replacing it with a sheet. The paper of the atlas was soft and fabric-like, its coloring worn to white and wrinkled at the folds. His scribbles on it had created ridges that were satisfying to touch. I traced our past thus far with the nail of my little finger, leaving no marks at all and noting that John's spelling was almost as atrocious as his penmanship. Then I traced our present location to the Valley. Less road lay ahead of me than I'd already traveled, and for some reason this frightened me.

His backpack sat on the armchair near the door. It occurred to me that I could look through his journal while he slept, the same way I read my father's. I was curious what he wrote in it. Whether he wrote about me at all or had any secrets. Whether he'd hidden the wrappers of a beloved candy he ate on the sly, flattening them between the pages.

I let it be.

30

I find it hard to believe I worked for the firm as long as I did. Ten years. School had given me a sense of progression and movement, week by week and semester by semester and season by season. Time moved differently in working life, and not only because of the nature of my career, which tended to blur private and public. It was all undifferentiated, days stretching into years that had no meaning beyond what comes of accrual. No part of childhood prepares you for the ceaseless noise of adulthood. I suppose people who have children and weddings and retirement and hobbies use these as beams and posts to structure time. Their absence is privilege and terror both.

Actually, I did have hobbies. My hobbies were keeping myself in incredible physical condition, sleeping around, and going to the range with Robert—always gun, never golf, no matter how he wheedled me. I'd often get dinner with him afterward or lunch if we met on weekends. I was careful not to be seen with him. He made it easy for me because he preferred to dine indoors even on beautiful days, sitting in the darkest, most private booth available. I also maintained a certain professional coolness toward him in the office. Still, people could tell we were friendly. He was always giving me vague career guidance, like *only take winning cases* and *keep your written communication with clients brief* and *never give free advice.*

"What are you charging me for this advice?" I asked.

"Tolerating my company," he said with a wink.

It's odd that we never slept together. He was my type in that he was a man, and I was his type in that I was a woman almost four decades his junior. But I was glad we didn't. It gave our relationship novelty and texture. I suspect sometimes he used me to manipulate other women, to stoke their jealousy or to make them feel safe around him. Yet he didn't strike me as a predator, despite his predilection for youth. He was so flagrantly himself, making no attempt to camouflage or conceal his intentions. The men who pretended to be good were the ones you needed to be careful around.

On my thirty-second birthday, Robert gave me a gift. I was surprised he knew it was my birthday. I'd almost forgotten it myself, the effect of that run of time.

He was unusually bashful about it. He took me to his favorite restaurant, a French place where all the waiters were men his age and called him *monsieur.* I teased him about this because I could tell it was important to him, that men who were in some sense his peers treated him with deference. Afterward he insisted on driving me home, though I lived only a few blocks away. He told me to open the glove compartment.

"Why?" I asked.

"It's a surprise."

"What kind of surprise?"

"If I told you, it would no longer be a surprise. You'll just have to open it."

He was wearing his warm-weather uniform: sunglasses, crisp button-up, khakis. He never wore shorts; not once did I see his knees. Beneath his receding hairline was a forehead pink from too much time playing golf without a wife to nag him about sunscreen. He had the patrician face of a man modeling an expensive watch. He was not tall, in fact was at least an inch shorter than me. He told me he was the same height Julius Caesar had been, which was a facially ridiculous comparison, but I forever after thought of him as a boy emperor. Like me, he'd been a long-distance runner.

I looked at him, thinking about how my adolescent self would have done anything to avoid being trapped in a car with a man even remotely like this. Thinking of all the words I would've called him at that age. I was appalled at my comfort around him and his money. It's one of the mysteries of my life, whatever change occurred in me that enabled me to tolerate him. Call it a character flaw.

"Should I guess what it is?" I asked, praying it wasn't something as embarrassing as jewelry or God forbid an engagement ring.

"Good God, woman, just open it, would you."

He was always calling me either *woman* or *kid*, both with a soft irony that made it impossible to take offense at either. I did as I was told. His glove compartment was immaculate. Inside was a mahogany lidded box with one of those cheap, stiff holiday bows you find at pharmacies around Christmas.

"Ha," I said when the box was open, its coffin-like sateen lining revealed. Inside was a water pistol, lightweight and in a child's neon colors.

"It's a stand-in," said Robert. "It'd be an honor to help you buy your first real handgun."

Robert knew people who knew people, and with his help, I'd just finished the monthslong process of acquiring a gun license. Of proving I was a person of good moral standing to keep a firearm in my residence. I didn't need anyone to buy me anything.

Still, the receipt of this gift felt like permission from a god I didn't believe in.

"You don't have to do that," I said.

"Hey, kid, you earned it," he said. "Besides, it's your birthday."

A few weeks later, after I'd got my purchase permission, he took me to his favorite dealer upstate as promised. I put the gun in its box under my bed. Then I became superstitious and thought lying above it might give me overzealous dreams and interfere with my sleep. I moved it to the closet in the bedroom, then to the closet in the adjoining bathroom, and then to a high shelf in the kitchen. I then told myself I was being ridiculous and, as a test of my will, moved it back to its original position under the bed.

That night, as I tried to fall asleep, it occurred to me that I should shoot myself with it. Not to kill but to maim.

Once I'd thought it, the idea followed me around like a dog, mostly quiet but never too far astray and occasionally barking loudly. Suicide had always been the plan, and I wanted a foretaste of what I was in for. To make it more tangible. To prove my idea wasn't just the fevered imagining of an unwell woman, but the serious commitment of a person who knew what kind of pain was entailed. It was a form of preparation. I felt strong and healthy, able to take anything.

On some days, I was aware this didn't sound like proof of anything, except maybe sickness or stupidity or terminal boredom. This is an underappreciated danger of guns in general, the way their unpredictable possibilities come to feel like inevitabilities.

I thought about it off and on for years. I had my condo soundproofed not solely for this reason but partly with it in mind. I figured it'd have to be a toe. I'd aim to lose the pinky, but if I had to lose the whole foot, I could live with that. Even if they had to amputate below the knee. I'd get a small-caliber bullet with a rounded nose to minimize the damage. Sometimes I'd lie in bed and practice my aim with the gun unloaded or just with my fingers, like playground cops and robbers.

Then Robert's career came to a predictable end. I was thirty-five; that's how fast time seemed to move. I thought I had a chance of making partner, particularly since I was one of the few women in the office who neither had nor hoped for children. I spent less time with Robert and more weekends in the office, pulling hours that would've looked insane to a person with anything even approximating a life to prove my worth.

When the first associate accused Robert of inappropriate conduct, I paid little attention. She was a newer hire. I'd met her briefly when she was assigned to assist with one of my cases. She was bright but fanatical and incredibly young; like me, she'd gone straight from college to law school. I thought she was histrionic in the way virgins sometimes were. It seemed to me that crying sexism while also working for a firm that protected the interests of exploitative global capital signified either naivete or cynicism more wolfish even than mine. When asked, I made anodyne comments that professed allegiance to both due process and a woman's long-overdue right to respect. Privately, I was a traitor to my sex.

I know, I know. Shouldn't I have been the first to believe a woman, knowing what I know? Shouldn't I have proudly taken up the cause, cut Robert out of my life, added him to the long list of killable men?

I can't explain except to say that I thought he was my friend and that I didn't think I was capable of such gross misjudgment. What do you do with a person who has been good to you but not to others? I could be loyal under the right circumstances. And it was never my intent to be a feminist hero. If I'd wanted to make a difference for women, I would not have focused all my energy on my nonessential father.

Besides, all Robert stood accused of was calling her sweetheart.

When I asked him about it at one of our increasingly rare lunches, over wide porcelain bowls of green soup dolloped with crème fraiche at that favorite French restaurant, Robert said it had been an embarrassing slip of the tongue.

"Better watch yourself, old man," I said. I was teasing but also serious. I'd trusted Robert to handle himself in a general sense. To hear him admit a mistake, even a minor one, was concerning.

"I do," he said. "I am a careful person."

"What does she think your punishment should be?"

"An apology."

"Apologizing seems easy enough."

"Never apologize," he said. He took a sip from his glass of Chablis, which was sweating like it was nervous on his behalf. "Admitting guilt is always a mistake."

"I don't know if that's always true now. The world's changing."

"No," Robert said. "It's not. Come on, Hester. You're smarter than that."

That was only the beginning. More women emerged with increasingly lurid accusations, reaching a quorum that was impossible to ignore. Some complaints tested the bounds of credulity. I doubt Robert ever cornered anyone in the coatroom at a holiday party; even when very drunk, he wasn't that desperate or indiscreet. But others were plausible, largely because they sounded like things he'd said or done with me.

The firm responded in keeping with the times, with multiple town halls and supra-mandatory trainings on workplace sexual harassment. Robert was placed on involuntary leave, a prelude to being dismissed or forced to retire. A discrimination suit was filed and later mediated. The partners were relieved he was on his way out. They'd never liked his style, his politics, his stubborn refusal to leave at the appropriate age.

He came to me shortly before being placed on leave. I came back from a conference room to find him already waiting in my office. I could tell it was him despite the opaque film on the office glass that ran from a person's knees to their head. He was sitting in his sharply tailored suit in one of the armchairs opposite my desk. He'd slid down far in the seat so that his pant legs rode up slightly, revealing the vulnerable curve of his ankles above his black leather oxfords with the gold floral print along the uppers and vamps. He was the only man I ever knew to wear sock garters. He could be a peacock in his quirky heterosexual way.

I walked in and shut the door behind me. I could tell without seeing his face that things were not good. Robert was a pariah by then; he wasn't a person you wanted in your office.

"Look what the cat dragged in," I said, approaching my desk. I dropped my armload of case files haphazardly onto it and then dropped myself into my chair. I was trying to keep the tone light.

"You see what they're doing to me?" he said. "They're trying to jam me up."

"Hm." I leaned forward to adjust the back of my blouse.

"It's extortion is what it is. Bullying. I've been with this firm forty fucking years. You know how much business I've brought in? How much money I've made these fat, lazy fucks? They should be putting my name on a fucking plaque. They should be dedicating fountains and fucking—fucking *streets* to me. They should throw me a fucking parade. My little toe is worth more than all these sad sacks combined."

"It's unfortunate," I said vaguely. We seemed to be having difficulty making eye contact.

"I wouldn't treat a dog like this."

"In their defense," I said, "I don't think they would, either."

Our eyes finally met. Robert had slunk even lower in the chair. I was surprised his spine still bent that far at his stiff age. The lights in my office were off because I hated the fluorescents and had disabled the automatic sensor. His eyes glinted in the dim, and for a moment I was afraid he'd cry.

"You've got to help me," he said. "You know me. You're a woman."

For some reason that was amusing to me.

"Am I?" I said.

"I get it. I was irreverent and disrespectful, and that was stupid of me. You were right, the world has changed."

He only said this to appeal to my vanity. "Don't say things you don't believe, Robert, it's insulting to my intelligence."

"They're making me out to be the devil, and I'm not. You know I'm not."

"Robert. Stop. Listen."

He stopped. I realized then the power I had. I'd shut up this man who had not once in his long life ever listened to any counsel but his own.

"You know I can't do that."

"Why not?" He sounded mortally wounded. I hadn't expected that. I thought he'd say he hated me, that I was an ungrateful bitch. That he'd storm out in such fury that the glass door of my office would shatter. That he'd behave like the oversize boy I knew him to be.

"It's not a winning case, Robert," I said.

He brought both of his hands up to frame either side of his head. He seemed to be puzzling it out, staring at the blandly expensive carpet in front of my desk. Eventually, he brought his hands down. He sniffed loudly, almost athletically, and raised his head, chin jutting out proudly.

"You're right," he said and got up and left. Even if I'd wanted to apologize, even had an apology been possible, I wouldn't have had time for one.

That night I went home and lay awake for a long time before I brought out the gun. I'd barely touched it since it had been given to me, treating it as a sacred object, too refined for the range and too rare for home defense, not that I had anything to defend against; not once in my New York years was I burgled or mugged or even jostled. I turned on the bedside lamp and loaded the gun. I admired it in the golden light, the craftsmanship, the fine work someone had put into it. The knowledge its maker had of how it would be used, at once intimate and vague.

Then, before I could overthink it, I aimed it at my foot and fired.

The pain was not an experience to be relayed in words. I missed my toes by a centimeter. The bullet went through my right metatarsal bones, traveled clean through, and lodged in the dresser beyond before coming to rest in its thick wooden back panel. I looked directly through the hole in my body and then fainted.

It was a dazzling amount of blood. The slippery silk of my bedding and nightgown did nothing to absorb it. My super later cleaned it up in my absence. He threw away the stained mattress and sheets and took the wounded dresser to the curb, dumping all the clothes inside, some of which were scorched, onto the floor for me to sort through. It seemed incredible that he still wanted to fuck me after that, after seeing how messy a person could be.

I don't know how long I was unconscious for. I have no memory of calling for help. The police accompanying the EMTs had to break down my front door. I have no recollection of this, either, and only know because I later got a bill for it from the super.

In fact my memory of all the ensuing weeks was poor. According to medical records—and presumably the police report, though I also have no memory of making any statements—I claimed it was an accidental discharge. That I thought I'd heard an intruder.

I had comminuted fractures of the fourth and fifth metatarsal with significant bone loss. They debrided me and grafted me and reconstructed me with wire. I was able to walk with assistance at eleven weeks, fully bear weight and walk with my normal gait after four months. My foot is disfigured and has a permanent ache, and there's a large scar on my thigh where they took the flesh for the graft. My doctor advised me against ever wearing high heels again, though I eventually did anyway, enduring the pain as penance. My doctor also told me I was lucky, that my recovery was impressively fast and that many people in my position were left unable to walk. I smiled, knowing more than he did about the degree of luck involved.

I tried to work from my hospital bed, needing something besides daytime soaps and opiates to occupy me. My attempts to make light of the wound by joking that I'd literally shot myself in the foot flopped.

"Stop it, miss, it's morbid," the super said when he came to drop off some items I'd requested.

I was still wearing the boot when I went back and was told I would not make partner. What doomed me was my connection to Robert, or the much-whispered-about circumstances of my medical leave, or being a woman, or maybe just that I was more obviously unhinged than I thought. I took the news with grace, or as much grace as I could muster with a pair of crutches and a medical device weighing down my right leg.

I was disappointed, but less than I would've been before. Trying to make partner was just a pastime, a diverting way to test my talents. My damaged foot had put everything neatly into perspective and made everything seem distant from me. At first I attributed this to painkillers, but the sensation persisted even after I left, poached by one of the firm's clients to go in-house. The unpleasantness of the experience did not weaken my resolve. If anything, it made me more certain.

Leaving that meeting, I hobbled by Robert's old office on my crutches. I wanted him to know to what good use I'd put his gift. His was the second largest in the firm, with a huge wall-mounted television and an antique carved desk he'd paid to have specially carted in, the wood that shade of rich mahogany he liked.

His office was empty. I later learned he'd finally taken his retirement while I was in the hospital. No fanfare, no party. The desk and the flowers he used to have delivered daily, lilies and tulips, were gone. The television, impassive box of nothing, was all that remained.

31

In West Texas, a handmade sign said THIS IS GOD'S COUNTRY DON'T DRIVE THRU IT LIKE HELL. Another sign warned us that dumping was illegal and incurred a five-hundred-dollar fine. Another advertised a place called HAPPY, THE TOWN WITHOUT A FROWN. Others warned us to conserve water in the severe drought.

Wouldn't it be funny, I thought, if my father left for cooler climes? If I arrived to an empty house? If he got a grant to go paint in Paris? I'd have to just sit there and wait for his return or hunt him down wherever he'd gone.

We stopped at a gas station only to find it had a broken ice machine and a flatbed parked out front with three decapitated rattlesnakes in the back. What few people we'd seen had odd teeth and dusty hair and an unpredictable number of tattoos. The harshness of the landscape accelerated the aging of the people who lived in it, fraying everyone like rope. John had me stop to take pictures of sinkholes that had formed near abandoned oil fields. The place seemed afflicted with a lack of belief in nice things; faith in God but skepticism for everything else.

We reached our last stop after dark. I thought this was accidental, the result of all the pit stops we'd made during the day. A former foundry, it was well protected by a tall, spiked fence. There might have been cameras or even motion detectors on the building and the trailer that squatted behind it, too. It was a Superfund site in the process of being converted into a strip mall.

I thought John would tell me to turn around, that it wasn't worth the risk, but instead he said, "Keep driving. Park a good distance away."

"You're up for this?" I asked. Barbed wire was a neat trick in the best of circumstances. John had taught me to find the joint where the latch post met the gate frame and to throw padding, a car mat or a thick coat, over the top and hoist yourself over. Doing it while injured seemed an invitation to further injury.

"Stop here," he said by way of an answer, indicating a road running along an old brick building with plenty of unoccupied parking spaces.

Once I stopped, he handed me a pair of large men's socks.

"What the hell?" I said.

"Footprints. Put these on over your boots."

"What do you have planned that I need to worry about footprints?"

"Just an extra precaution for a site this secure," he said, pulling on his own pair.

"Can we not just go somewhere else? It's dark anyway."

I nodded at his camera, that reliquary of criminal evidence, as he reshuffled items in his bag, including a collapsible tripod I hadn't noticed before. He said, "It'll be fine."

"Very convincing." Still, I rolled my jean legs up until they were knee height and put on the socks over my shoes as I'd been told.

Once we left the car, we stalked the perimeter of the fence until we found a spot far enough from the road that we felt comfortably anonymous. I'd brought my old faux-fur vest. I tried to fling it up and over the fence, but my aim was poor, and it came flopping back at us.

"Let me," said John.

"Wait."

I hooked my fingers into the fence's wires and hoisted myself up. The maneuver required the physical courage or at least the physical thoughtlessness of a much younger person, but I clawed my way to the top, reached down to have him pass me up the faux vest, tossed it over the wire, and crossed over. I still managed to scrape a long shallow line into the side of my calf. Blood beaded above my ankle, threatening the white of my double socks. All our accumulating damage struck me as a bad omen.

When I looked up, John had already made it over and was stashing the fur vest underneath a bush, covering it with loose debris, dried leaves and sticks. John inspected my wound and pronounced expertly, "Won't even scar."

When was my last tetanus shot? I racked my mind, my recent history of medical regularity, and remembered getting it from Dr. Sismor, the doctor who'd retired.

I followed John through the site. Bulldozers and excavators and backhoes and other vehicles I couldn't identify were parked in a loose ring on an open field. John and I observed them from nearby bushes like predators stalking prey. John knelt in the dirt beside me and from his bag extracted a crescent wrench and a burlap sandbag. That backpack was magically bottomless.

"What are you doing?" I hissed.

He held his finger up to his lips for silence, then, crouched low, hustled out into the open air. The sky was an odd mauve shade, an effect of the sodium lights of the town against the navy night, the city hall they needlessly kept lit around the clock. All the equipment was black by contrast, and John with it. I didn't see what he did or to which vehicles. I kept checking the time on my phone, cupping it in my palm to hide its light.

He was gone at most five minutes. He came back with the wrench in the empty burlap sack. He pushed at my elbow and said, "Move," in an urgent whisper.

I let him walk ahead, following his shadow. I didn't notice he'd stopped until I walked directly into him, my face pressed to the damp fabric at the back of his T-shirt, my mouth abruptly against the bony jut of his shoulder blade. He smelled like summer, which smelled like sweat and gasoline and wet grass and woodsmoke and the leather strap of his camera and the barest milky sweetness of the jacaranda tree we were standing under, its heavy blooming sleeves.

"What—" I said.

He held up his hand to silence me.

A radio crackled and blipped.

John tugged my arm. He tried to pull me behind the trunk of the tree even though it was far too narrow to conceal us, and besides, it was too late. The guard was right on top of us.

"Stop."

Surprise suppurated the guard's face. Trespassers were probably rare, except maybe the odd bored teenager. He belatedly thought to draw his weapon, which he pointed at us along with his flashlight. He said, "Don't move."

We probably could've outrun him. He was likely younger than me but looked considerably older. The weapon he carried was so gratuitous that I had a hard time taking it seriously: It was a child's toy, a movie prop. I hoped John would think this, too, or that my thoughts would transmit to him, but that's not how thinking works. John raised his hands. I thought about doing the same, then decided it was unnecessarily submissive.

"What are you doing?" the guard asked, sounding like he wanted to know. A dump like this held no appeal except maybe a curiosity better satisfied elsewhere.

"I'm a photographer," said John.

"What?"

"I photograph Superfund sites."

"Why?"

I willed John to come up with a convincing lie—he was a

government subcontractor, he had special permission from the state arts commission, anything—but, guileless, he just said, "It's a hobby of mine."

"What happened to your face?"

"Fistfight."

The guard looked at me like I was a grown-up who could better explain the situation on behalf of my incoherent child, but I only confirmed it with a nod.

The story seemed to confuse him enough that he was worried he should keep us around. He brought out the flex cuffs. I tried to gauge what could be done to convince him we were harmless. He seemed like the kind of person who owned a motorbike and a handgun collection, who had a proprietary and unnecessarily complex method of cooking steak and an interest in novelty fast-food campaigns. Who dabbled in writing excessively researched historical fiction with racy scenes that titillated him but that he later deleted because he considered himself serious. Who responded to sexual rejection with overly long, defensive texts.

I decided to be a dumb flirt. If it didn't seduce him, it might at least fluster or embarrass him. A do-you-know-who-I-am approach wasn't going to work here, I sensed. I wasn't anybody, not anymore, and even if I'd been, that man would've relished pretending he was too noble to care.

"You don't really need those, do you?" I said. "I'll be good."

"Protocol," he said, without meeting my eyes, and then tied my wrists together. I found this erotic, partly for the familiar vulnerability of being restrained but also for the sadness of his pretense to authority. For my role in helping him feel less pathetic. I read once in a popular magazine in Dr. Sismor's waiting room that women have dark, complex sexualities. I'd laughed aloud at that, drawing stares from fellow patients. I'm not sure now why it was so funny. Maybe because of its implication that men were simple and light, or because it seemed such a gross understatement.

Once the guard stepped back, I felt ridiculous, forty years old and restrained like a miscreant. He rifled cursorily through John's bag before escorting us to a white trailer. There wasn't much there: wood paneling, a boxy beige computer, a window crammed with an air-conditioning unit, a desk with a few television monitors for camera feeds. An American flag on a freestanding pole lurked limply in the corner like a voyeur. He had us sit in metal folding chairs opposite his desk. He pulled open a drawer and extracted a toothpick that he worked between his teeth while he stared at his computer screen, clicking his mouse at regular intervals.

He did not call anyone. That seemed encouraging.

I counted the seconds of silence. I tracked the movement of his eyes and tried to make out the reflection of the screen in them. He was probably playing *Minesweeper*, torturing us with waiting. His posture was erect, and I wondered if that was something someone had beaten into him a long time ago or something he enforced on himself.

"Officer," I said. "What's your name?"

He ignored me. Sunnily, I told him mine.

I said, "That's a lot of cameras. You have to watch them all?"

"Yep," he said, goaded into response because people abhor a conversational vacuum.

"Do you catch a lot of trespassers?"

"Some."

"Wow. I could never do your job."

His mouth quirked up into an almost smile, like *Of course you couldn't, you dumb cunt.*

I kept going. "You don't get bored?"

"Sometimes."

"I know what I'd do if I was stuck in a room by myself bored all day," I said and giggled for effect. I hadn't been this unsubtle since I used to walk around kissing drunk strangers in college. It was fun, like trying on an old dress to see if it still fit and finding it looked even better than before.

John seemed about to ask me what the hell I thought I was doing. I hoped he had the good sense not to.

"Yeah?" said the guard. The toothpick was dangling from his lower lip. It's a shame no one had told him to trim his sideburns.

"I can show you if you take these off."

Later I realized that I'd ripped this particular line from a budget porno I'd watched with May on her basement computer in freshman year, both of us shrieking with shocked laughter at the corny dialogue, the actress's frizzed-out platinum wig and ballooned proportions, the fact that all the men involved wore either backward baseball caps or backward sunglasses. I can't remember now how we found it. I thought we'd turn it off after the stilted intro, but neither of us wanted to be cowed by discomfort, and so we watched most of the thirty-minute clip, until our giggling turned to awed silence at the theatrical mechanics of it all. Her mother called us up to dinner, and I had to sit there twirling spaghetti with a soundtrack of moans still playing in my head.

The guard looked at me, then back at his computer, then back at me. I smiled. A stubborn flush clung to his cheeks. Then with an abrupt scraping of his chair legs, he stood up and marched John out of the trailer, John's elbow in one hand and John's bag in the other. John mounted a verbal protest that became inaudible beneath the hum of the air conditioner as soon as the door closed. I had a few moments of blissful stillness in that white office, watching the wind blowing through the trees in the grainy grayscale surveillance video.

The act itself was more awkward than anticipated. He left me cuffed in the chair and stood above me at such an angle that he was grinding against my shoulder. He muttered dirtily at me, and my eyes almost rolled out of my head, which he mistook as a sign of ecstasy. He didn't touch me except to put his fingers in my mouth, which was worse than what I'd expected from him, even though they tasted inoffensive, like salt and the cinnamon coating from his toothpick.

He groped at my shirt, pulling it up. I tried to lean away from his hand, but he was persistent, and I figured, well, serves him right.

His hand slowed over the bandage around my chest, but it seemed no real impediment. He tugged it upward, loosening what I'd bound so tightly that morning. I closed my eyes. I heard him say at some remove above me, "What the fuck is that?"

I didn't respond. I knew what he'd seen. I had a hard enough time facing it alone; I didn't need to look again now.

"Jesus," he said, sounding horrified. "You're a junkie?"

I can see how it looked like that, how the lesion resembled the kind of raw abscess you'd get after prodding needles into your body all day, a few inches of flesh that looked burnt at the edges, pink and lumpen within.

"Let me out," I said.

He released the plastic press on the cuffs. He was breathing heavily and wouldn't meet my eyes. He slumped into his chair with his hand shielding his face. I could tell he was ashamed; that, even beyond his bizarre and incomplete performance and my horrifying wound, he'd betrayed some private code of conduct.

I took some time to reorganize my bandages. I'm not an unenlightened person. I'm as positive about sex as I can be while still being, on the whole, a pessimist. But this experience was one that made me understand how some people arrived at the belief that sex should never be enjoyed or described but only exist for the quiet propagation of the species. Why ultraconservatives only ever fuck through a torn sheet.

I found John outside. His hands had been freed and were jammed in his pockets, and he was pacing anxiously, camera bobbing loosely.

"What was that?" he asked as I came down the wooden steps, and I hushed him imperiously, a celebrity brushing past a crazed fan.

We walked in brisk silence to the place where we'd come in, up and over the fence, and then we were free. I left my dusty vest behind, impaled on the fence's wire spikes. The cars parked at the edges of the street on the other side seemed somnolent, separated from their human drivers. A possum scurried out from beneath one of them and into a storm drain.

John caught up to me, grabbing my arm. "What did he do?"

I pulled free of his grasp. "Nothing. Barely had to do anything."

"Are you insane?"

The question made me smile. I liked John like this; he sounded uncannily like a normal person. "Did you or did you not tell me you're in trouble with the law?"

"I never asked you to do that for me."

"I wouldn't've if you had. Don't be ignorant, John. It's just sex."

He scoffed and turned his back to me, walking ahead of me like a teenager embarrassed of their oblivious mother. I kicked a foil wrapper of discarded gum across the pavement, feeling robbed of my victory and unable to tell what his problem was.

"You can thank me later. And by the way, thanks for the heads-up. That was a nice surprise," I called after him, referring to his little act of ecotage.

We walked in silence. I wasn't sure he'd get in the car, which seemed momentarily unfair, but he did. Once I turned off the cabin light and started the car, in the ill green dashboard glow, John said, "It's just. Uncomfortable having someone do that for you."

"I didn't do it for you. I don't want to get arrested either."

"What did he want from you?"

I looked at his still-swollen eye, trying to tell if there was more to the question, a certain possessiveness, though he'd expressed nothing like that before. He seemed simply concerned. I think I had unwittingly created circumstances under which John had become the first person in a long while to care about the state of my soul, both because he was inclined to treat all souls with care and as a form of attention to my particular person. And this though he probably knew my limitations, that I wasn't capable of reciprocity.

This was a singular realization. What were the odds? How likely was anyone to encounter a hitchhiker who not only wasn't a serial killer, but was in fact a species of ethical genius? I felt that old guilty feeling again, that I had somehow trapped or tricked this fundamentally good person into spending time with me. It wasn't my fault, I insisted to the voice in my head, and then I thought, *Why not?* Only much later did I wonder why anyone needed to be blamed at all.

"Just to see my tits," I said eventually and then laughed at my own crassness.

We hadn't found a motel, had figured we'd rely on luck, which proved stupid; motels were few and far between this far out, and the only one we passed had no vacancy. It got to be ten, then eleven, then after midnight, and then I realized I was half dreaming while driving, lulled to sleep by the oceanic radio static. I pulled over.

"I can't keep my eyes open," I told John. "You drive."

He took the wheel for a while, but after an hour or two, he braked, the jolt enough to wake me up.

"What are you doing?"

"Stopping. Need some shut-eye too."

"We can't camp," I said. I thought of the three rattlesnakes I'd seen, of waking up on the ground in John's too-small tarp to face glass-bead eyes and pixelated skin.

"In the car, we'll be fine in the car."

"There's no room. And it's cold."

"We'll manage."

John pulled his hoodie over his head and crammed it into the corner where the driver's seat met the window jamb, forming a lumpy pillow. He had practice at sleeping in adverse conditions. I missed the fancy hotel in Chicago. The comforts of civilization and three-hundred-dollar steaks. There must've been a stock pond nearby; I could hear frog song along with the crickets and the dry scrape of wind. The longer I sat, the more I imagined I heard: lizards skittering over rocks, javelinas gnawing shrubs, kangaroo rats leaping.

"John," I said. "Still awake?"

"Not for much longer."

"I can't sleep."

He shifted around in the front seat, rocking the entire car as he did. He said, "When we were kids, Dad made us play this game. He'd name a Bible verse, and then one of us would have to say the first word, and another of us the second, and another the third, and so on until it was complete."

"Oh?" This sounded psychotically wholesome, like those creepy family gospel groups of the seventies.

"Yeah, even now, I remember most of them. Go ahead. Pick a verse, any verse. I'll recite them. It'll be like counting sheep."

"I don't know any."

"You don't know any of the Bible books?"

"Leviticus."

"Leviticus what?"

"Um."

"Just name two numbers."

"You don't have to prove it to me. You could say anything you wanted, and I'd have to believe you. I mean. I trust you. And voices help me fall asleep." All those nights drifting off to the low muttering of the TV in my mother's bedroom.

"I think you're asking me for a bedtime story."

I remembered Caleb's teasing. *So cute when you act all edgy and dark.* I'd thought he just wasn't taking my darkness seriously because I was a woman, but maybe he'd described something more particular to me. A certain childlike insistence on knowing everything. Who would I be if I accepted how much I did not understand? Without headlights or streetlamps, I could see opalescent stars, half obscured by a gash of dust clouds. The wound at the start of everything.

"I guess I am."

"Okay. When I was seven, I went missing in the woods for four days."

"Really, truly missing?"

"Yes."

"What is seven, like, third grade?"

"Second."

"How'd you get lost?"

"*Lost* isn't really the right word. My family left me behind at a trailhead, and by the time they realized and came back for me, I'd wandered off."

"They left you?"

"Happens in big families. Easy to lose track in all the chaos. Plus my brother and I were having this argument about who was older, and I think he knew I wasn't in the car but didn't say anything and neither did my other brother and sisters, who were tired of the arguing."

My father used to leave me behind sometimes. No one thought much of it back then; even good parents did that kind of thing. He only started when I was eleven or twelve and becoming smug, criticizing the way he drove or messing with the dials just when the song he liked was about to reach the chorus. He'd drop me only far enough from our house to make the journey back something of a trek. What doesn't kill you leaves you behind the McDonald's eight miles from home. Sometimes the walks bordered on pleasant; other times, particularly in bad weather, they were humiliating. Normal people in normal cars gawking at my out-of-place body at the roadside, the occasional passing trucker hollering obscenely at me or well-meaning soccer mom trying to offer me a ride. My father somehow calculated that I'd never try hitchhiking or running away. He knew the limits of my bravery.

"Who was older? Were you twins?"

"No. I was the youngest. Kids have dumb arguments sometimes, don't you remember?"

"I was an only child."

"Figures. Anyway. They say if you're lost, the best thing to do is stay put because chances are, you're not too far from where you were, and so the searchers will find you quickly. But I didn't know that. I waited for what felt like a long time and then decided well, this is it, it's just me and the woods now, and I'm going to become, you know. A woodsman. I walked into the trees, looking for a place to sleep. I got lucky and found hillbilly bananas and elderberries and Juneberries. I leaned a bunch of sticks together and covered it with leaves. I tried to make a fire by friction like I'd seen in a movie, but it didn't work. It was September, warm still."

I tried to picture child-John, patron saint of the wilderness. One time after my father kicked me out of the car, I tried to stay out as long as I could to spook him, to force him to explain my absence to someone. By then, I wore bras and knew how to use tampons, though I needed neither just yet. I was tall for my age. I thought I could handle myself. I loitered in the small video arcade at the front of our town's grocery store, which was more of a deli and closed at six p.m. every day it was open at all, and then went to a neighboring field where ladybugs crawled over my knees. I counted passing cars and, once it got dark, stars. No one came looking for me, not even my mother. This was the only time I felt contempt for her, for what she allowed my father to do. What was wrong with her that she couldn't be rid of him? I lasted until midnight before I snuck back into the house through the sliding glass door on that never-finished deck, hungry and cold.

"Were you scared?" I asked John.

"Not until dark. I kept hearing this fox scream, this sound like a murder. Actually, maybe I was terrified and just don't remember. It's not a feeling you can access at all back in civilization, not even in memory."

I thought about how I'd shot myself in the foot. The pain was lost to me, the shape of it too big to hold long in my mind. I shuddered to remember it, but that was only in response to the image I retained of the wound when the nurses changed the dressing, ugly and livid, bursting and crisscrossed with black stitches like roads.

John continued: "The next day I was delirious, hungry and sleep-deprived and bitten by a million mosquitos. I drank out of a dirty creek and tried to make this primitive axe with a rock and a stick and a cord of tall grass. I didn't scream for help, but I did talk to myself. Like every now and again, I'd say, 'Mom,' like I could summon her. I tried bargaining with God, too. 'I'll eat my lima beans if you please just get me home.'"

"How far from home were you?"

"Forty-some-odd miles. As I later learned."

"I don't know what that means. Is that walkable?"

"Technically, if I'd known which direction to walk in. It would've taken a couple days. But listen, the part of the story that's essential is that at the end of the day, the sun going down, guess what crosses my path."

"What?"

"A wolf."

"No."

"Yes. Ten yards away, head down, looking at me with yellow eyes."

"A coyote, maybe."

"Shh. Listen. It was a wolf. I know it was. I can explain more, but just, for now, accept it was a wolf. I felt so calm. No impulse to run or back away. I read later that's what you're supposed to do: make yourself big and back up. We stared at each other a long time. It was the first time I ever thought the land wasn't just mine to be lost in. That there was some intelligence that had nothing to do with me or my family or people at all. Something ancient. I'd never understood what Dad meant in church when he talked about humility and grace, but I think I got it then, or close to it. And after I don't know how long, it blinked, licked its snout, and moved off."

"But how did you know it was a wolf?"

"It was huge."

"You were small then."

"I'd seen coyotes before, and this was way bigger. Coyotes are, what, two feet tall? This was twice that, easy. And its paw prints were different. More spread out. I saw when I tried to follow it. I had this idea that it'd adopt me into its den like I was a Kipling character or something. But it was dark by then, and I lost it. Eventually they found me. Everyone came looking for me—not just people from my town but also people from neighboring towns, the police. Even my uncle the motorcycle missionary came back."

"What's a motorcycle missionary?"

"What it sounds like. I was embarrassed to have caused such a fuss. They took me home. I didn't tell anyone about the wolf when they found me, not even when the local newspaper interviewed us about it. I was afraid grown-ups would look for it, try to kill or capture it."

"What was the interview? 'Local boy found in woods'?"

"Basically. Anyway, weeks later, I tried telling my mom. She said it was just a coyote. When I insisted, she said it was my overactive imagination or a hallucination brought on by bad mushrooms I'd eaten. I kept saying I was sure it was real; I swore it.

She said wolves had been declared extinct in Georgia for years and that lying was a sin. I started sneaking out with my dad's old Pentax, trying to find that wolf or others since I didn't know exactly where I'd been, couldn't get back there even if I'd tried. I figured I'd get a picture to prove it to her."

He sniffed and wiped his hand over his eyes as if to reset his facial expression.

"So you really still think it was a wolf?"

"You bet."

"That's a terrifying story."

"It's okay. It ended good."

"That wasn't some mystical experience; you're lucky you didn't die."

"Yeah," he said. "I'm still happy it happened."

I used to think misfortune was a great teacher, that I was somehow wiser for having suffered. I'd grown less sure of that. Maybe telling myself adversity had heuristic value just made me feel better about its meaninglessness. Abruptly, weirdly, I felt a tear escape from the corner of my eye, running down my cheek to my ear. My eyes were dry in the desert heat, I thought.

"That was a good story," I said.

"Do you believe it?"

"Believe what."

"That it was a wolf."

I thought about it for a minute. "Yes," I said. "I do."

32

In June every New Mexican sunset was unbelievable, full of gasping venereal hues that reminded me of the rack of expensive paints my father used to have. It was a solid, permanent rainbow. I'd wanted badly to touch them, though they were forbidden to me. When I eventually did, at great personal risk, the effect wasn't as magical as I'd hoped. The colors looked dull apart; only in the aggregate did they hold meaning.

Just one state remained between me and my father. I saw his life only in the rare glimpses he shared. In that respect, we each had an element of surprise for each other. Every night, I visited his site, looking for signs of his movements. He posted once during this time, an image of a painting he'd only just begun to work on, the colors barely blocked in, with the only accompanying text an all-caps, *I MISSED SOMETHING AGAIN, HAVEN'T I?* I used a metadata extractor to scrape the date and GPS coordinates of the place where the photo was taken: two days before the post, still in the Valley. I used to use an IP scrambler but no longer bothered. He'd never guess that I was pursuing him, never recognize the pattern in these random site views scattered across the country.

Only a little longer, I thought. John had so many plans. Wanted to see the site of the Trinity test, a place chosen for its flatness, its remoteness, its absence of weather. It was a plain full of sand

and grass. An obelisk marked the spot, that was all. Signs with bull-shaped pictograms warned us that it was an open-range area. Otherwise there was no indication that the basin downwind was full of mutated genes, that the ranch wells were full of alkaline water, that farmers still had to bathe in saltwater soap.

The heat had turned sand into knobby bubbles of green glass, filled with microscopic particles of the bomb's support structures, in a radiating circle around ground zero, the origin point of an entire generation's anxiety. The glass had been buried under dirt, but I thought I found a specimen. I pocketed it, ignoring the signs prohibiting its removal.

I was barely sleeping by then, afflicted with a dread that was controlled during the day but that later seeped up like ooze from the spongy earth. In fifteen-minute increments of dozing, I managed to have stunning dreams that felt like they lasted years. I wanted to die and be done with it, or else I wanted to live forever as a coward; I made up my mind and unmade it one minute to the next. A deep certitude remained, anchoring me, but there was enough slack in the line for me to drift with the changeable tides of mood.

I'd often awake in cold sweats, until I'd eventually have to get up and change my soaked compressive bandage. The veins on my left breast were huge and soft and bruised-looking. Sometimes I lay on the floor, door locked and top off, to give Beryl air. I'd pictured beryl as a mineral so darkly green it was almost black, but actually beryl is a name for many different varieties of stone, including emerald and aquamarine, found in every color raw. I must have been thinking of something else.

The lack of sleep is how I got the car stuck in a ditch. I drifted off, and when I woke up, the hood was crumpled like a boxer's nose, pressed up against the slope on the other side. I was suddenly eye level with some dry, dusty tumbleweeds scattered atop the other side of the embankment. The airbags had deployed and were rapidly deflating with a loud hiss. My chest felt like it'd been hit with a factory press, the pain on the left side so acute and nauseating that I leaned out of the driver's side and heaved. I felt the same way I had when I fell or got hit in childhood, the humiliating raw-edged urge to cry from the abrupt, the unexpected. *You're fine*, my mother would say, and I always had been.

John let out a low groan. He looked stunned, no worse. Blood colored his face, but it was just a reopened cut from the fight. At worst, we'd be bruised and achy tomorrow. I hadn't been going all that fast. The radio was still on.

While government-controlled anti-Christ schools teach of Before Christ and After Christ, they refuse to teach about Jesus Christ. They teach the big bang theory and evolution but absolutely censor any truth and reality to be taught. While the theories are just theories that are totally made up and don't make any sense, history books written on several different continents all talk of Jesus Christ.

"What happened?" John said.

"My fault."

"Are we in a ditch?"

"Sure are. Fuck," I said, groping for my phone.

"What?"

"It's dead."

A low hum of distant machinery suggested that, far out though we were, we hadn't escaped civilization. I opened my door. The car was astride the ditch, its front tires resting low on the far side and its rear ones on the side closer to the road, its undercarriage suspended a foot or so above solid earth. I rested one of my feet on the ground as though drawing strength from it.

The ditch had maybe once been used for irrigation before the drought. The sun was like a drunk at a party, menacing and vivacious. I wasn't sure how much water we had with us, John's canteen and maybe a few overheated bottles in the trunk, the plastic gone treacherously soft. One of us would have to go up to the road and wait for someone to pass. Or maybe one of us could set off on foot using John's atlas. I cursed again. If I died of thirst or heat exhaustion before I got to kill my dad, then I had only myself to blame.

I looked back over my shoulder. John hadn't moved, his head tilted back on the headrest and his eyes closed like he could just go back to sleep.

"Hey," I said, leaning fully back into the car and twisting my torso so I could snap my fingers in his face. "You aren't concussed, right?"

"No."

"Then what are you doing?"

"Praying. I'll help soon."

"Sure."

"Don't be cynical."

I was sick of being told that. If anyone had a manual on how to avoid being cynical, I'd read it, but it was a supporting pillar of my personality; take it away and you'd have nothing to bear the load.

I hoisted myself up out of my seat, puffs of dust rising where my feet made impact. Overhead, a bird spun in low, aimless arcs.

"Eagle?" I asked John, who, with the door open, could still hear me.

"Vulture."

The hum of the machinery grew louder and then abruptly stopped. A shadow fell over us. For one disorienting second, I thought John had summoned God. Shielding my eyes from the sun, I saw the silhouette of a man on a small tractor approaching the ditch. I could see few details about his appearance except his massive size, though the machine artificially inflated his height.

He called down to us but was inaudible over the roar of the machine.

"What?" I said.

He cut the motor momentarily, yelled, "Hold on," then coughed it back to life and disappeared. Several minutes later, he came back with a pickup truck, a winch, and two more men. I felt embarrassed at having to be rescued, and at needing assistance from so many people. Once again, without entirely intending to, I'd put myself at the mercy of strangers.

John and I clambered up the sides of the ditch and watched as the car was effortfully resurrected. The man introduced himself to us as Mr. Black. He shook first John's hand, then mine. The choice of order was likely random but felt deliberate, signifying the hierarchy of his respect.

Mr. Black's palms were calloused to the texture of rocks, but they had a noticeable tremor, and his face was stiff and impassive. His furrowed cheeks looked sand-blasted from sun exposure and the ruins of ancient acne. He had the most distinguished jowls I'd ever seen. He said he was the proprietor of the property. He had a serious voice, stentorian and slow.

"Thanks," I said, "for the help."

"Who was driving?"

"Me," I said.

He regarded me for a moment. His eyes were set back beneath his brow, which made him look like an animal peering out from beneath a porch.

"Ought to be careful on these roads. The straightness looks simple enough, but it'll bore you right off to sleep."

I said, "Pretty much what happened."

"Come up to the house," he said. "Get cleaned up. You look a little worse for wear. Jose's pretty handy around cars, too."

Jose nodded.

John and I looked at each other.

"If I can just get a phone, that'd be great. It's a rental," I said.

"Yes. Thank you. Very kind of you," said John.

We spoke simultaneously, cutting each other off. I felt he'd deliberately misread the look we'd shared. I'd hoped to keep my distance to the degree possible because I'm congenitally unfriendly and suspicious.

"It's nothing. Hop on up in the back."

I didn't protest, figuring there'd be a phone at the house regardless. We got into the back of his pickup truck, dirt and straw caked into the ridges of the flatbed. Jose rode in the back with us. The road was long and bumpy, full of dried mud and ruts, and we went slowly as it towed my hitched-up car. I kept my eyes on it. The gun was still in the glove compartment, and I worried that someone would find it and take it for themselves. Thieves are always the most paranoid about theft.

We passed endless rows of sorghum, russet-gold heads swaying, until we reached a cluster of buildings: a greenhouse and two long, low-slung buildings. A barn and a silo lurked in the back like awkward cousins in a family photo. I heard a goat bleat.

We stopped as we neared the buildings. A woman in coveralls was crossing the yard carrying a metal pail so heavy that all the sinew in her ropy arms stood out. People like me in New York paid one hundred dollars an hour for muscle definition like that.

Mr. Black got out of the truck and called to her.

The woman in coveralls returned. Words were spoken that I couldn't hear. From a distance, I thought she had no eyebrows or eyelashes, but they were just ash-blond, pale enough to blend in with her sunblock-smeared skin. Her hair itself was tightly plaited like a softball player's and locked in place by a blue kerchief.

John got out and I followed. We curtly exchanged names; hers was Arlo. She put the bucket down to shake my hand in a businesslike fashion and then led me off to one of the sloped-ceiling buildings. I didn't see what happened to John, but being separated from him was unnerving; I hadn't realized how accustomed to him I'd grown.

When I got inside, I realized it was a dormitory. Eight cots lay in a row, all tidily made. The sun made it through chinks in the rafters, backlighting cobwebs. It smelled of pine sawdust. Arlo brought me to bed, then told me to wait, and returned in a moment with a towel and other linens. All her movements were brisk and practical. I pictured us fucking—that interpersonal shorthand again—and imagined it would be intimately chore-like and slightly mutually repulsive, like milking a cow.

"I'll bring you a cold compress. Head off that soreness tomorrow. If you're hungry, I can run down to the kitchen. Toilet's out there, by the way," she said, pointing out the window to a dirt path.

"What is this place?" I asked.

"My father's farm," she said and blinked. Then she was gone. She came back up a few moments later with a brick of ice wrapped in a towel.

"Stay long as you like," she said and then left again before I could point out that she hadn't answered my question. The invitation was so terse I was convinced of its authenticity.

I sat on the bed, debating my options. The longer I debated, the lower I sank, until I was lying fully back, my neck resting on the ice, which was melting quickly into the sheets and lumpy mattress beneath me. A pleasantly musty, slightly ureic odor of dampened down pervaded. I could hear noises outside, people calling to each other, a metal gate clanking. I became hypnotized by the movement of the ceiling fan above, which was slightly off its axis, spinning wider than intended.

I fell asleep and woke much later, my head in a sopping puddle. Disoriented, I thought for a moment I was in my childhood bed, the peeling cornflower paint and the place in the windowsill by the headboard where I'd scratched my name with Dad's drafting compass. Mom was just downstairs, toasting the cheap, airy bread she always bought.

It took me a long time to find myself.

Outside the window, the sun was a low, portly pearl. I was unsure if I'd slept hours or years. I went to the outhouse behind the building, cursing dirty hippies and my sore muscles, my bruised chest, the golden, sap-like liquid seeping through my bandage. The crickets were deafening, and, leaving the outhouse, I realized why: They were visible on the walls of the place, crawling up the exterior, not so many as to alarm but more than I'd ever seen in one place at a time. I let one crawl into my hand, cupping it in my palm, and held its black glistening body up to the porch light until it hopped off into the night at John's approach.

I walked down to meet him. Someone had given him a bandage for the reopened cut. It bore a bright red stain that was difficult not to stare at.

He said, "Where you been?"

"I was asleep this whole time. What day is it?"

"Man. It's been like a week."

"Is that a joke? Are you being funny?"

"It's been like six hours."

"Where's the car?"

"In one of the barns. This place has everything, man. Greenhouse, dairy, root cellar woodshop, cold storage. Organic, fully sun-powered, you believe that?"

"The truck?" I said.

"Well. Almost fully."

"How do they get their water?" I asked.

"Don't know yet," he said. "I'll find out."

I didn't actually care. "Seems like we stumbled into your own personal Eden," I said jealously. I didn't think such a place existed for me.

"If I had the money to build something like this," he said, trailing off into an appreciative whistle at his own impossible dream.

"We shouldn't be here."

"What? Why?"

"They're a cult. They're Branch Davidians. Now we're stranded, and the Feds'll come, and we'll be caught in the crossfire."

John lifted his cap and scratched his forehead. "Doesn't that seem sorta unlikely?"

"This is how the plot of every horror movie begins. You have no sense of self-preservation."

"I just don't think they're a cult."

"Prove they're not."

"Prove they are."

"You don't find them weird?"

"People are allowed to be different from you."

"There's different and then there's the Mansons."

"All they did was help us out of a bad scrape—one *you* put us in."

"I need a phone, I need to call the rental place, they won't just let anybody touch a car," I said.

John laughed. "Screw it. You're rich, who cares? No one will know it's been worked on, and if they do, it's just money."

This made a suspicious amount of sense, especially since I wasn't planning to return the car anyway. I said, "Well, I want a phone regardless."

"Okay. So we'll ask for a phone."

John's loose grin made me uncomfortable. I didn't know what to do with him when he didn't seem as doomed and immiserated as me. I blew air out of my cheeks, thinking back to the crash, my mistake, my nodding. I was belatedly understanding that I might actually have even less time than the oncologist thought I did, and that made being stuck all the worse.

I said, "I'll give them money. I just don't want to spend however long it's going to take to fix it here."

Even without internet, I knew we were less than four hundred miles away from Dad, but only three days remained in the month. I'd have to extract myself from Arizona quickly. I could try to hitchhike, I thought, or walk straight without sleeping, arriving late and fully delirious from sweat and cactus spines and scorpion stings.

John laughed again. "They're not gonna want your money."

"Everyone wants money."

John stopped smiling. He looked at me intently and then surprised me by putting his hands on my shoulders. We'd never touched each other so purposefully before.

"You're tense. You don't like having to sit in one place and think, do you?"

"I don't need you to analyze me." I pulled back, but he pressed down on my shoulders, keeping me still.

"Slow down," he said. "Breathe. We might be here for a while. That's all."

He was pressing on a particular part of my shoulders that I hadn't even realized hurt. "Okay, I get it, I'm breathing. You can let go now," I said, trying to shrug him off.

"Close your eyes."

"I'm fine."

"Hush. Quit fighting everything."

He closed his eyes and kept his hands on me. I didn't complain or wriggle away, but I didn't obey, either; I had to keep at least that much for myself. I stared at his face, at the brown sunspots on the bony pink ridge of his nose. When this became too intimate, I stared at a fixed point beyond his shoulder, into a blurry, tangled knot of trees.

I felt an imbalance between us. I'd never be so bold as to presume I knew what John needed, or to presume I should be the one to provide it. If he'd been older than me—the way I was older than him—I would have been doubly cautious. He didn't feel the same reservations, but I didn't find that wrong, only unusual.

He opened his eyes. For a moment, he kept his hands in place.

The intensity had gone out of the sun; we were standing in faded shadow. Then he released me.

I cleared my throat, feeling that I needed to in order to transition out of the past moment. "They say how long it'd take?"

He shrugged. He looked neither disappointed nor pleased. "Didn't ask, only came out here to take a leak."

He shifted so naturally from quasi-spiritual to bodily needs. I moved aside to let him pass.

"See you at dinner," he said over his shoulder.

"Dinner?"

"The bell."

Just then, I heard a big, sonorous clang. I walked in the direction of the sound until I saw people and followed them. Everyone sat at long wooden picnic tables in the big barn. A man with a gin blossom nose and a Balbo beard. A tonsured type with too-forward teeth and an air of vegetarianism. A cloth-diapered toddler with a split thumb, two fingernails facing different directions on the same digit. A mannish older woman in a paisley vest with gold-framed lenses so round and thick they looked liable to pop. A gangly man wearing one blue sock and one gray. It was a diverse group, all ages and races, but everyone could be described as quirky and homespun.

It would have been funny to sit these people down at a meeting with the old firm. Cram them all into a sleek modern conference room, let them stink up the place. Robert would have shot them without remorse like old cattle. I don't know why we always hated the soft ones.

John and I were seated together. It was unclear to me if this was by the group's design or John's or simply happenstance. Before we were permitted to eat, Mr. Black led us in a prayer. The mannish woman, who sat to my right, took one of my hands, and John the other. As in other rare times of my life when prayer has been required, I kept my eyes open, relishing the opportunity for unfettered observation.

"And thank the Lord for shining a light on these two strangers," Mr. Black said at some point during his exhaustive rambling, nodding correctly in our direction with his eyes closed. I didn't understand why he'd be thankful for our presence unless they intended to butcher us on the barn rafters.

The prayer ended, and I was released. John carried on a conversation with Arlo. If he felt relieved to have someone other than me to talk to, I couldn't blame him. I tried to speak to the woman next to me.

"She can't respond," said a man from across the table. "She's taken a vow of silence."

She smiled at me like I should've figured that out.

I smiled back with no teeth and returned to my salad, the first fresh food I'd had in ages. In fact, it was probably the freshest food I'd ever had, short of all the apples I ate when I worked on the neighbors' farm as a teenager, shoveling manure medievally.

"Is that part of living here?" I said. "Vows of silence?"

He said, "She's a special case."

I stabbed my fork into a spinach leaf and felt the tine penetrate something thick and resistant. On turning it over, I found I'd impaled a golden slug, a small stowaway.

"That's good luck," he said. "The baby in a king cake. Don't eat it, though. Meningitis," he added, like I'd be tempted.

I widened my eyes with false enthusiasm, pulling the leaf off and resting it on the lip of my plate, as far from the rest of the food as possible. I didn't have much appetite anyway.

After the meal, as John and I walked together before splitting paths to head to our separate dormitories, I told him, "This is like summer camp for bullied adults."

I said this like I hadn't gotten bullied in high school. John hissed like he couldn't believe me, like I was more than he could stand. "Sour grapes," he said.

In the morning, all the other women were up with the sun and the birds. The parents of the toddler I'd seen the night before slept apart from everyone else, in a shack they'd built themselves. I'd learned at the dinner the night before that they'd met on the farm; in their previous lives, they'd been a divorced banker and a school administrator. They'd told me how their child helped them observe the world without interference from the ego, whatever that meant.

I heard the women rustling about, dressing, speaking quietly, maybe more hushed than usual for my benefit. It was stuffy in the dormitory, the windows closed to keep the worst of the crickets out. Despite the oppressive warmth, I stayed hunched, mostly hidden beneath my sheet, pretending I was still asleep so I wouldn't be forced into conversation or manual labor.

When I was certain they'd all left, I got up and peered out of the age-warped window panes, watching them file out away from the dormitory toward the barn or the fields. Their braids were all held in place with strips of the same cloth. I wondered if there was any universe in which I could make myself amenable to this place, snuff out my memories, live as a new person on honest sweat, self-invented and mythologized in the usual American way, the way the banker had.

I went out looking for the garage. I quickly found it. It was a plank shack with an open door. A radio on a worktable was turned to a norteño station. The car was inside, jacked up on a wooden ramp. A mutt lay outside, yawning and kicking up dust and flies with the rapid motion of its tail.

"Hey," I yelled over the music.

Jose rolled out from underneath the car on a dolly, also made of wood. His sleeves were rolled up to his elbows and covered in uneven streaks and smudges of black grease. He turned down the radio just enough that we could speak.

"Gracias por ayudar. ¿Qué tan malo es?" I said in my bad high school Spanish. I never bothered softening my American accent.

He sat forward, elbows on his knees, and then pushed himself up to standing, limber for what I thought was his age.

"Not so bad," he said in good English. "Tie rod replacement, wheel alignment. The rest? Just some dents."

"I can live with dents. How long?"

He shifted his head from side to side and pursed his lips, considering. "Few days. It'd be faster, but I got other shit to do around here."

"Puedo pagar," I said, implying that if he hurried, I'd make it worth his while.

"De nada," he said. "But it's gonna take the time it takes."

He was wiping down the ratchet he carried with a blackened rag at the crowded worktable. I could see I was interrupting the master in his studio.

"Mind if I get some stuff out?"

"No, 's open."

I grabbed my bag from the back seat. His worktable was positioned to the left of the car, so his back was to me, and I was able to extract the gun unseen and put it in my bag. We were in open-carry land, but I had a feeling it was better to keep it secret.

"One more thing: There internet here?"

He shook his head no.

"Too slow, too pricey. Mr. Black thinks it's the, what he call it? Taller del diablo."

I bit my cheek to keep from laughing. I guessed in a sense he was correct. In a different age, it would have been much harder for me to find my father, to keep prodding at this festering wound.

"Yeah, okay. Where is Mr. Black?"

"In the fields with everybody else. We all work the same. That's a rule."

Walking back to the room, I could see more of the property: beehives, greenhouse, arched metal storage sheds, field beds, chicken coops, a whitewashed barn, the composting outhouse. Every roof was laden with solar panels and more filled a meadow. An orchard of trees I couldn't identify looked desiccated, but otherwise the place seemed surprisingly green.

Sure enough, Mr. Black was in the fields with the rest of them. He worked ponderously, pushing a two-wheel tractor with a tiller attachment and wearing big yellow earmuffs. Evidently the tractor was a technological innovation Mr. Black didn't think Satan had a hand in. From a distance, you couldn't see his tremor; he looked sturdy.

I spent the entire day in the loft. I stalked the aisle between the rows of beds, shamelessly looking through each woman's cubbyhole of belongings. One woman had a box of Guatemalan worry dolls. Another had a jagged jumble of bobby pins on top of a deck of sun-faded tarot cards and a plastic baggie of old weed. The last had a diary written in elegant cursive. I took it with me back to my bed. I lay on my back—any other position was impossible thanks to Beryl. It mostly contained accounts of unpredictable weather, reports of hours slept, discussions of various minor ailments, and almost always a final assessment of the value of the day, good or bad. I was hunting for lurid details, signs they were all having ritualistic sex in the corn shed, but if that was happening, the writer didn't deem it exciting enough to document. In fact, there were no truly private details or thoughts at all.

I heard footsteps on the stairs. I slid the diary beneath my pillow and closed my eyes, feigning sleep. It was Arlo, hunting for an item in a wicker basket she pulled from beneath her bed. It was her diary I'd been reading, I realized. When she stood to leave, she said with the unmistakable disdain of the healthy and wholesome for the selfish and weak, "We can always use more hands." I kept my eyes closed, though she clearly knew I was awake. She waited a moment as though confirming that I really was that brazen, then turned on her heel and left.

I stayed there all night, didn't even go down to dinner. I wanted to establish that their way of life was not superior, that not everyone would want to join their little utopia. I wanted, of course, to be right. I pretended to still be asleep when they all returned. They turned off every lamp at night, the property pitch-black but for the porch light.

Hours later, bedsprings creaked. I heard a door click shut, the sound sharper for the fact that whoever opened it had been careful not to let the hinges whine. Bare feet padded soft on the steps, and another door pressed open. I twisted in bed and leaned forward until I could see out the window, my eyes barely clearing the dusty sill. Two figures were walking away from the sacred circle of that one light, their backs receding into the dark. Arlo in her nightgown and John.

I was no longer that girl, that object of romance, maybe never had been and never would be again, for John or anyone else. I was glad for John even as I realized this. I imagined it was something like what a parent feels when they see their child happy. Complex, bittersweet. This attachment to him made me feel less his chauffeur and more a thief of his time. He belonged here, and I belonged nowhere, having made myself an exile. I had to let him be. I had to let him pursue what he'd pursue.

I thought I'd sleep, but I was wide awake, attuned to every branch shaking in the wind, to every cricket chiming in with its stridulating song. It's only the male crickets who sing; the females can't. I don't know why I know that.

Far into the deepest part of the night, I got up and went outside. I have no memory of this. I have no memory of taking off my clothes, of unwrapping my dressing. I have no memory of getting down onto the cracked parch at the edge of a sorghum field. No memory of covering myself in earth like it had some power to cure me, like burying myself in my own grave. Of turning it to mud with tears.

I remember the ache in my breast, my hollowness. I remember the drought-borne crickets forming a dome of silence around me. I remember being on my knees and seeing all the women standing at a distance like at a vigil, a few of them holding candles, no flashlights or phones, all together in shabby nightgowns, whispering among themselves and staring at me with gibbous eyes. Where the men were, I didn't know. Arlo was there, at the front of the crowd. I must have cut a frightening figure, wild-eyed and filthy, with earth in my teeth. There was something gone wrong with me, something much the matter, something beyond my control. I'd never felt death with such clarity. It was happening; I was passing unseen from the earth; there was no escape.

Arlo came to me, put one hand on mine where it rested in the dirt, the warm yellow light of a flame in her other. Then the other women were surrounding me, lifting me up. I went passive as soon as I was touched. They all carried me, arms braced beneath my body in a slow, careful shuffle. Women with candles flanked us in a mock processional. White, then a flicker of dark, a susurration of cotton, low voices and creaking wood, the chirp of a bird early to rise.

I woke in the morning, clean and clothed and alone in my borrowed bed in this hay-smelling loft. I could've sworn it was a dream, and I was relieved, and then I saw the dirt beneath my nails.

33

When I turned thirteen, my mother and I spent the day at an amusement park with whirling lights and cotton candy on tight paper cones and older girls walking around in bikini tops to show off the colored crystals in their belly buttons. I rode a coaster alone, whipping around in brain-damaging loops, trying to pick my mother out of the crowd of onlookers. The park had a pool, and my mother waded into the shallow end with all her clothes on, and I was not embarrassed. My period—my first—started abruptly, sparse blood blotting the tan mesh crotch panel of my swimsuit. We stopped on our way home for tampons and for my mother to pick up a miniature cake with my name written on it in blue gel frosting. The letters glowed gold in the candlelight, the scent of all thirteen blown out.

Dad wasn't there until later. After dinner there was a scene. I don't remember how it started or why. I don't remember if the birthday or my father's lateness had anything to do with it. I don't remember why I didn't flee like usual. Most of what I have from that day is impressionistic, images and moods like beads with no logical string to hold them together.

One image: my father holding my mother against the wall by the front door, next to the coat rack. Her begging him to stop because I'd see whatever happened next.

A second image: that old BB gun in the attic. I knew BBs weren't for killing. I also knew that occasionally people did die from them. That, like anything, they could be deadly under the right circumstances. I call this the first time because the intent was there if not the means. Getting that gun was the action of a dreamy, morbid, lonely little girl who got most of her ideas from old movies, Peggy Cummins or Karen Steele or Rita Hayworth. My hands were steady and I was not afraid. That's a lie, I must have been terrified, but that's how it is in my mind, so that's how I'll tell it.

He turned to me, laughing. He wasn't at all livid. He seemed not to think it was a big deal. He seemed to think we were overreacting. He seemed to know we wouldn't follow through, because women don't.

I pulled the trigger. A final image: the holes in his shirt, bloodied a maraschino red like the cherries on my cake, like the stain in my swimsuit. Red was the color of the day. I wish I'd coolly re-aimed and done it again. Instead I panicked. I threw the gun at him and then ran out the back door and into the woods.

He ran after me. I thought of all the children he might've had before or would have after me and whether he'd ever give himself up for any of them, ever acknowledge himself bested. If it was something particular to my mother and me that made him like this.

There are more images, actually. The contours of every leaf on every tree and bush. The hum of every insect, which is a sound, not an image, but which was so loud and overpowering as to become visual. Many years later, the drugs I took from his cabinet gave me the same feeling, and I sat outside my seminar, admiring the symmetry of discrete branches of trees on the green while I waited for Caleb.

Dad caught me, wrapping his arms around my waist and pulling me down into the dirt. He was on his back; my shoulder blades pressed into his chest. Bits of decaying leaves clung to our hair, and the earth was crawling with worms and beetles, like the soil was alive and we were already dead.

We lay there a long while, panting. I kept waiting for him to get enough energy to curse or to crush me. He rolled us over so that he was on top of me, his legs pinning mine in place and his hands pushing down my shoulders. I thought for sure that was it, he was going to do the unforgivable. I was so certain of it that I almost invited it, my hands limp in the dirt beside me. I even tucked my skull back into the dirt so he'd have more of my neck to strangle.

When I was small, we used to play a game. I'd beg him to lie down on top of me. I'd be on my back on the bed, and he'd form a bridge over me, elbows above my head, like I was a road or a river. Then he'd pretend, with great fanfare, that the bridge's engineers had been negligent, that the structure could no longer support itself, and he'd collapse on top of me, crushing all my air out. I'd think I was dying until he'd raise himself up, resurrected. And then, breathless and giggling, I'd ask him to do it again.

In the woods, though, he just slapped me gently on the cheek. His hand lingered there for a moment, thumb under my chin, and he shook my face a little, like he was trying to knock some idea out of my head. He stood up and held out his hand and called me stupid but in a way that sounded almost admiring, and he said, "We're going to have to work on your aim," as if I'd missed him.

I felt a confused pride at his use of *we*. I'd forced him to see me, provided a friction he didn't usually encounter. I thought that might make him interested enough in me to turn me into one of his art projects. I could never hate him all the way through like I wanted to.

I took his hand. We walked out of the woods together, fingers clasped, sweating and mosquito-bitten and dirty. The police were already in front of the house, I could tell by the flashing lights on the silvery undersides of the surrounding treetops. My mother had finally called them, finally done it. Finally admitted our unmanageability.

When we reappeared, the officers surrounded Dad, separating us. When they swarmed him, I kept reaching out for him with the hand he'd been holding, calling after him, *Daddy.* I felt he was being taken from me, though that's what I thought I'd wanted, though I'd wished worse on him, wished we weren't related, wished he'd drop dead. My friend's father held my other arm and patted my head until Mom came, and I clung to her for what felt like years. Dad was quiet as he was led away. I don't know what to make of that, the lack of sniveling or raging or counter-accusing.

Mom and I did not discuss that night again. All I knew was that he did not come back. What happened to him in the aftermath was a lacuna in our family history; by the time I wanted to fill the gap it was too late. Even had I known, no punishment he received would've satisfied me. How could I trust anyone else to make him understand, to deliver the message the way I wanted it said?

I'm not sorry this happened to me. Does that make sense? I don't know. I think it's beyond sense. I'm not the same person I was then, the earth not the same earth. I didn't inhabit the same body as that child; that would never happen to me. But I have come to love this memory because it is part of me. To believe that, without it, there would be no me.

I knew that, in the end, when I met Dad, he'd tell me it didn't have to be like that. That we could have another ending. But I'd given it more thought than he had, and I knew we could not.

III

FOREVER CHEMICALS

34

"Good news," John said.

We'd been at the farm three nights. I hid the whole time in that stuffy attic, acting like the ill person I was, standing up only to visit the outhouse or refill the jug of water I'd taken from the car to keep by my bed. After my episode, the women began bringing me plates of food and glasses of a cold tea I never drank because it tasted like pond muck. They were hushed and respectful, like the nurses in the ward where my mother spent her last days.

John was standing at my bedside. I wasn't sure what he'd heard or seen of my episode. I sat up a little, appraising him. He looked good, a solid sun-brown. Working outside and eating three meals a day suited him. He was mostly healed, the bruises faded and the cut on his nose just a dry, dense scab I wanted to pick for him. It would heal into a scar for which he could invent a better history but probably wouldn't, being so upright and honest.

"Jose says the car's ready. We can leave any time," he continued.

"We?"

"What, you don't feel well enough?"

"I'm fine," I lied. "I just figured you'd want to stay. You seem to like it here."

Every night we'd been there, the routine had been the same: the step on the floor, the creaking. John chewed his lip and looked out the window.

"That's true. But I can come back."

I clutched the side rail of the bed, reaching for something firm. I couldn't tell if he was attempting to do me a kindness or if he wanted to continue his work. At what point would he consider his collection finished? Probably not until America stopped polluting itself.

"Did you hear anything the other night?" I asked.

"Like what?"

I scanned him for signs of dissimulation, but he looked straightforward as ever.

"Nothing. Probably just the cows."

Maneuvering the car felt good, possibly better than when I'd first driven it off the lot. I'd missed the radio, the nattering that supplanted my thoughts. The whole place came out to watch us go, this big send-off. I half expected them to weep and wave kerchiefs over our departing halation of dust. I've claimed to never feel shame, but I couldn't look at Arlo, at any of the women who'd appeared unbidden to help me. Never had I been so out of control except in childhood, beyond memory.

I sat behind the wheel of the car, picking away the dirt that still lingered beneath my fingernails while John made his farewells. Arlo approached the car. I tried to pretend I didn't see her, but when she knocked on the window, I was left with no choice but to roll it down. She leaned to my level, elbows resting on the door in a way I found overly familiar.

"Are you feeling better?" she said with an unplaceable accent I hadn't noticed before—something soft, almost European, like she'd been raised elsewhere.

I tightened my thumbs around the steering wheel, thankful that my sunglasses put a protective barrier between me and the world.

"Very," I said.

"Good. Rest is important."

"You're right."

The ensuing silence was long enough that I could see each second approaching and then fading from view. I watched John shake hands with each gathered person, sometimes bestowing upon them a firm upper arm grip or a shoulder clap. I wondered how he chose who got which type of flourish.

"Is it true that you and John are only friends?" she asked.

I turned and looked at her. Somehow I hadn't thought sturdy country girls were susceptible to jealousy. She was watching John too, allowing the wind to blow her hair across her cheeks and eyes. The weatherstripping at the base of the window was running a fine pink line into the skin of her arms. I entertained the idea of lying to her, but instead I said, "I'm not even sure we're friends. I'm just giving him a ride."

She nodded, squinting at the dust. "I didn't tell him about your time in the dirt. If you were wondering."

"Okay," I said, appalled at her phrasing. *Your time in the dirt.* Like I was one of her farm animals.

"That's not quite right. I told him you had a sort of night terror. But that's all. He didn't seem surprised."

"We sleep together. I mean, we have slept in the same hotel rooms. Separate beds. We've never—you know. It's not that kind of thing."

She stood up, arms crossed over her belly so that her face was out of view. From above, I heard her say, "I don't know that I believe you. It sounds pretty weird, whatever kind of thing it is."

"It is," I acknowledged.

She lingered, maybe waiting for an apology from me, or a

word of thanks. I could give her neither, but I could at least be honest. She crossed paths with John, who by then was walking toward the car. They exchanged words that were not for my ears, their faces inscrutable, and then John came to the car, and we were ready.

35

I wanted to move quickly then, but in Arizona I had to change our paths often to avoid road closures, the helicopters spewing red haboobs of Phos-Chek on the trees below. We took the long way round, wending through suburbs. Every house was a ranch or a mission style or some combination of the two. It was the type of architecture you only saw at old Taco Bells out east. I had this idea that everyone was living in a drive-through, like I could pull up to their living room window and order a chalupa.

We got into towns with three churches and no bars or tattoo parlors. Dairies that advertised themselves with sculptures of milk cartons, neighborhoods where some houses had tinfoil on the windows, neighborhoods offering oxtail barbecue, African hair braiding, pawn shops, shoe hospitals that did "shoeshine and dying," a shirtless guy with a tattoo of a gun tucked into his waistband, a barefoot woman with a parakeet on her shoulder outside a salon advertising the BADDEST NAILS & SWEETEST HAIRSTYLEZ. Nurses in turquoise scrubs stood guard over a table laden with water bottles in the shade created by a Salvation Army tent. We stopped at the Grand Canyon, where the air reeked of mineral dust and sand verbena. I was moody and quiet and strange, and John was treating me gently, like radioactive glass.

Life wasn't so bad, I thought, surveying these scenes, even in its degraded state, its decayed landscapes. If it were, I wouldn't be bitter about Dad outliving me. Or maybe it was that bad, and Mom and I had been blessed with an early departure. Maybe Beryl was a gift. Maybe I was doing Dad a great service.

Early one morning, before John woke up, I went for a long walk to smoke and call the oncologist from a gas station pay phone. I let the cigarette burn down between my fingers while I cradled the phone between my shoulder and ear.

"Hester," he said. "I'm glad to hear from you."

"You are?"

"Yes. I was very disturbed by our last conversation. Where are you now?"

"I'm just calling to tell you I think you were wrong."

"About what?"

"About my prognosis. It's okay, I'm not going to sue or whatever. Like you said, these things are hard to predict. I just thought you might want to know."

"I see. I take it you got a second opinion?"

"I was in Oklahoma recently. Well. A couple weeks ago. I'm actually not sure when it was. Anyway, I went to this place owned by the Quapaw tribe. This old creek where the government milled lead and zinc to make bullets and left these big piles of white chat. Do you know what chat is? It's this waste that looks like sand. And it coated the creek beds and all these families used to picnic on it, not knowing it was all lead. When they figured it out, they had to abandon the town. Some of the houses still have lace curtains up. It's been like seventy-five years."

There was a pause during which I could hear the oncologist breathe.

He said, "I'm afraid I'm not following. You think environmental factors made you sick? Is that what you're trying to say?"

"Do you think I'd be like this if the world didn't make it so easy? Like. Was I always going to be like this?" I asked.

"Hester. I need you to do something simple for me. Can you hang up, take a deep breath, and call 911 immediately? Do you think you can do that for me? You can call me right back after."

I tried to parse the graffiti scratched into the glass of the booth, wondering when anyone had last used it, last thought to deface it.

"Don't you have a poem for me? I know I made fun of you, but I actually liked those eternal words. I liked those eternal words a lot," I said.

There was another long silence. He sighed, sounding chastened and dismayed.

"This is a bit embarrassing, but I'm afraid nothing is coming to mind."

"That's okay. Thanks anyway. I'm hanging up now to call 911. I'm dialing 911 as we speak. My fingers are on the buttons."

I dropped the phone, left it hanging off the hook, and finished my cigarette. Then I went back to the motel.

36

When a property is listed, it goes quickly. Doesn't it feel good to be among like-minded people?

The last place we visited was Las Vegas. I knew it was the last place. I didn't tell John, who thought we were going there to see an old railroad refueling station. It was only because I was so bad at goodbyes, I thought. It wasn't because I wanted to keep my options open. It wasn't because I still might have changed my mind.

I had an agenda for when I got to a city. A proper city, not some Podunk with fifty thousand residents packed in at density but an actual place, the kind with its own cultural ecosystem and access to goods and services of a certain cachet.

My first stop was the hotel. I booked the priciest suite in the priciest hotel I could find, over John's protestations. The second stop was the gym. I bandaged myself so that I could barely breathe, ran on the treadmill as fast as I could for as long as I could, until my vision was spotty and my nerves jumpy and my bad foot throbbed.

The next several stops consisted of various salons. I had my hair trimmed and dyed and pressed and blown until it shone with no hints of silver or brass. I had my eyebrows threaded and my body hair waxed off in violent honeyed strips until I was dizzy and shivering. I had my cuticles pared and my calluses pumiced and my nails shaped and varnished clear. I had a catastrophically expensive facial, then went to an old-fashioned tanning salon, the kind people think went extinct in the 1990s. I washed my hands, applied an ointment to Beryl, cut a bandage to her size, and sat baking under the ultraviolet glow as long as I could tolerate it, which was not at all long but still enough to develop the light patina I wanted.

I'd forgotten the aggressive maintenance a conventionally attractive body needed. My aestheticians were well maintained themselves, advertising their own services. They all had boyfriends named Jared or whatever and seemed to have at least one child from a prior relationship. I liked their chatter, their complaints about intemperate weather, the wild antics of their worst customers. One of them, the waxer, asked me if I had a special occasion and seemed so disappointed when I said no that I almost wished I'd told her the truth.

I took my suitcase of terrible clothes and left it outside a shuttered Goodwill where other people had abandoned clothing and children's games and books in an undistinguished heap. I kept only an oversize men's button-up and a pair of black jeans. I went back to the white marble boxes of expensive shops lining the strip and bought myself a dress, simple and abbreviated and very black, and expensive underwear and thick-soled shoes, also black. No jewelry, no makeup. I stood in the gilt mirror of the dressing room deciding if I looked the way I'd envisioned, severe and uncompromising as punctuation, the meanest em dash.

Lastly, I went to a gun shop. The man who sold me the ammo had a tattoo of a diamond under his eye and a smartwatch on a bracelet made of gold bars.

He asked, "This a gift?"

"Why, do you do gift wrapping?"

"We can slap a bow on there, sure."

Which I thought was strange until a calendar on the back wall reminded me it was Father's Day.

On my way back, I mentally organized my remaining possessions. The ammo, the gun. My computer, phone, and keys. I imagined them laid out on the bed and admired the picture they made, simple and tetric.

One of the beds in the room held John, barefoot and mapping out where in Nevada he wanted to go. A comical number of gold-fringed pillows dwarfed him. I wondered if he liked the comfort of material culture despite himself. If a lizard part of his brain couldn't resist silk sheets, rejected his supererogatory life.

"Planning?" I asked.

"They opened this lithium mine, it's a disaster," he said with a degree of vitriol that was unusual for him.

"I thought lithium was good. Electric cars, et cetera."

"Any mining's bad. The answer is a car-free society."

A car-free society! I thought.

John continued talking, something about *protestors* and *sabotaging equipment* and *two-person job.* I dropped my shopping bags on the glass-topped dresser and went to look out the window. Our suite was high up. The room was strongly perfumed like an old heiress, and the windows were free of streaks. Deep arteries of traffic were slashed by pedestrian bridges and layered with the turrets of a palatial hotel, a fake Statue of Liberty, unvariegated suburbs, asphalt and concrete and neon. People once came here hunting gold and silver. They dug out ores and extracted bits of gold and silver by grinding them up and mixing them with water and salt and bluestone and mercury and heating them all in an iron pan. A hundred million ounces were lost, flowing down the Carson River to a reservoir that now emits mercury vapor.

"Look how far I can see," I said. "This city just goes on and on."

John said, "Contamination makes sprawl worse. Developers can't afford cleanup costs, so they skip over already built-up land for fresh soil. The more sprawl, the more people drive, the more water they use."

I turned and looked back at his array on the bedspread. I could read his descriptions of places I'd never see: the Utahn Moab pile, an Idahoan mink farm, a Montanan wood treatment plant, an asbestos-tainted military barrack in Oregon. American Redoubt country.

"Forget this. Come downstairs," I said, nudging his shoulder. "We're in Vegas, I want to do Vegas things."

He looked up at me without remark on my sleek new hair or sleek new legs.

"You'll come to the mine tomorrow?"

"Of course."

He silently bent to put on his shoes and followed me out into fountains and lights and pools and malls and an omnipresent invitation to spend money. I knew John hated it, knew he hated the artificiality, the money, the excess of false cooled air. The fun. He didn't bring his camera, like he didn't want it tarnished by the place. He kept shaking his head at that pinnacle of centuries of human enterprise, that birthplace of the buffet.

We wandered away from the antiseptic glistening Strip and passed a huge ruby high-heeled shoe covered in a thousand tiny lights rotating on top of a pole. A stilted robot voice told us the walk sign was on to cross Fremont. Gnawed chicken bones and empty fifths of vodka littered the bus stops. I thought a woman was kneeling to pray, but she was just trying to get a better angle on her camera. A couple stood on the median on the strip, jostled by indifferent tourists; the woman wore a sandwich board that said JESUS EXISTS BEYOND A REASONABLE DOUBT, and the man wore one that said WARNING GOD-HATERS! I thought it was cute that they matched.

"Is that the kind of pastor your father was?" I asked John.

"Sort of, when he was younger."

"What changed?"

"He went to prison. I think it taught him to be quiet."

I let this information settle for a moment, like waiting for a freight train to pass. "What was he in for?"

"It's a long story."

I was running out of time. Soon there would be no opportunities to extract the information I wanted from him.

"My father has a long story, too," I said.

"Hm."

"I'll tell you if you tell me first."

He glanced around at the sunny pavement. "Now?"

Though it was a bright and surveilled place, the city had a sense of privacy. We had strayed far from the wending pedestrian bridges that knit the Strip together. We were across the street from a wedding chapel / nightclub, waiting for the light to change on a six-lane highway. On the intersecting street, a pregnant woman in a tube dress sat in front of a tamale truck with her cell phone to her ear.

"Yes, now."

We walked a quiet while together. He seemed to be gathering all the words he needed.

"Remember my story about getting lost?"

"Yes."

"I didn't tell you all of it."

I looked at him with raised eyebrows. We were walking beneath an overpass, the shade in sharp contrast to the light beyond. There was no sidewalk, just an aluminum guardrail separating the concrete slope from asphalt, floor and walls and ceiling all tagged with graffiti, color in surround sound.

John said, "There was a man. I thought he was there to save me, but he wasn't. That's where they found me. At his cabin."

I turned my eyes from him, licked salt off my upper lip. Keeping my gaze on him would have damaged us both, I felt. Instead I scanned the road ahead, looking for a path forward.

"Later, my father found him and shot him dead on his front

porch. He went away a long time. He's only out now because he got sick."

I had many obvious questions but knew how impossible it was to talk about these things, to provide answers you didn't want to give. How discussing the past is a kind of betrayal of it. I didn't even ask whether the wolf was real or just a kind of parable, though I later wondered.

"Oh, John. I'm sorry." It had been a long time since I'd told anyone that.

"I know."

"Your father was a righteous man," I said with not a little jealousy. I wondered what he'd felt when the deed was done. If it was like I imagined, operatic and triumphant.

The air reeked of car exhaust. I decided looking at the ground made me a coward, so I looked at him again. I was a few steps ahead of him so that I had to look back, admiring the odd undersea quality to the light, the way his eyes shone with suppressed emotion. His mouth was in a tight thin line.

He said, "A waste. He should never have done it."

I frowned. "Why?"

We'd emerged back out into the sun. He didn't answer me but instead coughed to clear his throat and said, "You said you'd tell me your father's long story."

I felt too ashamed to tell it to him in full, afraid to seem puritanical, hyperbolic; too in love with my own suffering or somehow in competition with his.

"He hurt my mother."

"That's not a very long story."

"It's hard for me to describe."

John nodded. "You think he's changed."

"No."

John looked askance at me. "Then why see him?"

I sucked in my cheek, struggling to articulate an approximate truth. The heat of the day was stunning, spirit-stealing. I said, "A reckoning."

John hissed as if struck. "You mean punishment."

"I don't think of it that way," I said, not caring that it sounded absurd.

"Would prison have been punishment enough?"

"I don't have to explain myself to you. You're just some stranger. I don't even know why I picked you up."

"Simple," he said. "Because you were lonely."

"Fuck off."

"You know nothing good can come from this. You're perpetuating his logic. He treated you as something to be dominated, and now you'll do the same to him. You don't have to. You don't have to act on his terms. Don't you want to spend your time on something more worthwhile?"

I was angry, but the anger had nowhere to go, an electrical impulse swimming in circles beneath my skin. I heard his words but wasn't sure what he was saying, what he knew of my plan, what I might have revealed to him without knowing it.

"You don't understand. It's this old idea of mine, I can't let it go now."

I didn't want to be my father, who started a family but never finished it, the same way he started and abandoned paintings. I didn't want to break my own promise.

"I swear you can."

"And do what?"

"What you're already doing."

"With you?"

"If you want."

I thought of all the weeks I'd spent with him, all the delays. I tried to picture doing this or some version of it until my end, like penance for my glib years of material comfort and lonely accumulation. A memory came back to me of the surreal night at the farm:

my teeth chattering as disembodied hands wrung cold water from my hair in the dark. I couldn't be that vulnerable again. I needed to reclaim some dignity for myself, some of my old sangfroid. It would be just like a woman, I thought, to fall apart now.

"You're only saying that because you want my car and my money."

John laughed. It surprised me how good-natured the laugh was, how free of scorn. "You know that's not it."

"Well, it can't be because of my charming personality."

John turned solemn and nodded. "No," he said. "It's not that either."

We'd returned to society, riding an escalator to a pedestrian bridge that had no roof or cover on the assumption that it would never rain. I stood a few steps above him, looking down. A digital billboard loomed above us, turning our skin blue, then red, then white, then blue again. Tourists milled about in ill-fitting shorts and oversize paper shopping bags. The pain in my breast crackled like static.

I abruptly asked, "Do you forgive him?"

"Who, my dad?"

"What? No, the man in the woods."

"Yes."

"How?"

"'Nothing human is alien to me.'"

I thought I recognized the quote. "Is that Terence?"

John nodded. *See*, I thought, addressing the doctor in my head, *I finally got one right.*

"I don't know what you think you have to forgive your father for. But do you?"

John thought about it, hands in his pockets, looking down at our shoes. We reached the top of the escalator and slotted into place with all the other foot traffic, walking side by side.

"It took longer because he was closer. But yes."

"They know what you're up to? Your family."

"They know I'm on the road."

"I've never seen you call them."

"I don't."

"How come?"

"I just never belonged there."

"How do you mean?"

"Sometimes love is better from a distance."

I decided to pretend I knew what he meant.

We took the monorail and then followed a series of tunnels and covered bridges back to our hotel. You could travel an impressive interval in a sealed space that iced out nature with air conditioning and advertising, posters and screens on surfaces horizontal and vertical. I could feel myself being watched on security feeds. A separate network of storm drains existed, parallel to and below us, where the homeless lived, drinking tawny port under the shadows of tourists through street grates above and praying rain didn't come and wash them away. No one watched those spaces, there being no profit in it.

"I want to gamble," I said as automatic doors parted for us.

I expected John to complain, but he nodded again and said, "Of course."

A drunk sang along to Merle Haggard on the casino floor, tapping his cane in time with the twangs. I decided I wanted to be drunk, too, drunk enough to sing and not care, drunk enough to forget my name, Dad's name, my whole history. Killing Dad seemed stupid, suicide the clumsiest experiment. I don't know why revenge plots are so commonly accepted. These simple stories by the lazy and uninspired.

John declined to participate, watching me at some remove as the machines lit up my eyes and the drinks I ordered lit up my dumb rat brain. He looked like a lost little boy, a child put to bed early only to wake in the middle of a party, when the adults were all shambolic and changed. I don't know how I looked. Bad, probably.

I wore my gas station sunglasses at the blackjack table because I'd forgotten to buy more stylish ones. I held a huge icy drink in my hand, a comically sized plastic cup with a comical volume of alcohol in it because although this hotel had airs, it was as crummy as the bottomest-budget affair on the strip. I remembered the chickens Dad was raising and laughed aloud though I was alone. I was stuck in a circus of sensation, the lights and the movement, the electronic dings of the slot machines, the music piped in from the overhead speakers, the shuffle of cards and the chatter of voices, Spanish and English blurred to inseparability.

For a moment, John went off somewhere, maybe the bathroom, or maybe just to get a breath from my methodical and relentless self-destruction. I was, for the moment, unsupervised.

I wanted to die, I wanted to be loved, I wanted to kill someone or be killed. I wanted to reach my destination and to never arrive. I wanted to leave like I'd never wanted anything else, and I wanted to stay, too. I wanted to take every drug I'd ever taken all at once. I wanted to shred my passport and renounce my citizenship and spit on the flag, and I wanted to weep to the national anthem. That part about twilight's last gleaming.

A man sat next to me, his white hair gelled into a swoop that looked purple beneath the dancing blue and red lights. He had a private, curling mouth, permanent twin dimples beneath eyes that were too close together, and a work shirt tugged loose around the collar. He put his hand on my leg like I'd just told a joke and he'd gotten confused about whose knee to slap. I didn't admire the approach, but it was so corny that it became funny. Besides, I didn't mind. I turned to smile in his direction and then realized with some alarm that I'd slunk low enough in my seat, gone off-balance enough, that I was going to slide right out of it. A moment of ungainly fear came, but nothing happened because John was there to catch me. How I'd miss him, I thought, this plowboy next door, this prince of earnestness, this maligned Marabout.

"I think that's enough," John said, tugging at my shoulders. "Come on."

We stood on opposite sides of the elevator. I was leaning on the wall, cheek pressed against the mirrored surface, the plastic arm of the sunglasses crushed into my temple and my hand on the rail for support. There was no music, no porter, just a soft bell that indicated our arrival on the correct floor. I had spins like I hadn't had since I was a teenager, but it wasn't unpleasant; if anything, it was nostalgic and novel, like a trip to a planetarium. He walked me to my room. I wasn't walking straight, but I wasn't stumbling, in that liminal space between function and dysfunction.

"It's so dark," I said.

"Take off your sunglasses," he said.

"I like the darkness," I said, not wanting to admit I'd forgotten they were on my face. When we rounded a corner, I took them off and crammed them into a golden trash can, its metal flap ajar and biting at the back of my hand.

I reached our door and leaned against it with relief, this solid, unmoving thing. The silence was immense and soft, both the hallway and its quietness luxuriously carpeted. I snickered. The key was in one of my pockets, or at least I hoped it was, but I let John fumble for his. He'd already rescued me once tonight, the pattern of helplessness established. I was already in the hole.

"You're going to be too sick to go to the mine tomorrow," he said, sounding disappointed. Part of me felt like laughing again, but another part of me felt guilty, like a neglectful parent.

"Sorry," I said before I could think about it. He nodded. He wasn't taking me too seriously now that he'd insulated me from further damage. He thought this was the standard messiness of a woman who ate cake out of plastic tubs in motels and hated her father with adolescent causticity. It made me unbearably sad, though I was the only one who knew it was the end. Though I'd done this by design.

"Can I ask you a question?" asked John.

"You can ask me anything. Anything."

"Why are you called Hester?"

I knew the answer and would find it momentarily, floating in the air, catchable on the tongue. In some sense, I'd succeeded in getting drunk enough to forget my name, my name that was possibly the last thing my parents had ever agreed upon. I almost said actually it's Beryl.

"Okay. To bed," he said, bringing his hand up from his pocket with the key. I'd heard that if you ask for a replacement, hotels just give you one that's not programmed for a specific room, can open any door in the place. Lose the key and open a million possibilities. He leaned forward and pushed the door open slowly so I'd have time to right myself.

I dropped onto the bed with all my weight. I threw my arm over my face and felt him removing my shoes and folding the blanket over me. I liked that I couldn't see him do this. It reminded me of those times as a kid I'd held my eyes shut after long drives. The strength of Dad's arms carrying me to bed.

I sensed John grab one of the upturned glasses on the dresser and go to the tap. I lowered my arm and looked around, picking out shapes in the room illuminated only by a golden wedge from the half-shut bathroom door. The pressure of my arm had left blots on my vision. I waited until they steadied themselves and then reached for the remote.

On the TV was an old black-and-white movie. The actors all

looked purposeful and bright, like they knew the future only contained color. I don't think I'd seen it before, or if I had, I couldn't think of the name, but when John came back I said, "Look, it's this movie. I love this movie. Come watch it with me."

He put the water down on the nightstand and got in.

37

I dreamed that night I was in the hospital where my mother died, the one where nothing more could be done. I sat with my arms looped through the rail at the side of the cot. The morphine drip never seemed enough even when it was more of a flood. She was awake and knew she was dying, and I'd called for a nurse, but they weren't there, not yet. I wanted them to come and give her drugs. I couldn't bear being around her. It was easier when she was asleep, and I'm not ashamed to say I wanted the easier thing.

I had this feeling of color. The specific graying blue on the wall of her bedroom late at night when we'd fallen asleep with the TV on, just where it edged to black in the corners behind furniture. I had an ocean of that color in my lungs and throat and back, heavy and vast and dead still. I couldn't tell if it was a hollow feeling or a full one, only that it made everything impossible.

"Promise," she said.

"She's coming," I said, too loud, as if she were already a great distance from me. "Okay? Mom? The nurse."

She grabbed my hand. Her eyes were wild and wide, the skin around her lips gummed and cracked. After she was gone, I spent minutes scraping the gunk away from her dead mouth, as if it mattered, until the doctor came and told me they needed the body, such a strange choice of words.

"Promise."

"I did, I already did."

"Again."

She dragged me in, dragged me down, deeper into that gray-blue color, into the unbearable weight of it, and reminded me what I'd said. That I'd try. That was what she wanted from me.

I said, "Please."

I said, "Mom."

I said, "Help!"

She only tightened her grip and said again, "Promise."

So I did.

38

I left before dawn. It was dark enough that the sky was plum-colored, with the neon signs of the strip still aglow and the distant mountains all gray-blue-pink. The sound of what little traffic I saw outside was muted by the glass and our height.

We'd fallen asleep during the movie. I'd awoken at some point during a late-night infomercial for a psychic claiming to have connected a client to their dead mother. I hadn't slept after that. I spent most of the night thinking I was wasting my last chance at sleep or thinking about a psychopathy test I took online with May in high school for a laugh, throwing the results on purpose, or thinking about writing a letter to John, whether and what I should explain, and at a certain point I just gave up, got up, packed Beryl down, and dressed in the dark with an odd feeling that I'd died in the night.

John was face down on the bed, arm hanging over the side so that his knuckles brushed the carpet. He wasn't even under the covers. Sleep had ambushed him. My eyes had adjusted to the dark. I could see the shape of his wallet in his back pocket, scuffed and soft like everything he owned. I leaned over and extracted it, pausing when he stirred only for him to snuffle his nose deeper into the pillow. I got his identification. John was not his real name. That should not have surprised me. I'd known he was younger than me but would never have guessed by how much. I could've been his mother if I'd had him at seventeen.

I thought I'd made it out clean, but when I reached the door, he asked, so sleepily I almost thought I imagined it, "Where are you going?"

He'd rolled onto his back. In the dark, I could see only the impression of his face, the dark slash of his mouth. The wells of his eyes.

"Nowhere," I said. "You're dreaming."

And then closed the door.

At the front desk, I requested a printer and two witnesses. The hotel was one of those full-service places that hosted business conventions as well as ordinary gamblers, so half the clerks were notaries. It was early to make such a request, but as with almost everything, a liberal application of money opened possibilities.

The lobby was airport-sleek and well lit, the polished floors reflecting the chandelier lights and velvet stanchions. The bar at the far end never closed, a lone old cowboy haunting the counter to watch QVC on the curved flat-screen television that hung above the liquor bottles like a bad halo.

You need a notary if you want to make your will self-proving so it moves through probate faster. If no one learns anything else from me, there's that, at least.

I entered John's name into the will I'd written. The remainder I split between Magda, the super, Caleb, and May. That was how sad my life had been, that those were the people I felt closest to, who had the most reasonable claim to my money. I wore my reading glasses and hoped brushing my teeth three times had been enough to make me look officious. I was probably still drunk.

The younger desk agent had one earringless gauged ear and hair weaponized with gel. He said as he signed his name, "Sorry, you're not, like . . . ?"

He was too tactful to say it but not too tactful to broach the topic. The other agent, a middle-aged woman, elbowed him.

"Not what?" I asked. "Going to kill myself?"

He said, "It happens sometimes."

"You're off the hook."

"People come here to die more often than you'd think."

"Mostly the usual, though," said the woman.

"The usual?" I asked.

"Getting hitched and losing all their money," she said.

"Sometimes all three," he said.

"Lucky for you," I said. "Otherwise no business."

"That's right," he said, punctuating his sigh by thwacking his stamp on my will. "Lots to do here in Lost Wages."

I had them send the original to my lawyer's office back east by mail and digitally. I didn't want to log into my old accounts and see the tally of unread messages in bold. It had nothing to do with me.

By the time I left, the sun had arrived with a vengeance. Despite the drunkenness or blossoming hangover, I felt clearheaded and alive. I stopped for coffee, creamed and sugared, and a new pair of sunglasses. I still could've turned in any other direction, driven into any other life. Any explanation of myself I offered to the people I'd once known or the people I'd yet to meet would make more sense than this. But who would I be if I did that? There was no solid ground there. I had to be harsh with myself or face a dissolution worse than death.

I thought, when you were close to the end, that every detail was supposed to become hyper-vivid. I started looking out the window, willing this percipience to happen. The sun was rising behind me, casting long shadows around buildings and lending color to the six empty lanes ahead. Farther out, the highway wended its way through suburban divisions, each house the texture and color of sand and separated from the road by tan barriers. Palm trees and cacti stood stiff and overexposed as cardboard cutouts. I passed malls, a sandstone movie theater, a fairground. The types of places where mass shootings might happen. A man in a reflective vest stood alone plucking trash from the shoulder.

The night before, while I gambled away a minor chunk of the inheritance John didn't know he had, he told me about alluvial basins pocked with nuclear craters. About particles that fell in radionuclide-tinged snow on mountains hundreds of miles away. I'd pictured unlucky drunks looking up from rolling dice to watch through rattling panes the upwardly unfurling mushroom clouds. The ice in their drinks all ashake.

Okay, listen up, you guys. So for you, those of you with Facebook, I'm going to do a shout-out to our followers. We now have over fifteen thousand likes. Give it a look on there. Guess what. I got a CD, we're gonna give it away. This is all Hopi Big Buffalo Songs, Volume II. *We'll take the fourth caller, fourth call is free, give us a call. Don't start now, hold on until the song starts, okay? Okay. Askwali for listening.*

39

The drive took almost exactly two hours. I was there. It was happening. Nothing had permanently diverted me. Maybe if I'd done this when I was younger, found John in an earlier phase of my life, that could've changed my mind, but I was all gristle and bone and dust now, no fertile ground for new ideas.

I stopped at the base of his unpaved driveway, which led up a long slope to the house. The house was a flat, single-story adobe, postage stamp–size. Huge windows looked out on the endless valley below. A wind chime dangled under the eaves. The new wife's touch, I thought. An aboveground water tank stood guard outside. There was no garden, no landscaping; things you forgo in a desert. On the eastern side of the house stood the chicken coop I'd seen in photos, with a few in their nesting boxes and others strutting and pecking at the dirt. A truck was parked out front, new and shiny, a car for someone playing at rugged country life.

My cell phone buzzed. I didn't recognize the number. I hoped it might be John calling me from a pay phone, though I couldn't remember ever giving him my number.

"Hello?"

"Is this Hester?" said a man's voice.

"Speaking."

"I'm with the police department, calling to let you know we

recovered your car. Officer pulled a gentleman over for speeding, realized his plate didn't match the make and model, rest is history."

"Wow. Great," I said.

"The prosecutor wants to hold it in case it goes to trial, so you won't be able to pick it up just yet. But you'll get a call soon."

"Is there—was there an urn in the car?"

"An urn?"

"For ashes. It's an urn shaped like a car. In the car."

"I'd have to check the voucher. You know, it's pretty rare for them to find stolen property this long after the fact. And in good shape, too. I mean, he made some, well. Let's call them modifications, that I'm not sure you'll love, but the thing still has all its bits and pieces. More than I can say for myself at this age."

He laughed at his own joke. I pressed a hand to my temple, fighting waves of nausea. I may have emitted a gasp of discomfort or dismay.

"Ma'am?" he said.

I don't know what I said in response. I was trying to form a sentence but had no way of knowing whether the sounds that came out of me were words or not. I hung up and threw my phone into the footwell as if it had bitten me. I rested my forehead on my steering wheel and breathed in and out, in and out, until I felt steady enough to leave the car. The heat was astounding, eyeball-searing. The gun was tucked into my waistband holster, concealed by my too-big button-up men's shirt and too-big pants. I cracked my knuckles because I thought it would help my hands stop shaking.

The slope leading to the door was not unlike that of my childhood home, which had sat atop a lonely hill, shy of the road below. As a child, I'd thought the steepness of the hill was why my relatives never visited. That it was a geographical problem. More likely, it was because they all hated each other, at least on my father's side. I never met him, so I don't know where this comes from, but when I picture my paternal grandpa, I see him falling down a set of basement steps in a fit of drunkenness, his cheek, which had been mangled by a German S-mine, finding relief on the cool concrete floor. Grandma, withdrawn and partly deaf, continues making dumplings at the kitchen table upstairs, palms spectral and floured, while my aunts and uncles chase each other outside in the violent games of children. Dad hears his father's thump but keeps drawing primitive breasts in chalk on the attic floor.

No answer came when I knocked on the door. I heard what I thought was the sound of running water. I tried the knob and the door came open. Limited fear of intruders out this far, where you had only sand and sagebrush for neighbors.

The house looked more sturdily built than I'd imagined. A door opened into the dine-in kitchen. A half-drunk carton of milk sat on the table, an old habit of his I'd forgotten until that moment, the way he used to drift around the house drinking from it so that Mom had to buy a separate gallon for cereal. Unopened mail was scattered everywhere, along with sugar packets, a jar of peanut butter scraped empty by a serrated knife, a can of coffee grounds, an assortment of lighters in what seemed like every shade of blue, an open carton of strawberries, a clear glass plate on which rested an unidentifiable dust thick as ash, paintbrushes, a lidless saltshaker emptied and filled with white daisies that, on closer inspection, were plastic. I checked a piece of mail to confirm I'd come to the right place, but I didn't need to; the disorder was familiar. More proof that nothing had fundamentally changed.

I could see into the living room from where I stood. A small TV was on, the end of *Planet of the Apes* when Charlton Heston realizes there's no Earth to go back to. What had looked online like a full working studio was just one corner of the living room where his old drafting table stood, surrounded by paintings. Canvases in various stages of completion were stacked on the floor or leaned in rows against the wall. They were all landscapes now, suns and cacti and dunes, but still looked gynecologic to me.

I heard running water again. He was singing, off-key and higher-pitched than his natural voice. Hadn't I wanted this to be efficient, with minimal fuss? Already this was too messy, too personal. I sat on the couch. The wife seemed to be nowhere. Out running errands, maybe. I was glad for that.

The shower cut off. His singing was muffled on and off as he moved around with a towel. Sometimes he devolved into muttering or whistling. I wondered why he didn't have a dog.

After a minute or two, he came out, striding across the living room on the way to what I assumed was the bedroom, not realizing I was there. His naked body was a shock, with a belly ponderous enough to obscure his genitals, the sticklike limbs of the advanced in age, and the skin of his flattened, puddled ass wrinkled as a rag. His hair had gone white at the front and pale gray at the sides, still unruly. A scar ran down the center of his chest, a remnant of some surgical procedure about which I knew nothing. I was forty years old, and he was over sixty by then, and the acuteness of that difference was stunning. More than twenty years, a whole human life between us, the buffer of a generation.

I had the feeling again that this was a mirage. I'd fallen asleep, and my body was miles away, my car upturned and the wheels spinning to a stop. I'd drunk myself to death last night. This was a nightmare. I was back in Vegas with John, slot machines tinkling stories below us, the morning promising us lithium. I was still in a hotel somewhere in America, my world not yet so badly narrowed.

He reemerged some moments later, dangling a long, unlit cigarette from his lips. He was looking down, tucking the tails of his shirt into a belted pair of pants with the fly left open. I felt a bolt of contempt bred by intimacy and familiarity. I was cheating, leaping ahead; you shouldn't be able to experience that feeling so quickly with a person you hadn't seen for years.

"Dad."

He looked up. I wasn't sure he'd know me after all this time. He kept the cigarette in his mouth but didn't move or speak, the ends of his belt still pulled taut in each hand. I watched recognition dawn over his face, then doubt, then settled acceptance, all in a span of a few seconds. He was close enough that I could see the color of his irises, which I'd forgotten were the same as mine. He didn't run. Maybe the thought occurred to him and he didn't because he was old now, too tired or frail for flight.

"It's. Been a long time. I. You. Want a drink? Milk or Coke," he said.

I didn't respond. He concluded his belt and sat in the nearest chair, which was so deep his torso slanted far from his knees. He looked like his body had grown burdensome, its size and weight. He spoke more slowly than I remembered, too.

"You don't really want to do this, do you? You're not the sentimental type. Even when you were a kid, I could see that. You're like me that way."

"Those sunsets are pretty sentimental."

"You came all this way just to heckle me?"

I said nothing. The moment didn't feel right, but I wasn't sure what would make it so. An appliance chirped in the kitchen, an inane announcement of its readiness.

"It never sat well with me. The way things went after you left," I said.

"Your mother was an unlucky woman."

I laughed. "You were the luck. It was you."

"You know, she called me once, when she was sick, and asked me to come back. I said no. I knew how bad that would be for you."

"You're a terrible liar."

"She kept her own secrets. From me and from you."

I registered a heaviness around my belly and wrists and ankles. It was deep fear, a double-edged paralysis that kept me from both collapse and decisive action. It originated in what felt like my bones; my mind and mouth were separate, clear, bizarrely calm.

"If she called you, it was only because she was delirious," I said. "And if you said no, it was only for yourself."

"She put ideas in your head. I'm not the villain you think I am."

"Then what are you?"

A long silence elapsed. He picked up a dusty, abandoned-looking glass of water from the end table next to him and took a sip. With wet lips, he said, "You wouldn't be so hard on me if you had your own family. You don't know what it's like."

Since he'd lied to me, I lied right back. "I have a son."

I doubt he believed me. I didn't elaborate and he didn't ask. We fell quiet again. I watched dust motes drift through the stale air, the way my breath disturbed their paths.

"We had," he began, and then paused to consider his words. It seemed he was still stuck on my mother. "Differences."

"That's what you call it? Differences? How about the new wife, you have differences with her?"

He looked at me as if surprised, and then his face started to crumple. *Oh God*, I thought. It was like watching a machine collapse in on itself in a way you know will wound some unwitting worker.

"She left," he said, his voice high-pitched and hoarse. "No idea she was thinking of leaving."

I wondered if there existed any person famous or impressive enough that he'd stop bawling if they walked in at that moment and told him to. If anyone could command as much attention as himself.

"Oh, give me a break," I said.

"She's pregnant. She's got no right."

A revealing way of putting it. I wasn't certain it was true, but

I wasn't certain he had cause to lie, either. I hadn't even thought she could still have children. There's something unseemly about the way life perseveres in inhospitable places.

"You don't like children. Not that way. Or was that just me?" I said.

He kept sniveling, one hand over his eyes, just to show I was wrong, a performance designed to prove it was no mere performance.

I stood and went to the window. It was shadowed in his house but bleach-bright outside. A blue-tailed lizard darted across a rock. In the distance was a jagged line of purple-and-ochre mountains where gold had once been found, ghost towns and empty mines long since turned over to coyotes. Red dust was everywhere, fine as school chalk and whipped up into devils by the wind. It was hostile country, fighting any humans trying to tame it. In the distance I saw a huge plume of black smoke and something troubled me about that, but I couldn't think what. I could've asked him anything, any confirmation of my memories, but I didn't want or trust his answers. Instead I asked, "You like living out here?"

His reflection in the glass pulled out the front of his shirt, lifted his glasses, wiped his eyes on the turned-out collar, and then dropped the lenses back into place. His reflection sniffed in one nostril, then the other, by pressing one side closed with a single finger. He cleared his throat. I realized he could probably see the gun at that angle.

"Good for my arthritis," he said. "Lonely, though."

Left to his own devices, I doubted he'd stay put long. He couldn't entertain himself. He needed attention, an audience and preferably a captive one. I wanted to know the circumstances of the pregnancy, if it had been her wish or his, if he had been careless or selfish or calculating. Bringing a life into this world can be as terrible as ending one.

His cigarette had extinguished itself. He was spacing out,

looking at some distant spot on the floor, the edge of the threadbare Indian rug, rather than at me. The television had gone to a commercial for a casino, then a car salon.

I stood there, loathing. I wasn't even sure if I was loathing him or myself or his dumb chickens or his art. It was a directionless sensation, not at all like my old anger. It was strange, after all those years spent building up to this idea, this totem, to feel no urgency. I'd made an island of trash, and a rising sea had washed it away. I wondered what else I could do instead. If he'd apologize at gunpoint, or even just if I asked. Or if he'd paint me, and what his painting of me would look like. What it would reveal or hide. The gun felt remote from me, a gag gift, an object distorted by wormhole physics.

I stared at the inscrutable scratchings in the dust left by the birds. So bright out there and so blue within, a light like being underwater.

"The baby," I said. "Is it a boy or a girl?"

Then he grabbed me from behind.

It startled me. Despite all my effort and forethought, I'd expected a different outcome. I'd expected the universe would punish my hubris with a random, absurd accident. I'd expected to be kidnapped by a cult, to have the tumor growing over my heart explode, to crack my neck and stroke out. If I reached him at all, I'd thought, for whatever reason, that he would submit to my punishment with quiet dignity. That was my insane, naive belief. That he'd recognize his sins and accept retribution.

Under the rubble of my life, I was as full of hope as anyone else.

There was no dignity, though, on the tile floor where I'd fallen. He'd grabbed the gun from the back of my waistband. It went off while we grappled over it. Neither of us was prepared for the recoil. The bullet flew into the television screen, which went black and spat out shards of glass and gray smoke. The gun flew from his hand and skittered away toward the door, beyond reach.

Never in a thousand years had I thought there'd be a physical fight, both of us so awkward. Dad lunged in the gun's direction, and I kicked him as hard as I could. Then we struggled for real, with fingernails and teeth and elbows. I struck his heavy body, his egg-shaped belly, above me, trying to keep him from controlling my arms and reaching the gun. Broken glass crunched under my back, cutting holes into my shirt and skin.

He lost one of his house shoes at some point, a slip-on sandal with a stiff rubber sole, and I reached for it and beat him about the head with it. We slid nearer to the drafting table, and when he reared back to dodge my blows, he struck the edge of it, hard, with his head. Pens and brushes rained down, and a row of half-closed, pint-size, round metal paint cans that tottered near the edge fell, covering us in fluid acrylic, titanium white and cadmium yellow and ruby lake.

I bucked and rolled, trying to wriggle free. Probably no more than a few minutes had elapsed, but we'd been fighting for years, decades, an awful dance to the longest, slowest song in the universe. Not many people ever see this side of their parents, this animal will. Not many people are as stupid as I am.

He got his hands around my throat. This was no joke, the weight of his hands pressing down harder than I would've thought possible. This was the worst mistake I'd ever made. I should've listened to John, to Robert, to Caleb, to May, to Magda, to my mother, to my super. Anyone except myself. Mom had been in this position, a tidy circle we were drawing here as if with a drafting compass. I scrabbled at his shoulders, groped to my sides for anything, anything. My ears went silent, then filled with the ringing of a tuning fork that got louder as my vision fried and frayed, black flowers blooming and wilting, a whole life cycle before my eyes, thinking on loop of my mother, the lightless circle of her dying mouth.

I heard a shot.

The sound was so loud and stark, it obliterated all other perception. The full weight of his body collapsed on me. I pushed at him, revulsed, wanting to scream but having no voice. My eyes were blind, but my limbs knew to scramble, my hands slip-sliding through paint and blood. The difference in temperature between these two fluids was worse than the sight of them. One of the overturned paint cans had stayed on the desk and dripped onto the floor.

Never had drawing breath been more painful or more sublime. I wanted hills and mountains and rivers and lakes and basins and steppes and all the webbed asphalt America had to offer in between. It didn't matter if it was irradiated and filled to spilling with lead and arsenic and scorched and parched or flooded or swept away. It didn't matter if nothing could stop it from being broken and useless and degraded. All my pride was gone. I would endure anything, bear any agony. I felt giddy and so, so alive. I'd done it. Somehow, convolutedly, I'd found happiness. It had taken me so long, but I'd kept my promise, and it didn't matter what happened next as long as it kept happening.

I turned. A woman stood a few feet away, holding the gun. A strange contrast of light through the open front door gave her a low-toned glow, a full-body halo that showed every wrinkle, every wispy hair escaping her ponytail. She was just at that stage of pregnancy when it becomes obvious. Her dress, baby blue except where it was darkened with sweat, looked more like a child's nightie. The cross she wore looked even bigger than it had in pictures.

My dad's new wife. New ex-wife.

She put the gun down on the table. Then she adjusted her dress, tugging down the hem at either side. She pulled out a chair, sat down, plucked a few strawberries from the carton, tore off the stems, and ate them one by one. Her hands shook.

"What?" she said, noticing the way I stared. "I have a craving."

She ate a few more. "I was just coming by to pick up some of my things. Don't think I want them now. I know who you are. He never talked about you, not once. I had to figure it all out myself."

She chewed, then sucked at her fingers and wiped the clean spit on her dress. She said, "I met him at my church. Isn't that a trip?"

She pointed to the fresh marks ringing my neck, a galaxy of popped capillaries. "You're going to want to ice that. You want some water? You might not be able to drink, but you can hold it in your mouth, and it'll feel nice. Talking's gonna be hard, so don't. Just nod yes or no. Quiet's good anyway because I'm going to need it to think."

I'd come to rest with my back against the wall. I could not look to my right, where the body was. I didn't want to see if he was alive or dead, didn't want to see where he was wounded, didn't want to know. Beryl was going insane, throbbing and vicious. My ears felt full of song. I looked up, seeing the sky from an odd angle through my father's window, seeing the dark cloud blotting out the sun, a respite from the wild heat.

I attempted to speak, but instead I croaked, swallowed, and winced.

"Don't talk," she said. "One thing at a time."

I nodded without understanding.

She picked out seeds and pulp from her teeth, then ran her tongue over them. Neither of us looked at the insane mess in the corner.

"Bastard," she muttered.

And then I fainted.

Reinvent yourself with one of our sixty programs in areas like IT, health care, business administration, and early childhood education.

Ask yourself what you will miss more: Your children or your cigarettes?

Is it truly possible to love thy enemy?

Freedom isn't free. Salute your armed forces.

About 1.3 billion dollars will be devoted to earmarks.

Recibe diez dolares en dinero estrella por cada cincuenta dolares gastados.

Today's environmental roundup: Wildfires continue unabated in several US states. Lake Powell has reached record lows. A billion gallons of coal fly ash slurry were released into the atmosphere after an ash dike erupted, creating a mudflow wave that knocked three homes off their foundations in North Carolina. We may be underestimating the melting of Greenland's ice.

In better news, scientists have discovered a new type of octopus.

40

I've been here for a while.

I'm trying to be pleasant with the nurses. Most of them don't trust me. I assume they've figured out who I am and what my story is from the local news. It's also possible I just give them a bad feeling. I could be paranoid. Pain medication can distort your perception.

When I came to at my father's, the wife was gone. For all I know, she was a figment. I hoped my father's body was a figment too. It wasn't. I forced myself to look, to behold what I'd wrought. His head was turned away from me. It was a terrible thing, the stillness of him. Without seeing where he'd been struck, it seemed possible he could get back up. That it wasn't final, that I could undo what had been done.

I called for help. Help took a long time, local services having been called to deal with an explosion at a lithium mine across the state border. I stayed in my father's house with my consequences for a long time, his landline pulled down by the cord and resting next to me on the floor. From where I lay, I could watch the sky going smoke-black through the front door, which had been left wide-open. I was covered in paint and blood and water and ink, all combined into a nameless new color. I see it still in the fine lines of my hands, the soles of my feet.

The gun was on the table where the new wife had left it. I could've used it on myself. I didn't. Death seemed the quickest exit, offering an ease I didn't deserve. Harder would be to live with what I'd done. To cede control and let whatever existed beyond it decide when it had had its fill of me. This might be as self-serving and deluded as anything I've ever thought or felt. Most likely, it's not a question I'll get to decide.

When the law came, I told them that during the struggle, he'd hit his head and that I'd used the opportunity to get the weapon back. I said I stood alone and shot him from the doorway before collapsing. I omitted the wife. The story was a lie that told the greater truth about my guilt. I was dying anyway and felt the wife deserved that chance. I have no idea what has become of her or her baby.

I hired attorneys. I paid them to direct my life, to sell my house and chattel in New York, to explain me in court, to tell me how to be. It was wonderful to let someone else direct the particulars. Like being dead but more expensive. Out on bail, I went into treatment. Beryl was removed, along with the rest of my breasts. I asked if I could keep her, my only creation. To my surprise, the surgeon agreed, as long as I paid to have her properly stored. A clerical error resulted in her disposal anyway; in the end, she was autoclaved and landfilled.

My sickness has spread. They've told me that with the right combinations of poisons, I could live awhile yet. My lawyers are considering using my illness as a defense; secondary metastasis to certain areas of the body can manifest in behavioral changes. The Beryl strategy. No one knows about my weeks of trespassing with John. I almost wish they did, that I had proof those weeks were real.

I'll be discharged soon. I have no home. It's expensive, all these lawyers, all this uninsured care. I'm watching my account dwindle to nothing. This does not trouble me. I think I'll be relieved to reach zero.

When I got my effects back from New Jersey, I found the journal Magda had given me. There are daytime stretches when hospital televisions show nothing good, just soaps or news about climate protests in Copenhagen presided over by bored cops in neon vests. In those narcotic hours, I fill the pages. I didn't intend to—in fact, it was stupid to, could be considered a voluntary statement—but once I started, it was hard to stop. Mine's a story best forgotten, a tale with little instructive value. A past that only makes the possibility of a better future more remote. Yet I feel compelled to tell it.

It is strange to win but have it feel like loss. To live in wrongness. The value and renown of Dad's work has risen posthumously, acquiring a new audience thanks to his macabre demise. His works will never end up in a landfill now. Maybe he would have considered that a worthwhile trade. Maybe he regretted the past the way I do now. I don't know, I didn't ask him. My aim was never quite true, no matter how I worked at it.

All that is gone. I have none of that anger left. I have been remediated of it or traces of it linger imperceptibly, forever chemicals just under the surface, uncapturable except by nature and time. I studied the abyss, I thought I'd mapped its dimensions, thought I'd readied myself for its embrace. Having gone to its edge, I came back humbled. It is beyond fathom and should cow any man.

I don't dream. Opiates take some of the fighting spirit out of the subconscious. I've only had one, the night before surgery. John and I were in a darkroom. I have no idea how photographs are developed beyond what I've seen in movies, yet my mind set the scene. Somehow I knew we were in the basement of my father's old housing development. I expected John to yield glossy ribboned negatives of barren brown soil, but when he drew the prints up from their toxic baths, I saw they were portraits of my mother.

I should've listened to John or gone with him. I want him

at my bedside. Not to grant me absolution, but just to have his decency within reach. The other day, one of the nurses came to check my drains during a news segment about the estimated cost of the damage from the lithium mine. Lithium is unstable, prone to corrosion and fires when exposed to water, but the news described it as an explosion. Every outlet detailed the evacuations, how the smoke could be seen for hundreds of miles, how it had contributed to existing wildfire plumes so large they made their own lightning. All were vague about the underlying cause.

The nurse shook her head, muttering as she worked, "Where's *my* 3.2 billion dollars, huh?"

I watched her as she fussed with the various tubes tethering me to life. "What do you think went wrong?" I asked. I just meant about the mine, but the question took on philosophic dimensions, as if I were asking her to explain everything since the first fish shimmied ashore 370 million years ago.

She continued her work without looking at me. "Bet you anything it's the Chinese," she said, this being one of the more popular quasi-conspiracy theories proliferating.

The screen switched to a stream of the menacing black cloud, by then burning uncontrolled for weeks. We both watched it, transfixed. A ding from my infusion pump drew the nurse out of her reverie. She said, "I'd stop worrying and turn this stuff off if I were you."

I won't stop. A novel feeling for me, worry gives purpose and drive to my days. I don't know if John went to the mine as planned. I don't know if he was there when it happened. I don't know if he caused it—whether accidentally, through mischief, or deliberately, through knowledge I hadn't known he possessed. Such chaos seems unlike him, but if I've learned anything, it is how little I know.

I wait for signs of him the way you wait for sightings of rare species to confirm they are not extinct. He's a rare breed, the last hitcher in America. I like to picture him getting picked up by the new wife. The two of them starting the cycle over again. Ending up back at the farm or somewhere like it. Raising the baby unpressed by the past.

Unlikely, I know. But hope is my obverse of worry.

I don't know why he wanted me to come with him. I always complained about how dull his Superfund sites looked, all the vast, mute dirt and plain, tall grass. Maybe he wanted me to see a lithium mine. They can be beautiful. I've looked them up online. They're visually quite dramatic, with their patchworks of square brine pits, which come in shades of green and blue, the same color as a TV screen in a dark room.

ACKNOWLEDGMENTS

The following is a nonexhaustive list of all the people for whom I'm thankful:

My editor, Caroline Zancan, for her invaluable feedback, vision, and patience with me; Leela Gebo, editorial assistant, for keeping me honest; Marinda Valenti, copyeditor, for her sharp eye; Hannah Campbell, production editor, for putting it all together; Emily Mahar, for her gorgeous cover design; Henry Holt and Company at large, for taking a chance on me; and Samantha Shea, my incredible agent, for seeing the potential in this manuscript.

I also owe thanks to Mary Beth Keane, for her encouragement when I was a student at Barnard College and publishing a book seemed a distant dream; Joshua Henkin, director of Brooklyn College's MFA program, for his generosity and priceless advice; Helen Phillips, Julie Orringer, and every other teacher I had during my time at Brooklyn College, for their kindness and wisdom; Kimmel Harding Nelson Center, for providing me with time and space to write; Maddie Crum, for building our little writing community and for all the nights at Guero's; Alexandra Tanner, Michelle Lyn King, Erika Recordon, Andrew Blevins, James Chrisman, and Jessie Shabin, for reading this book in its earliest iteration; Jenzo Duque, Emily Neuberger, Wesley

Straton, and all the other gifted, inspiring writers I met through Brooklyn College; *AGNI*, for providing me with indispensable editorial experience and community; Eve Gleichman, for publishing my first short fiction in *Guernica*; Anna Dorn, for loaning me the bravery I needed to begin the querying process; Mark Chiusano, for his guidance in finding an agent; Lura Chamberlain, for her friendship and insights into the lawyering life; Anne Osherson, for all the long walks in Prospect Park; and Beth, Carol, Ron, Anna, and Becca Breslaw, for keeping me supplied in crosswords, chocolate-covered matzoh, and laughter.

Writing this book would not have been possible without the love, patience, and stability provided by my family: Sarah, Dan, Andrew, Emily (B. and C.), Tom, Pete, Courtney, Jack, Vivian, Ingrid, Nathaniel, Alexander, and especially Sue and Michael. Much love to my parents for making me the writer I am today, and a special word of gratitude to my sister, Susie; I would be a much worse version of myself without her.

Lastly, I'd like to thank my husband, Daniel, whom I love beyond words.

ABOUT THE AUTHOR

Ariel Courage is a graduate of the Brooklyn College MFA program, where she was editor in chief of the *Brooklyn Review*. She's currently an assistant fiction editor at *Agni*. Her short work has appeared in *Guernica*, *New Limestone Review*, and *The End*. She was also a 2019 Kimmel Harding Nelson resident.